Praise for Total War Rome: Destroy Carthage

'Delivers historically accurate fiction by the bucket load. After only a few paragraphs of the novel's prologue it becomes abundantly clear that *Destroy Carthage* is a book written by a Roman history enthusiast for Roman history enthusiasts . . . Gibbins clearly understands the immense levels of fear, excitement and adrenaline that pump through each Roman soldier, and the surgical brutality of their battles'   Sega-addicts.murnaumusic.com

'Gibbins delivers the last battle in superb scenes of the horrid surprises of war, and although he rewrites an alternative death for Hasdrubal, the general defending Carthage, his work rings true. "Carthage must be destroyed" is the endgame of this novel, but the road to that Roman victory is the true reading enjoyment'

Kirkus Reviews

'Simply stunning . . . Gibbins effortlessly creates a rich atmosphere. In my opinion, *Destroy Carthage* is definitely one of the best historical novels of the year. Gibbins has done a stunning job piecing together various historical sources to create an extraordinary tale of Scipio and his role in the siege of Carthage'   Upcoming4.me

'Gibbins really shows that he knows his history, from weapons to siege engines and other units, but also its geography. It's a great feature and an even greater pleasure to read'

TheBookPlank.blogspot.com

TOTAL WAR
ROME
THE SWORD OF ATTILA

TOTAL WAR
ROME
THE SWORD OF ATTILA

DAVID GIBBINS

THOMAS DUNNE BOOKS
ST. MARTIN'S PRESS
NEW YORK

This is a work of fiction. All of the characters, organizations, and events portrayed in this novel are either products of the author's imagination or are used fictitiously.

THOMAS DUNNE BOOKS.
An imprint of St. Martin's Press.

TOTAL WAR ROME: THE SWORD OF ATTILA. Copyright © 2015 by David Gibbins. All rights reserved. Printed in the United States of America. For information, address St. Martin's Press, 175 Fifth Avenue, New York, N.Y. 10010.

www.thomasdunnebooks.com
www.stmartins.com

Library of Congress Cataloging-in-Publication Data

Gibbins, David J. L.
    Sword of Attila / David Gibbins. — First U.S. edition.
        p. cm. — (Total war Rome ; 2)
    ISBN 978-1-250-03895-1 (hardcover)
    ISBN 978-1-4668-3425-5 (e-book)
    1. Attila, –453—Fiction. 2. Huns—Fiction. 3. Rome—History—Empire, 284–476—Fiction. I. Title.
    PR6107.I225S96 2015
    823'.92—dc23

                                                                2014044384

St. Martin's Press books may be purchased for educational, business, or promotional use. For information on bulk purchases, please contact the Macmillan Corporate and Premium Sales Department at 1-800-221-7945, extension 5442, or write to specialmarkets@macmillan.com.

First published in Great Britain by Pan Books, an imprint of Pan Macmillan, a division of Macmillan Publishers Limited

First U.S. Edition: January 2015

10   9   8   7   6   5   4   3   2   1

Historical Introduction

The fifth century AD was one of the most momentous periods in history, a time of violent upheaval and war that marked the transition from the ancient to the early medieval world. Almost five hundred years after Augustus had become the first emperor, and eight hundred years after Rome first embarked on her wars of conquest, the Roman Empire was a waning star, no longer on the offensive but struggling against barbarian invasions that threatened to consume it. Already the unthinkable had happened: the city of Rome itself had been sacked by a marauding army of Goths in AD 408. Much had changed from the glory days of empire three centuries earlier. Rome was now Christian, with a new hierarchy of priests and bishops. The empire had been split in half, with two emperors and new capitals in Constantinople and Milan, both of them riven by dynastic feuds and infighting. The Roman army had changed almost beyond recognition; gone were the legionaries of old, replaced by men likely to have been of barbarian origin themselves. And yet there were still those among the Roman officer class who harked back to the days of old, men steeped in the traditions of the Caesars and the great generals of the Republic, men who believed that the ancient image of Rome could be thrust forward one last time to marshal the army against the forces of darkness that were bearing down upon her, so that if there were to be one final battle they would march forward, upholding the honour of those legionaries and generals of old.

For many, only death and destruction lay ahead. The bishop Augustine forsook earthly pleasures and looked only towards the promise of heaven, to the City of God. The monks of Arles believed that the biblical Apocalypse was upon them. And yet, for the first time in Roman history, we see writers of the day absorbed in what we might term 'grand strategy'. Should Rome appease the barbarians, offering them concessions and land, or should she stand up to them militarily? This debate preoccupied all levels of society, involving even the lowliest soldier in a level of strategic thinking that had been rare among his legionary forbears. The main commentator on the years covered in this novel, Priscus of Panium, was himself a diplomat and much concerned with this issue. His work only survives in fragments, and he had little interest in military detail – my reconstruction of the great sieges and battles of this period required even more imagination than the second-century BC battles described in my previous novel, *Total War Rome: Destroy Carthage*. Nevertheless, just as the historian Polybius was an eyewitness to the destruction of Carthage in 146 BC, so Priscus himself went to the court of Attila the Hun and gives us an extraordinarily vivid picture of what he saw. It is from him that we learn of the myth that the Huns were born of Griffons, of their bloody funeral rituals, of the cult of the sword, of all the reasons Rome had so much to fear from this terrifying new enemy that brought the western empire to the precipice in the middle years of the fifth century AD.

A more detailed summary of this period and of the late Roman army can be found in the Author's Note at the end of this novel, where there is also a note on the historical and archaeological sources.

THE BATTLE OF THE CATALAUNIAN PLAINS
as depicted in this novel

River

ROMANS
Aetius

VISIGOTHS
Theodoric

R I D G E

OSTROGOTHS

HUNS
Attila

GEPIDS

Attila's
Wagon Laager

Schematic depiction, not to scale

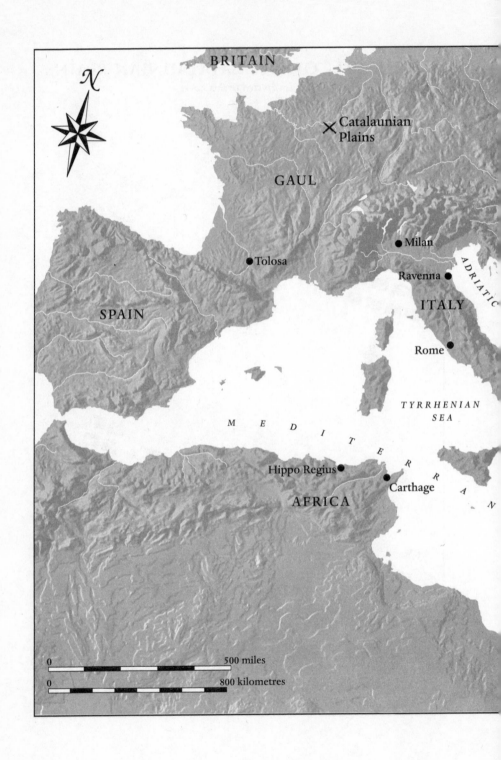

THE MEDITERRANEAN WORLD
5TH CENTURY AD

HUN
CAPITAL

River Danube

BLACK SEA

SEA

Adrianople
GREECE   ✕   Constantinople

AEGEAN SEA

ASIA MINOR

IONIAN
SEA

Athens

E
A
N

S
E   A

SASANIAN
EMPIRE

Alexandria

EGYPT

Glossary

Late-Roman terms used in this novel:

Caesars – Generic term for the early emperors, up to Hadrian

Centurion – A time-honoured rank for the senior non-commissioned officer (NCO) of a numerus (see below)

Comes – 'Count', the commanding officer of a limitanei (frontier) army

Comitatenses – 'Companions' a field army

Dux – 'Duke' the commanding officer of a comitatenses army

Foederati – Barbarian war bands allied to the Romans

Limitanei – A frontier army

Magister – General in overall command of the armies of a diocese or province

Magister Militum – Commander-in-chief

Numerus – Military unit varying in size from under a hundred to several hundred men

Optio – Rank similar to corporal

Sagittarii – Archers

Saxons – Generic for the north Germanic invaders of Britain

Tribune – The officer commanding a *numerus*

Characters

These are actual historical characters unless otherwise indicated.

Aetius – Commander-in-chief of the western Roman army

Anagastus – Roman general under Aetius, along with Aspar

Andag – Gothic henchman of Attila

Apsachos – Fictional Sarmatian archer in Flavius' *numerus*

Ardaric – Commander of the Gepids, under Attila

Arturus – Semi-fictional British warrior monk

Aspar – Roman general under Aetius

Attila – King of the Huns

Bleda – Eldest son of Mundiuk

Cato – Fictional *optio* in Flavius' *numerus*

Dionysius – fictional Scythian monk, teacher of Flavius
    (and grandfather of Dionysius Exiguus, to whom AD dating
    is usually attributed)

Erecan – Daughter of Attila

Eudoxia – Wife of the emperor Valentinian

Flavius – Fictional tribune, nephew of Aetius

Gaiseric – King of the Vandals

Gaudentius – Goth grandfather of Flavius and father of Aetius

Heraclius – Greek eunuch in the court of the emperor Valentinian

Macrobius – Fictional centurion, friend of Flavius

Characters

Marcian – Emperor in the East who succeeded Theodosius

Maximinus – Cavalry tribune in the eastern army

Maximus – Fictional soldier in Flavius' *numerus*

Mundiuk – King of the Huns, father of Attila

Octr – Brother of Mundiuk and Rau

Optila – Hun bodyguard of Erecan, along with Thrastilla

Priscus – Scholar and emissary of Theodosius to Attila

Quintus – Fictional tribune, nephew of Flavius

Quodvultdeus – Bishop of Carthage

Radagaisus – fictional Visigoth commander under Thorismud (and grandson of Radagaisus who invaded Italy in 405)

Rau – Brother of Mundiuk and Octr

Sangibanus – King of the Alans of Orléans

Sempronius – Fictional soldier in Flavius' *numerus*, a veteran of Britain

Theodoric – King of the Visigoths

Theodoric – Youngest son of King Theodoric, and brother of Thorismud

Theodosius – Roman emperor in the East

Thiudimer – Visigoth commander under Thorismud

Thorismud – Son of King Theodoric of the Visigoths

Thrastilla – Hun bodyguard of Erecan, along with Optila

Uago – Fictional senior *fabri* tribune in Rome

Valamer – Ostrogoth commander under Attila

Valentinian – Roman emperor in the West

When a certain cowherd beheld one heifer of his flock limping and could find no cause for this wound, he anxiously followed the trail of blood and at length came to a sword it had unwittingly trampled while nibbling the grass. He dug it up and took it straight to Attila. He rejoiced at this gift and, being ambitious, thought he had been appointed ruler of the whole world, and that through the Sword of Mars supremacy in all wars was assured to him.

JORDANES

(c. AD 550), XXXV, 83, quoting the fifth-century historian Priscus,
an eyewitness to the court of Attila

They are lightly equipped for swift motion, and unexpected in action; they purposely divide suddenly into scattered bands and attack, rushing about in disorder here and there, dealing terrific slaughter . . . you would not hesitate to call them the most terrible of all warriors, because they fight from a distance with missiles . . . then they gallop over the intervening spaces and fight hand-to-hand with swords, regardless of their own lives, and while the enemy are guarding against wounds from the sword-thrusts, they throw strips of cloth plaited into nooses over their opponents and so entangle them that they fetter their limbs.

AMMIANUS MARCELLINUS

(c. AD 380), XXXI, 2, 8–9, on the Huns

PROLOGUE

The Great Hungarian Plain, AD 396

The two Roman prisoners lurched forward, their chains dragging through the wet snow on the slope leading up to the meadow. A harsh wind whipped across the plateau that surrounded the ravine, bringing a sharp bite of winter to those gathered for the ceremony. High above them eagles soared, flown free from the wrists of their masters, waiting for the flesh and gore that would be left for them when the ceremony was over. Around the edge of the meadow great bronze cauldrons sizzled over open fires, the steam from their contents rising to form a thin mist over the people. The rich aroma of cooking meat, of beef and mutton and venison, wafted down the ravine over the circular tents of the encampment, past the spring where the holy water began its journey to the great river two days' ride to the west, at the place where the land of the hunters ended and the empire of Rome began.

The younger of the two prisoners stumbled forward and leaned against the other man, who shouldered him upright and spoke harsh words of command in a language unknown to most of those watching. They wore the ragged remains of what had once been Roman *milites* tunics, stained brown with rust where the chainmail had been, their feet unshod and bloody from days of marching shackled to each other. The older man, grizzled, gaunt, his white stubble broken by long-healed scars on his cheeks and chin, bore weals on his forearm where long ago he had cut the mark of his unit, 'LEGII'. He stared defiantly ahead as his captors pushed him forward; it was the look of a soldier

1

who had stared death in the face too often to be afraid of what he knew must lie ahead of them now.

A horn sounded, shrill and strident, setting off the eagles far above, their raucous cries echoing up and down the ravine. A wagon lumbered into view pulled by two bullocks and surrounded by horsemen, their lances held upright and their bows slung over their backs. They wore leather trousers and tunics, the fur turned inwards against the cold, and they sat on saddles cushioned by slabs of raw meat that oozed and trickled blood down the horses' flanks; the meat protected the animals from saddle sores and provided tenderized food for the men on the long hunt into the steppe-land that would follow the ceremony. The horsemen also wore gleaming conical helmets over wide-rimmed hats of fur with earflaps that could be tied down against the bitter wind of the plateau; over their tunics lay elaborate armour made from small rectangular plates sewn together, acquired by exchanging rare pelts with traders from far-off Serikon, the land the Romans called Thina. From those traders too came the silk that the women in the gathering had wound around their heads, and also the fiery magic that the archers would launch into the sky to signal the end of the ceremony and the beginning of the great feast that would follow far into the night.

The lead rider cantered past the cauldrons through the throng of people, coming to a halt in front of a towering brushwood pyre, not yet lit, that rose to twice his height in the centre of the meadow. He pulled on his reins, the embossed gold leaf on the leather flashing as he did so, and turned around to face the approaching wagon, leaning forward and whispering to his horse as it whinnied and stomped, calming it. When the wagon had stopped he thrust his lance into the ground and took off his helmet, holding it by his side and staring impassively. His forehead was high and sloped from where he had been bound as an infant; his dark hair was tied tightly on top of his head, his long ponytail now falling loose where it had previously been coiled under the conical peak of his helmet. His skin was deeply weathered, and he had the narrow eyes and flat nose that were characteristic of his people; wisps of beard fell from the corners of his mouth. A livid scar ran diagonally across each cheek from temple to chin, long healed but mottled and purple in the frigid air.

He drew himself up on his saddle, his hands on his hips. 'I am Mundiuk, your king,' he said. His voice was harsh, grating, like the cries of the eagles, the words ending in the hard consonants of a language meant to be heard and understood above the howling of the wind. He pointed at the cart. 'And today, if the signs are right, you will see your future king.'

He reined his horse aside, and the boys who were leading the bullocks coaxed them forward until the cart was within the circle of people. It had high wooden sides, its interior concealed from view. As the boys unhitched the bullocks and led them away, four men approached from behind; two held burning torches, another, the firewalker, was dressed in protective leather and carried a heavy bucket, and behind him came the shuffling figure of the shaman, his eyes white and unseeing, dragging the sun-bleached scapula bone of a bull. The firewalker went up to the pyre and tipped from the bucket a load of the heavy black tar that bubbled up from the ground in the ravine, walking around the bundles of brushwood until the bucket was empty and then returning to stand beside the shaman.

Behind them came Mundiuk's personal guard: Alans, Saxons, Angles, renegades from the West, men who would be loyal to the highest bidder, whose fealty he had bought with the gold he had received from the emperor in Constantinople in payment for staying east of the great river. Employing mercenaries was something he had learned from the kings of the Goths, rulers he had courted before crushing them. Once he had become more than a chieftain, once he had become a king, he had learned to trust no one, not even his own brothers. The horsemen of the great plain, his Hun warriors, were the best fighters who had ever lived, but each one of them was a king in the making, used to ruling all that he could see across the steppe-lands stretching to the horizon. And mercenaries would fight to the death, not because of loyalty but because they knew that for a mercenary, surrendering meant certain execution.

The boys who had led the bullocks away had returned and now stood on either side of the cart. Mundiuk nodded, and they unlatched the wooden sides, letting them fall down. Inside, two women crouched in front of another lying on her back in the last stages of labour - Mundiuk's queen. Her face was covered by a veil and she made no sound, but the veil sucked in and out with her breathing and her hands were clenched and white. The other women in the gathering began ululating, swaying to and fro, and the men began to sing in a deep-throated chant, rising in a slow crescendo. There was a movement on the cart, and then one of the women suddenly knelt up and stared at Mundiuk, pointing at the pyre. He put on his helmet and cantered his horse backwards. *It was time.*

He took a burning torch from one of the men and reined his horse around towards the pyre. In one swift movement he swung it over his head and released it, watching it crash and disintegrate in a shower of sparks. At first nothing seemed to happen, as if the pyre had absorbed the flame, but then an orange glow suffused the centre and lines of flame licked out along the splashes of tar, racing around the edge in a ring of fire. The flames leapt up the brushwood and reduced it in seconds to a smouldering mound, revealing an astonishing sight. In the centre, as though it had risen in the clutches of a god, was a gleaming sword, its long blade pointing up to the heavens, its gold-wrapped pommel held on a scorched stone pedestal carved in the shape of a human hand. It was the sacred sword of the Hun kings, brought here by the shaman for the ceremony of renewal, ready to be spirited away

4

again and to await rediscovery just as it had done a generation before when Mundiuk himself had been the future king.

Mundiuk reined his horse around again, the gold trappings resplendent in the reflected flames. The women were still huddled down over the recumbent form in the cart, but in front of it one of the boys who had been standing on either side had stepped forward. By tradition, the task ahead would go to this boy, Bleda, the king's eldest son, whose birth had not been accompanied by propitious signs, but who would be the sword-companion of the future king. Bleda stood uncertainly, his head still bound in coils of wool, his right eye drooping where Mundiuk's sword had slipped on the boy's tears while he was making the cuts on his cheeks borne by all Hun warriors. His arms and legs were swathed in damp cloths, and he looked fearfully at the fire. 'Go,' one of the other boys urged. He began to run forward, yelling in the cracked voice of an adolescent, and then leapt into the embers, his yell turning to shrieks of pain as he scrambled through the flickering pile to the sword. He slipped, and then grabbed the hilt, wrenching it off the pedestal and turning back, stumbling out of the embers towards Mundiuk. He was gasping, his eyes streaming and his hands scorched, but he had done it. A woman hurried out and tossed a bucket of water over him, leaving him sizzling and steaming. He held the sword by the blade and lifted the pommel up to Mundiuk, who took it by the hilt, raised it high and then bellowed, the sound echoing up and down the ravine. It was the Hun battle cry, a cry that brought terror to all who heard it: a cry of death.

Mundiuk touched the freshly whetted blade, drawing blood from his finger, and stared at the two Romans. *One would live, and one would die.* It had been the way of the ceremony for as long as his bloodline had ruled on the great plain. Bleda knew that it was his right to choose. The older Roman scowled at the boy, straining at his chains. Bleda stared back, and then raised his arm, pointing. Mundiuk needed to test the man's mettle, just to be sure he was the right one. He took the club from his saddle that he used to dispatch game, cantered forward and swung it hard against the man's mouth, hearing the crack of broken bone. The man staggered back, but then came upright, his lower jaw shattered. He spat out a mouthful of blood and broken teeth, and glared defiantly at the king. '*Futuere*, barbarian,' he snarled.

Mundiuk stared back at him. He knew what that curse meant. But it was good. These were not like the snivelling eunuch emissaries from Constantinople who had been the only captives they could find for Bleda's birth ceremony, men who had made the mistake of travelling to Mundiuk without gold, who had begged for mercy in their high-pitched voices and who had soiled themselves in front of his queen. When he had seen them face death like that, as cowards, he had known that the signs would not be right, that the gods would not will Bleda to be the next king. But this time it was different. These two were soldiers. They had been captured three weeks before in a raid on a fort on the great river, the river the Romans called Danubius; they had fought like lions but had been lassoed and shackled in their own chains, those they had used to enslave others. Mundiuk's brothers Octr and Rau, who had led the raid, had taunted them about the legendary marching ability of the Romans, but still they had marched on. Mundiuk had seen the scars on the older man's arm, the mark of the legion. Only the toughest would do that to themselves. Octr and Rau had done well. His blood would bring Mundiuk's son into the souls and minds of the greatest enemy his people had ever faced. The other would serve the future king as a slave, and teach him all the tricks of their warriors, their swordsmanship and tactics – he would teach him how to fight like them and how to think like their generals.

He nodded, and the men who formed his bodyguard kicked the two prisoners forward onto their knees. The blood welled up in the older man's mouth, but still he stayed upright, staring ahead. He growled to the other in the language of the Romans, words that Mundiuk understood: 'Remember our comrades, brother. Remember those who have gone before. They wait for us on the other side.'

The young soldier was shaking, his face ashen and his eyes bloodshot, the look of a youth who had begun to realize the unimaginable; he was not to know that he might be spared. In his shackled hands he held something, grasping it so tight that his knuckles had gone white. He raised his arms up towards the fire, working the object up between his fingers until it was visible, a crude wooden cross that looked as if he had made it himself. He held it silhouetted against the flames and began mouthing incantations, the words of the brown-robed priests who had once long ago made the journey to the people of the plain to show them the bleeding god of the cross, a god who seemed to them to be one of weakness and capitulation, a god whom they despised.

Mundiuk saw the cross and became enraged. He changed his mind; the other would be spared. He bellowed, held up the great sword and leapt off his horse, pushing Bleda aside and striding towards the young soldier. In one sweep he cut off both of his hands, sending the cross cartwheeling into the fire. He threw the sword up into the air, grasped the hilt as it came down blade-first and drove it straight through the man's neck and torso into the ground, pinning it there. The soldier belched blood, his open eyes glazed, and then he slumped over, his wrists spurting red and his head lolling forward. Mundiuk bellowed again, pounding his fists on his chest, and his men bellowed back. He put his foot on the man's shoulder and pulled out the sword, wiping the blood from it on his cheeks, licking the flat of the blade. He picked up the Roman by the hair and decapitated him, hurling the head into the fire, and then thrust his blade into the centre of the torso, ripped out the heart and holding it high, squeezing it until all of the blood had gushed down his arm and over his tunic, letting the final drops trickle into his mouth before throwing it back down on the body.

He had remembered the words of the shaman. *To kill the victims once was not enough. For the sacrifice to work you must kill them many times over, again and again, until the gods were satisfied, banging down their tankards in the heavens with each blow, their spilled beer mingling with the gore of the victims.*

Behind him men threw more bundles of wood on the fire and the firewalker placed the bull's scapula in the embers. Mundiuk held the sword high, its blade shining with blood, and turned towards the cart. The men roared in anticipation and the women began to chant. One of the women in the cart turned and held up the baby, a boy, and the noise increased to a crescendo. Mundiuk scooped him up in his left hand and held him aloft. He stared into the eyes, slits of darkness that seemed to bore through him, reflecting the fire. The omen was good. The baby had not yet cried. *He must bleed before he cries.*

He raised the sword until the tip brushed one cheek, streaking the baby with the soldier's blood. Mundiuk remembered the words he had been taught. *The blood of the enemy will mingle with the blood of the king. Only then will you know your enemy, and know how to defeat him. You will become one with him.* He pressed the blade in, cutting through the boy's cheek to the jawbone, and did the same on the other side, watching the droplets of blood cascade off the blade into the air, hearing the chants turn to ululations, seeing the flames rise up above the pyre. The baby still had not uttered a sound.

He looked to the sky. The cries of the eagles had increased to a crescendo, shrieking and rasping, drowning out the crackling of the fire. The smell and heat of the entrails had excited them. Far above he could see the ripples of cloud streaming to the west, like an unstoppable river torrent. One of the eagles, the largest, had separated itself from the rest and was swooping down in ever-decreasing circles, the rush of its wings sounding louder each time it swept over the meadow. Mundiuk quickly stepped back, and his men pressed against the people to make space. Suddenly the bird tucked its wings and dropped down into the circle, aiming straight for the bloody torso and the Roman's heart. With its prize in its talons it flapped its huge wings again, lifting the heart from the body, dragging a ribbon of entrails along with it as it rose and flew off to the east, to the distant eyrie in the mountains where it would gorge on its share of the feast.

Mundiuk breathed in deeply, savouring the coppery smell of fresh blood. The omens had been good. *The sword had spoken.* He handed the baby back to the woman below. He himself had seen the carvings of eagles in the cliff above the Iron Gates, near the ruined bridge and the fort on the river where they had captured the Romans. The eagles had once been sacred to the Romans, their image carried aloft on standards above the soldiers in the carvings; but it was said that after the Romans had failed to take the lands beyond the Danube the eagles had flown away in disgust, returning east to their ancestral eyries, seething with dishonour and betrayal. The soldiers in the forts on the river now followed the god of the cross, a god not of war but of peace, a god whom Mundiuk could only regard with contempt. And now the eagles had found new masters, horsemen who would one day sweep all before them in their drive to bring the eagles their revenge, led by a king who would tear the heart out of Rome itself.

There was a commotion by the fire, and Mundiuk turned to watch the shaman and the firewalker use a stick to pull the scapula out of the embers. They doused it with a bucket of water, making it hiss and crackle. The shaman knelt down beside it, muttering to himself, and the other man guided his hand to the flat of the shoulder blade, its surface scorched and covered with fine cracks. For a few minutes the shaman traced his fingers over the bone, reading it as only he knew how, muttering, occasionally raising his sightless eyes towards the heat of the fire, then looking down again. After a final pause he struggled to his feet, helped by the firewalker. He took his staff and hobbled towards Mundiuk, the whites of his eyes flickering red with the fire. Mundiuk laid the flat of the sword across his shoulder, feeling the wet slick of blood against his neck. 'Well, old man?'

The shaman raised his hand. 'You must take the sword and bury it in the pastureland above the great lake, below the eyries of the eagles. If when the boy has come of age a shepherd brings a bull before him with a bleeding leg, then the boy will know that the sword has risen and is awaiting him where the bull was injured. If when he finds it the blade is burnished and shiny, the edges sharp as if freshly whetted, then the sword is yearning for blood, and he will know his destiny.'

Another eagle swooped down from on high, crying raucously, taking a morsel held up for it by the shaman and flapping heavily off to the west, bringing in its wake a gust of cold air that drew the flames flickering towards the king. Soon the rest would be following, swooping down to rip away morsels. Mundiuk went to his horse, grasped its mane with his free hand and leapt on, still holding the sword. One of the women passed the baby back to him, swaddled now, its face cleaned of blood. He held the sword behind him with one hand and the baby in the air with the other, so that all could see. Every muscle in his body was tensed, and he felt the battle lust surge through him. He stared again into the eyes of his son, and at the raw wounds on his cheeks. 'You will learn the ways of our people,' he said. 'You will learn the way of the bow, of the sword and the lasso, of the horse. You will learn the language and ways of our enemy, not to converse with him but to learn his tactics and his ways in war, to know how to destroy him. Your army will travel faster than the news of its coming. Only when the rivers run red with the blood of Hun warriors and their lifeblood is extinguished will your conquests cease.'

The shaman limped up to the horse, his arms stretched out in front of him; then, finding the reins, he held them and raised his sightless eyes towards the rider. 'What will you name him?'

Mundiuk stared at the sword, the sword that bore an ancient name in their language, a name that few had ever dared speak, and then stared at the boy again.

You will bear the name of the one who scarred you. You will become one with him.

You will not just be a leader in war.

You will be the god of war.

He raised the boy high, and bellowed out the name.

'*Attila.*'

PART ONE

CARTHAGE,
NORTH AFRICA

AD 439

1

A dog howled, a strange, unearthly sound that pierced the still air of the morning and echoed down the barren valley between the desert and the sea. The man on the parapet stood up, his cloak wrapped around him against the cold, thankful for his sheepskin boots and the woollen trousers and tunic that he wore under his chainmail, and listened hard. Sound travelled far across the treeless African hills, but this was close, no more than an hour's march away. He glanced at the men trying to sleep in the trench behind him, restless, uneasy, as if the dog were entering their dreams, and for a moment he wondered whether he too were in a kind of netherworld, his senses numbed by cold and lack of sleep. But then the howling began again, not just one dog but several, an eerie crescendo that rose and wavered like a gust of wind, and then died away again. This time he knew it was real. He felt a sudden chill down his spine, not of cold but of something else, and quickly clapped his hands together and stamped his feet. He knew that many of the men would be awake now, their bleary eyes watching him, the night sentries spaced down the line looking to him for orders. He must keep his nerve. *He must not show his fear.*

'Pass the word along. The cities of Africa Proconsularis to the west have fallen. Bishop Augustine is dead. The army of the Vandals is coming.'

The soldier who had brought the message paused to catch his breath, his face pinched with cold and his eyes bloodshot and exhausted beneath the rim of his helmet. Flavius stopped clapping his hands and stared at him, his mind struggling to take the news in, and then nodded, watching as the man stumbled over the forms of men still sleeping in the trench towards the next sentry, repeating his message in a hoarse whisper. *The western cities have fallen.* Flavius clapped his hands again, trying to control his shivering. The daylight hours were tolerably warm, but the African night in early spring was still bitterly cold, keeping him awake for the brief time he had allowed himself to lie down and try to get some sleep. He climbed the rough earthen side of the parapet they had piled up the evening before and stared out to the west. Hippo Regius had been the last bastion on the African shore before Carthage, the ancient city whose western walls loomed out of the mist less than a mile behind him. For almost six hundred years Carthage had been in Roman hands, the centre of the wealthiest province in the western empire. And now even Bishop Augustine had forsaken them. Eight years ago, when the Vandals had taken his bishopric of Hippo Regius and made it their stronghold, there had been rumours that he had starved to death during the siege, but his fate had never been confirmed; now they knew it was true, that he had finally abandoned his earthly city for the City of God, the only place where he could find protection against the coming onslaught.

Above him the sky was reddening, streaked with the sunlight that was just appearing over the horny-tipped mountain to the east of Carthage. The air still smelled like the night, damp, humic, on one side suffused with the tang of the sea, on the other side with the gritty reek of the desert. Polybius more than five hundred years before had written of the taste in the air before Carthage, a taste like blood, and Flavius thought he could sense it now, an acrid coppery odour that seemed to rise with the dust above the hills. They were wedged between the two worlds, between the sea and the desert, defending a narrow corridor in which would soon flow a torrent of death, as if the floodwaters of a great river were building up in the hills and ravines to the west, about to come rushing down upon them, unassailable, impossible to resist.

He picked up his sword, buckled it on under his cloak and then raised his helmet, seeing where the gold leaf of a tribune's rank that he had ordered in the workshop in Milan had already become dislodged and soiled, even before he had seen any action. He stooped over, spat on it and began rubbing it with a corner of his cloak, and then looked around as someone came up from the direction of the cooking fire behind the ridge. 'You don't want to do that, Flavius Aetius,' the man said, speaking Latin with the rough accent of the Danube frontier. 'Unless, that is, you want to make yourself conspicuous for the first barbarian spear-thrust.'

'The men should see my rank and know who to follow,' Flavius replied, trying to sound stern.

The other man snorted. 'In this man's army, everyone leads from the front,' he said. 'It's not like the army of your revered ancestors of the time of Scipio and Caesar, full of feathered helmets and polished breastplates like those you see in the sculptures in the forum of Rome. In this man's army, if a tribune wants the respect of his men, he leads *primus inter pares* – first among many. That way, if he gets killed his unit doesn't falter, as those around him fill the gap and another takes his place. And if you want to show your men who to respect, you should smear that gold leaf with dirt and sweat from digging the trenches and then with sticky gore from the bowels of your enemies. I bet they didn't teach you that in the *schola militarum* in Rome. Think about it, and then get some food. I'm going to inspect the men's weapons.'

Flavius looked thoughtfully at his helmet, and then at the other man as he left. Macrobius Vipsanius was heavily muscled, shorter than the usual Illyrian, the almond shape of his eyes betraying some distant lineage from beyond the Scythian steppes. As a centurion he seemed as Roman as they came, yet in his blood he was a barbarian. Flavius himself was hardly much different, being descended on his mother's side from the ancient *gens* Julia, but on his father's side from a Goth warlord. Many of the soldiers were like that now, a result of integration and intermarriage, of appeasement and land settlement inside the frontiers, of the need to recruit more and more barbarian warriors to keep the Roman army up to strength. Barbarian chieftains such as Flavius' grand-father had admired the Roman martial tradition and sent their sons to military school in Milan and Rome, but there was always something that set those men apart, some kind of edge, some-thing that Flavius had seen in his father and uncle and hoped he had himself. It was a restlessness that had driven other barbarians who had not sent their sons to Rome, who had not admired her ways, to burn and ravage their way across the empire, to do what some thought impossible and make the sea voyage across the Pillars of Hercules from Spain to Africa, transforming and adapting like some great shape-shifting beast, to begin their relentless march along the African shore towards Carthage. And everyone knew that the march of the Vandals was merely a portent of things to come, that for every tribe that Rome appeased, for every warrior band integrated, there was another more belligerent force lurking behind in the forests and on the steppes; and that behind them was a power like nothing ever seen before, a warrior army bent solely on destruction that threatened to eclipse Rome not by settlement and treaty, but by fire and the sword.

Flavius had first met Macrobius only three weeks before when he had disembarked at Carthage with the other new tribunes and been put in charge of the reconnaissance *numerus* of the city garrison, his first field command. Half of the officer candidates who had gone through the *schola militarum* in Rome with him had been veterans like Macrobius, men who had risen from the ranks and been recommended by the *comes* of their frontier force or the *dux* of their field army. The military council of the emperor had deliberately sited the *schola* in the old city not just to remind the cadets of the past glories of the empire, but to keep them away from the imperial courts at Ravenna and Milan where the privileged younger cadets like Flavius might draw on patronage to ease their way through the training programme and gain favours. Macrobius himself would have scorned the *schola* and been wasted in it. He was a born centurion, superb at making a fighting unit out of the eighty-odd men of a frontier *numerus* but preferring to leave the life-and-death decisions to a tribune he respected. He relished his ancient rank – one derived from the fact that his parent unit was the famous Twentieth Legion Valeria Victrix, once the pride of the Roman garrison in Britannia, but with the withdrawal from that province thirty years before, now reduced to a unit of the African frontier army. His soldiers joked that he was the last centurion of ancient Rome. Given the likely outcome of today's events, they might well be proved right.

In the weeks before Flavius had arrived, Macrobius had been given the task of scratching together the reconnaissance unit from among the frontier troops of the desert who had come streaming into Carthage with the threat from the west, their forts abandoned and the frontier contracted to the defensive perimeter they were now occupying within sight of the walls of Carthage itself. The numbers in the city garrison were desperate: fewer than a thousand men of the depleted Twentieth Legion along with the equivalent of three *numeri* of frontier *limitanei*, a little under three hundred additional men all told. Even within the city the garrison was stretched hopelessly thin, with large sectors of the city wall manned only by sentries, scarcely enough to alert the garrison commander of an approaching enemy let alone mount any kind of serious response. With no hope of further reinforcements, the defence of Carthage was now a matter of upholding Roman prestige and honour, of fighting to the death, and of suicidal bravery and doing enough against the odds to ensure that history did not remember the end of Roman North Africa as an ignominious rout and a massacre.

Flavius put these thoughts from his mind and focused on his men. Unlike the volunteer legionaries of the past, they were almost all conscripts, with the exception of the Illyrians from the Danube, who represented the nearest that Rome still had to a professional cadre motivated by a martial tradition. Yet Macrobius had shown him that even the least promising no-hoper could be knocked into some kind of shape, that there was always some strength to be found somewhere. The greatest strength of this army of Christian Rome lay in the compact size of its units, for they were less complex to manage than the old legions and better suited to dispersed deployment and small engagements. Flavius had paid the soldiers a bonus in gold *solidi* out of his own pocket, always a good start for a new commander, and with Macrobius to guide him, he had tried to build up their *esprit de corps*, telling them of the old generals and wars, of Scipio Africanus and the Roman capture of Carthage; he had told them that there was no reason why they should not be as good as the soldiers of the Caesars, and that even then it had been the frontier auxiliaries, like the modern *limitanei*, who had done the brunt of the soldiering.

In the three weeks before their forward deployment to this ridge Flavius had joined with the men as a common soldier while Macrobius had trained them, relentlessly marching them in the African sun, leading them on practice reconnaissance missions miles into the wasteland to the south of Carthage; they had used Numidian guides to teach them how to find water and a semblance of warmth at night, something Flavius himself had signally failed to do over the past few hours. He remembered all the training, all of the exercises, and slapped his hands together again for warmth, looking along the crest of the ridge where they were dug in. Beyond the dip it was cut through by the road to Carthage, the route an attacker would have to take from the west. Half of his men were dug in on one side and half on the other, and behind them he could just make out the shallow ravine with the water hole and the cooking fire, the wispy smoke from breakfast preparations curling above the rise. The smaller the unit the easier it was to keep an eye on the men, he thought wryly to himself, and the easier they were to feed; there was something to be said for the size of his command.

He watched as Macrobius worked his way towards him beside the trench, running his finger along the men's sword blades, licking his finger when it drew blood, leaving the blade unsheathed to be sharpened when it did not. Despite Flavius' inexperience, he knew that Macrobius respected him for volunteering for the forward unit when none of the other officers in the garrison would do so, and in turn Flavius respected Macrobius for seeming to care nothing that Flavius' uncle Aetius was *magister militum* of the western Roman empire, second in power only to the emperor Valentinian himself. Out here, on the front line, old-fashioned patronage and family connections were of no consequence, and all that mattered was whether a soldier had the courage to stand his ground and fight to the death for the man beside him. Flavius had begun to understand that nurturing this quality among his men was more important than all of the tactics and strategy he had learned in the *schola militarum* in Rome, and that his success as the leader of a small unit like this in the little time he had would depend on listening to Macrobius and heeding his advice.

Macrobius returned to him, wiping his hand on his jerkin and blowing his nose into the dirt with his fingers. 'If this was a training exercise, I'd crucify them,' he grumbled. 'More than half of their swords had spots of rust on the blades. If the edge is dull, they may as well use the flat of the blade for all the good it will do them.'

'All of the remaining oil had to be used for cooking last night, and without a good oiling the blades rust in hours,' Flavius said. 'Where's the farrier?'

'With the *optio* at the fire. He's setting up the grinding stone now. I'll see that the men sharpen their blades when they go for breakfast.'

Flavius jerked his head towards the southern end of the parapet, where he could see the messenger returning. 'Have you heard the news?'

Macrobius nodded grimly. 'A straggler first brought it in about an hour ago, while you were asleep. They've been coming in from the west over the past few hours, mostly Numidian slaves who can barely string two words of Latin together and are too shocked and exhausted to tell us much. We need to find someone with authority who can give us good intelligence.'

Flavius put on his helmet, stepped up to the highest point of the parapet and stared over the ridge. Refugees had been trickling in from the west ever since the *numerus* had deployed to this place, survivors of the towns and cities that had fallen to the Vandal army all the way from the Pillars of Hercules. Macrobius came up beside him, his grey stubble glinting in the dawn light and his Pannonian felt cap compressed in the shape of his helmet, solidified from years of wearing it beneath. Together they scanned the horizon to the west, the folds and valleys still obscured by the early-morning shadows. Macrobius squinted and pointed. 'Over there, about two miles away, to the south-west. Coming from that direction marks them out from the other refugees, as anyone wanting to evade capture would have swung south from the western cities and made their way east towards us along the edge of the desert – harsh terrain where they'd be less likely to be pursued. They might be escaped citizens rather than spared slaves like those Numidians. Three, maybe four people, and two animals.'

Flavius followed his gaze, seeing nothing. 'Your eyesight is better than mine, centurion.'

'I've served for twenty-two years in the *limitanei* frontier army, ten of them out here in Africa on the edge of the great desert. You get good at spotting distant smudges in the dust.'

A half-asleep-sounding voice grumbled from among the recumbent forms lying behind them in the trench, most of them now awake, 'Join the *limitanei*, they said. See the frontiers of the empire, they said. Eat boar and venison every day, take your choice of local women and select a hundred *iugera* of prime land as a retirement present. Never have to raise your spear in anger. Meet fascinating barbarian tribesmen.'

'Too right,' another growled. 'Fascinating, that is, in the few moments you get to see them in a blur of warpaint and screaming as they hurtle out of the forest towards you. Then, if you're lucky enough to survive, you get shipped to the other side of the empire to this place and told to dig a trench and wait for the same thing to happen again.'

'And meanwhile, the *comitatenses* field army are skulking in the towns and around the emperor, growing fat and rich at our expense.'

Macrobius cocked an eye at Flavius. 'Have you heard that one before?'

'About the *comitatenses*? It's all I ever hear,' Flavius said.

'The *comitatenses* say the same thing about the *limitanei*. Each one thinks the other is second-rate. If it isn't a grumble about that, it'd be something else. It's the same with soldiers the world over. Gripe, gripe, gripe.' He turned to the men, speaking more loudly. 'And looking at you lot, I might just agree with the *comitatenses*.'

'And we never get paid,' the first man added, blearily getting up.

'We haven't been paid since my father's day,' the other one complained. 'If it wasn't for the bounties given by the emperors or the odd generous-minded commander wanting us actually to fight for them, we'd be no better off than slaves.'

'You'll get yours, Maximus Cunobelinus,' Flavius said. 'I was true to my word and gave you each a bonus of five *solidi* when you passed inspection as a unit, and you or your families will get five more when this is over. That's equal to two years' pay. I sent instructions to the chief accountant of my uncle Aetius in Milan to receive entreaties from any woman or child whose name accords with the list that I sent him two weeks ago from Carthage. Your families will be well looked after.'

'What about yours, tribune? Who gets your bounty?'

Flavius cleared his throat. They knew perfectly well that he received no pay, that his income came from the wealth of his family. 'A tenth of my gold goes to the Basilica of St Peter in Rome, for the glory of God.'

The soldier blew his nose messily on the ground. 'The Church has too much money, in my opinion. Jesus was a poor man like us, and he had no need of priests with fancy vestments or towering marble basilicas. We're the true soldiers of Christ, not the priests.'

The other man, a Sarmatian archer named Apsachos, grunted and got up. 'Anyway, gold *solidi* are of no use out here. I don't see a market anywhere in this godforsaken desert to buy food. And I'm starving.'

Macrobius dropped down into the trench and stood in front of the two soldiers. 'Well, then you're in luck. The cooking fire smells ready to me. As you're the first to get up, I'm detailing you and the rest of your section for first call at breakfast. There's a haunch of venison and a bowl of broth for each of you. Take your swords and get them sharpened. When you're done, come back here and I'll detail off the next section. And remember, if I see any of you pissing or shitting anywhere except in the latrine trench you know what your next job will be.'

The two soldiers jumped out of the trench followed by the dozen or so other men who had been slumbering nearby, all wide awake at the mention of food. Macrobius made his way up the trench to the *optio* of the next section. The waft of boiled and roasted meat had made Flavius salivate; he suddenly realized how famished he was. One advantage of being in a forward reconnaissance unit was that his command included a detachment of *sagittarii* like the Sarmatian Apsachos – archers were as useful for foraging as they were in battle. The previous evening in a wooded oasis they had cornered and shot three of the European deer that had been stocked there centuries before when the Romans had first taken over those lands after the Punic Wars, making them into a vast hunting preserve. Flavius had thrilled to the chase, forgetting the coming onslaught, his exuberance taking him back to his boyhood years when he learnt to hunt with his father and uncles in the forests of central Gaul. The deer would provide a hearty breakfast for all sixty of the men ranged along the hilltop, and the cook had made a hot drink from the broth.

Flavius tried to ignore the rumbling in his stomach and the knowledge that hot food would help against the cold. *Primus inter pares* or not, one thing he would not do was to go ahead of his men to the cooking fire. Despite their griping and ribald humour, these were some of the toughest men left in the African garrison, and they all knew that this meal was likely to be their last. If he were to lead them to their deaths in battle, he would at least have the satisfaction of knowing that he had fulfilled his responsibility as a commander and provided for their families and their stomachs.

He swallowed hard and looked ahead. The men not yet at breakfast were already standing to along the parapet, silent, swords loosened in their scabbards and spears ready, the archers holding their bows unslung, all of them staring at the horizon as Flavius was, looking for the first hints of what was to come. He saw one man make the sign of Christ, and he glanced back at the huge wooden cross that had been erected outside the walls of Carthage, standing there like the cross of the crucifixion that was still said to tower over the rock of Calvary in Jerusalem. The Carthage cross had been made from charred timbers found outside the walls from buildings destroyed when Scipio took the city, and it seemed to stand there now as a symbol of past glory, as a talisman against the coming evil. And yet the cross was behind them, invisible when they turned to face the enemy, as if

Christ himself were fearful of straying too far forward into the jaws of hell, as if the thin line of soldiers had been thrust into a hinterland where even the power of the Lord would be swept aside by the violence of war.

He thought of what the soldier had said about the wealth of the Church and the poverty of Jesus. It had been over a hundred years since the emperor Constantine had thrown away the mantle of the old gods and embraced the cross – years that some in secret were no longer calculating *ab urbe condita*, meaning since the foundation of the city, but *anno domini nostri iesu* – in the year of Our Lord Jesus Christ. Flavius himself had been taught Greek by the monk Dionysius from Scythia, and it was he who in secret had come up with the new dating system, the little monk whose books he used to carry while he had scurried to and fro between the Greek and Latin libraries on either side of Trajan's Column in Rome, selecting works of Christian virtue to be copied in the *scriptoria* and others to be discarded as amoral and corrupt. On hearing of his appointment to Carthage, Flavius had revisited the Greek library in order to consult the military historians, and he had been shocked by the gaps on the shelves; he had taken away Polybius' work on Carthage in order to preserve it from the monks, on the ostensible grounds that it would be needed in the field as a training manual for the fighting to come.

It was a changing world, and not just in the libraries. The old patrician families were still there, the senators and equestrians, the ancient *gens* like his mother's family, but their power was in name only; the new aristocracy consisted of the priests and the bishops. Christians for generations now had been able to worship openly, free at last from centuries of persecution; the old temples had been converted into churches, and new basilicas had been completed. Yet many eschewed those places and continued to worship privately in their houses or in secret underground rooms, in caves and catacombs. For them, the promise of Christianity had been of a religion without priests, a religion of the common people, and the Church of Rome and of Constantinople was nothing more than the old religion in a new guise, with arcane rituals and fear of divine retribution and obligatory paths to salvation that enslaved the congregation to the priesthood. And for the emperors and the generals, the peace-loving prophet of the Gospels was no longer sufficient to gird the Church for its role in the war of all wars, for the coming darkness; Christ needed now to be armoured, to be recreated in the image of Mars Ultor – the Avenger – to be placed in front of the soldiers on the battle-field to dissuade them from dropping their arms and following the path of Augustine to the City of God where the priests could hold no sway and the only emperor was the true divinity.

Flavius turned and saw the distant cloud of dust that Macrobius had spotted to the south-west, and took a deep breath. There were no priests here today, and there was no flaming cross for the soldiers to follow. What mattered now was not the smiting power of the Lord or the mercy of Christ but the small superstitions and rituals that had kept soldiers' courage up since time immemorial: snatched prayers, a lucky charm, a statuette of a loved one tucked into a pouch on a belt. He pulled out the little silver cross he wore around his neck, held it tight for a few moments and then folded it back under his chainmail. The time had passed even for that. All that mattered now was to keep his nerve, to keep fear at bay, to focus on cold steel and battle lust and the desire to kill.

2

Flavius pulled the last tendrils of meat off the leg of venison with his teeth and tossed the bone away, wiping the grease from his stubble with the back of his sleeve. He already felt better, and could sense the beginning of something like warmth spreading through his body. He turned away the offer of wine, fearful of becoming drowsy, and instead took the drink that Macrobius had passed him – *catha*, an infusion of leaves from the eastern desert that the frontier soldiers had learnt from the nomads to drink to keep themselves awake. He drained the wooden bowl and passed it back to Macrobius, who took a wad of the leaves and shoved them in his cheek, chewing them and spitting out the pieces of stem. He eyed Flavius, speaking with his cheek full. 'Once you've developed a taste for this stuff, the infusion isn't enough,' he said. 'You've no idea what it's like spending months in a desert outpost trying to keep awake.'

'Now I think I understand why your night vision is so good,' Flavius said. Since taking the drink the light seemed sharper, clearer, as if his point of vision had been projected forward slightly. He pointed to the south-west. 'They're coming now, up the rise. No more than two *stades* distant. Should I order the men to stand to?'

'Your call, tribune.'

Flavius looked down the line. 'The final section can continue eating. The rest stand to behind the parapet with helmets on and swords drawn. *Sagittarii* to be spaced at five-man intervals with an arrow ready to be drawn. They are only to shoot on my command.'

'*Ave*, tribune.' Macrobius conveyed the order to his senior *optio*, and the clunk of armour and swords could be heard down the trench on either side as the men stood at the ready. He turned back to Flavius and the two men marched up to the parapet and stood again on it, Macrobius with his feet planted firmly apart and his hand on his sword pommel, his helmet now in place over his felt cap. Flavius loosened his sword, feeling the dust of the air in his mouth again. The group of refugees came into view, three men and a mule, slowly making their way towards the parapet, the man in front holding up a cross that looked as if it had been hastily made from two branches and some cord. There was a shuffling and muttering among the soldiers behind Flavius. 'The Vandals claim to be Christians too,' one of them said. 'We shouldn't trust that cross. I say shoot them.'

'Only some of them are Christian and it's a pretty strange sort. Anyway, that one in front is wearing a cassock. He's clearly a monk.'

'Shut it,' Macrobius snarled out of the side of his mouth, 'or I'll have both of you out there for target practice.'

The man in the cassock came to within twenty yards of them, and then passed the reins of the mule to one of his two companions, both of them Nubians wearing little more than loincloths. The man took off his hood, revealing the long hair and beard of a penitent monk. He raised his hand to shade his eyes and then scanned the parapet, spotting Flavius' helmet and advancing a few steps towards him. The archer behind Flavius drew his bow, but Flavius put out his hand and stayed him. 'Identify yourself,' he demanded.

'I am a man of God.'

'We can see what you are pretending to be,' Macrobius snarled. 'Where do you come from?'

'I come from Hippo Regius. I am Arturus, Bishop Augustine's scribe.'

'Arturus. That's a pretty funny kind of name,' Macrobius said suspiciously, drawing his sword half out of its scabbard. 'Sounds Vandal to me.'

'It's British.'

Macrobius snorted. 'What's a British monk doing in the African desert?'

'Unless I mistake your accent and appearance, I could equally ask what an Illyrian, possibly even a Rhaetian from the Danube with something Scythian about him, is doing out here.'

Macrobius' nostrils flared, and Flavius put out his arm to restrain him. 'Tell us what has become of Bishop Augustine.'

Arturus paused. 'We left Hippo Regius in secret when the Vandals appeared on the western horizon. We lived in hiding in a monastery close to the great desert, working on his final writings. When he entered his final illness he ordered me away, to preserve his books. They're here, in my saddlebags. I took a southerly route on the edge of the great desert, known to my Nubian companions, to avoid being pursued, but fortunately the Vandals lingered in the cities to pillage and burn and showed little interest in those who had escaped; they know they will get us all in the end. As for Bishop Augustine, I can only fear the worst.'

'We hear he is dead.'

Arturus bowed his head. 'I confirmed the rumour among the refugees that he had died in Hippo Regius. It is as Augustine himself would have willed it.'

Flavius eyed the man, trying to weigh him up. 'What of the Vandal army?'

'You will know that they are led by King Gaiseric. You will also know that Bonifatius, *magister* of the African field army and *comes Africae*, has gone over to the enemy, so that almost all of Roman Africa is already in Gaiseric's hands except for here at Carthage. Gaiseric went back on his word and slaughtered most of the *comitatenses* who gave themselves up to him, so there is no augmentation of his force as a result of Bonifatius' treachery, but it makes little odds as Gaiseric has more than twenty thousand Vandal warriors at his disposal, all of them drunk on blood. He also has almost a thousand Alans.'

'Alans?' one of the men said, his tone hushed. 'Out here?'

Arturus nodded, his face set grimly. 'Gaiseric now styles himself *Dux Vandales et Alanes*. The tribal chieftains of the Alans are subordinate to him. He uses them to spearpoint his attacks. They stand feet taller than the rest – blond, blue-eyed giants. Everything and everyone has fallen before their onslaught.' He paused again, squinting at the Roman soldiers. 'But if you're interested, I know a way to kill them. If you've got the guts for it.'

'That's a bold assertion for a monk,' Flavius said. 'And also a pretty astute tactical assessment. Are you one of Augustine's converts? A soldier-turned-monk?'

A gust of wind, hot and dry, lifted Arturus' cassock, and Flavius saw a glint of metal beneath, the sheath of a sword that looked like an old-fashioned *gladius*. He narrowed his eyes at the man and jerked his head towards the sword. 'You monks engage in close-quarter fighting, then?'

Arturus stared back, his eyes cold and hard, and then swept open his cassock so that the hilt was there for all to see. 'You weren't at Hippo Regius,' he said quietly. He pulled out the sword and placed the flat of the blade on the palm of his hand. It was an old sword, its edge irregular where dents and dings had been ground out, but the clean parts were gleaming and sharp. A smear of dried blood covered the blade near the hilt, where it had coagulated in a thick layer. 'I haven't had a chance to clean and oil it properly,' he said. 'We've been on the move continuously since I left Augustine, and I've had a few encounters with Vandal marauders.'

The Sarmatian Apsachos standing behind Flavius unsheathed his own blade, a much longer sword, and held it so it glinted in the haze. 'Thrust the blade into the sand,' he said. 'That's how we used to clean ours when we were based in the desert. It does the trick in seconds, and polishes them as well.'

Arturus jerked his head back to indicate his two companions. 'The Nubian warriors believe that to thrust your blade into the sand is bad luck. They believe that to do so would be to pierce the skin of Mother Earth, that the wells would dry up and your enemy would be upon you. They wipe down their blades and clean them with olive oil. They may be heathen and superstitious, but out here I'm inclined to go along with them.'

Apsachos looked at his sword blade, grunted and then resheathed it. 'Well, that's just great,' he muttered. 'As if things aren't bad enough out here without an ill omen.'

The shadow of a smile passed across the monk's lips and he turned to Flavius. 'In answer to your question, I've always favoured close-quarter fighting over the arm's-length tactics taught to Roman infantrymen these days. Using those long swords and thrusting spears in massed formation to repel a charging enemy is all very well as long as the enemy doesn't break through your lines, and anyway it's not the kind of fighting that's in my blood.'

'Which is?' Flavius said, looking at the monk quizzically.

The man paused, looked down the line of soldiers and then lowered his sword, holding out his right hand. 'Gaius Arturus Prasotagus, former commander of the *Cohortes Britannicus* of the *Comites Praenesta Gallica*, the field army of the North.'

Flavius looked the man in the eye, made his decision and then took his hand. 'Flavius Aetius Secundus, tribune of the *protectores numerus* of the Twentieth Victrix legion, the forward scouts of the Carthage garrison.' He swept his hand along the trench. 'These are my men.'

Flavius sensed Macrobius tense and saw him slide his hand down again to his sword hilt. 'Wait a moment,' the centurion growled. 'Wasn't that the unit that deserted in Gaul? That went over to the barbarians? That killed Romans?' There was a general movement among the soldiers, their eyes fixing suspiciously on the monk, weapons being drawn. Flavius held up his hand. 'Let him have his say. And he is now a man of the cloth.'

'Or pretends to be,' Macrobius muttered.

Arturus reached up and pulled down the cassock at his neck, revealing an old scar that ran from below his left ear across his neck to the opposite collar bone. 'When I was six years old, the Saxons came across the sea and overran the shore fort where I lived, slaughtering my mother and sisters and cutting my throat, leaving me for dead. My father was the garrison commander.'

Flavius turned to the soldier behind him, a grizzled veteran even older than Macrobius who had been kept with the unit because of his skills as an archer. 'You were there, weren't you, Sempronius, in Britannia at the end?'

The man lowered his bow, leaned over and spat. 'I was there, all right. A teenage recruit with the *classis Britannicus*, the British fleet, manning the shore fort at Dover. We were the last to leave, having overseen the withdrawal of all the troops from the northern frontier and the other shore forts. There was no glory in it. It was not even a fighting retreat. We withdrew under cover of darkness, poling off our transport barges from the very place where Caesar had landed almost five hundred years before. Those were the days when Rome was led by strong men. We were led by that weakling emperor Honorius, who abandoned Britain and left the civilians to their fate.'

Arturus listened gravely to the man and then nodded. 'If the garrison in Britain had been retained, things could have been very different. They wouldn't have been able to repel the Saxons, but they might have persuaded the Saxons to reach an accommodation, to accept a land grant as the Visigoths accepted it from the emperor in Aquitaine. Britain would still have been a province of the empire, and Saxons would have been sending their sons to Rome to be educated just as the Goths do now from Gaul. Instead, the emperors depleted the British garrison to fight their own wars of succession and to bolster their own bodyguard, weakening Britain and providing a tempting target for invasion. By the time of the final withdrawal the British garrison was little more than a skeleton force. Britain was lost not through barbarian pressure but because of the obsession of the emperors with their own security and the threat of usurpers.'

'The emperor Valentinian is different,' Flavius said. 'He will strengthen Rome again.'

'Perhaps,' Arturus said. 'But I don't see him out here standing behind a cross, leading his men against the greatest threat the empire has faced. Losing Africa with her revenue and grain would be a far greater loss than the sack of the city of Rome itself. Yet the emperor sits with his court in Milan, and all I see before me now is a young tribune, a centurion and sixty-odd men of a *limitanei numerus*, a pebble to hold back a raging torrent.'

'That's us,' one of the men muttered. 'The last-ditch *limitanei*.'

'Rome needs generals like Gaiseric,' Arturus asserted. 'Men who are both kings and war leaders, men like Julius Caesar or Trajan of old. Without them, Rome may win battles, but she will never win wars. And the Vandals are not the worst of it. Behind their northern homeland, in the forests and on the steppes of the East, lies a greater force of darkness than anyone here could imagine, building up strength for a confrontation that will test the empire to its very limit.'

Flavius gestured at the weapon Arturus carried. 'That sword? A legacy from the past?'

'My father was left for dead too that day when I had my throat cut, the Saxon dead piled around him,' said Arturus. 'I managed to crawl over to him and in his dying breath he gave me this sword. He had told me that as long as the sword was carried by a soldier who was descended from its original owner, Britain would resist invasion. I became the boy follower of a *comitatenses* unit, and then was adopted by the soldiers, and two years later, when I left Britain with them, I still had the sword with me. Its original

34

owner was a soldier of the Ninth Legion who had been among the first to step ashore with the invasion force of the emperor Claudius, over three hundred and fifty years before.'

'So you *are* a Roman,' Macrobius snarled. 'That makes the crime of desertion even worse.'

'What does it mean to be Roman?' Arturus said, looking around. 'Who of you here is Roman, truly? Yes, you fight for a Roman army, against barbarians. But you are also Sarmatians, Goths, Illyrians. I have Roman ancestry, but my father's family were mainly from the British kingdom of the Iceni, my mother from the Brigantes. And after Honorius had forsaken us, we no longer called ourselves Roman. We called ourselves British.'

'So why the cassock?' Flavius asked. 'Why aren't you back in Britain, fighting the invaders? There are rumours of continuing resistance in the mountains in the west of the island.'

Arturus re-sheathed his sword and closed his cassock. He put his hands up to his face, sweeping them down his cheeks and over his beard, and remained still for a moment. Flavius saw for the first time how weather-beaten and filthy he was, and how tired he looked. He let his hands drop to the crude wooden cross that hung around his neck. Macrobius remained unmoved, his hand still resting on his sword pommel. Arturus raised the cross and kissed it, and then looked again at Flavius. 'When I left Britain I was determined to return, to take up my father's sword against the Saxons. My mission for Bishop Augustine is not yet finished. I must take his books to a place of safety, to a monastery in Italy. But I will not flee Carthage without facing the enemy in battle. I offer my sword to you.'

'You still have to tell us how to kill the Alans,' one of the men muttered.

Flavius looked at Arturus. They did not know the full story yet, the story of how he had come to leave his unit in Gaul, but there was little time for that now. 'Your offer is accepted.'

Arturus nodded in acknowledgement, and then gave Flavius a

steely look. 'And now, if we are to fight for you, my men and our mule need water.'

Flavius watched Macrobius lead the group towards the watering hole, dropping down into the trench and leaping up the other side, his hand on his sword hilt, still clearly not giving Arturus the benefit of the doubt. He turned back towards the west, pondering what Arturus had said. He remembered as a boy in Rome being overawed by Augustine, the hell-raiser they had all wished to emulate, and being as perplexed as everyone else when he suddenly gave up wine and women for the cassock. Some came to see it as a strength, as evidence that he had the willpower to do away with worldly vices, but others viewed it as a weakness, as a sign that the cloth itself was a temptation that men of action should resist in order to do God's proper work on earth – leading the armies of Christ against the barbarian enemy.

Flavius cocked his ear. He was sure he had heard it again, the sound that had haunted him as he had lain there a few hours before, battling the cold, drifting in and out of consciousness, a sound from the west that had risen and undulated above the snoring and grunting around him. Noises had seemed louder, more acute, since he had drunk the infusion of the *catha* leaf that Macrobius had given him, and he wondered whether this was that same heightened awareness experienced by those who cannot sleep, whether his imagination and the memory of that sound in the night were playing tricks on him. And then he heard it again, and saw others stop what they were doing and listen, as a wave of tension seemed to rustle down the trench. It was a dog baying, and then others, echoing from one end of the western horizon to the other, the noise a lot closer now than it had been when he had heard it earlier. This was not just the yipping and howling of wild dogs – it was something different, more orchestrated, and it sent the same shiver down his spine that he had felt less than an hour before.

He tried to ignore it, and focused his mind on the tactical plan that he had worked up with Macrobius over the past two days. Everything depended on the men of the *numerus* keeping their nerve, and letting the enemy get as close as possible. Concealed among the hillocks behind the trench were five *onager* catapults loaded with fireballs, tensed and weighted so that the balls would burst on the sloping ground less than a hundred yards in front of the trench. They would only have time to fire once, and the artillerymen had doused the machines with naphtha to ensure that the fireballs, as they were lit, would ignite the catapults as well and prevent them from falling into enemy hands. A team of *fabri* from the Carthage garrison had also dug a ditch in front of the catapults and filled it with pots of naphtha, ready to pour out and ignite after the fireballs had exploded, to protect any surviving men of the *numerus* who had fallen back towards the walls of Carthage.

For a line defended by fewer than a hundred men it promised to be an extravagant show of force, more impressive than anything the Vandals would have encountered as the depleted garrisons of the western African shore had fallen one by one to their advance. But Flavius and Macrobius were under no illusions about its effectiveness. Once the Vandals realized the puny size of the force set against them, the momentary check caused by the fireballs would only redouble their fury, and the only chance for those of the *numerus* who could get back to the walls of Carthage would be to escape with the rest of the garrison by sea. But Flavius knew that putting up a planned defence was not merely a heroic gesture; what was at stake was the tattered remains of Roman military prestige. That had already taken a battering with the betrayal of the *comitatenses* commander in the West, and it would suffer a further blow if word spread to the other enemies of Rome that her army could not even be bothered to put up a token resistance against an assault on Carthage, a city whose conquest by Rome six hundred years before had launched the empire. Flavius felt that if he and Macrobius and every last man of the *numerus* fell taking a Vandal or an Alan warrior with him, then he would have upheld his pledge to his uncle Aetius when he was appointed as tribune always to maintain the honour of Rome and that of the soldiers under his command, to ensure that his actions were remembered by history not as the dying gasps of an army, but as a final act of valour and fury.

Macrobius had come upon to the parapet beside him and was listening to the eerie howling coming from the hills in front of them. 'I've heard that sound before,' he growled. 'It was while I was serving under your uncle on the Danube frontier twenty years ago, when the Vandals first came out of the forests.'

'They're called the Alaunt,' Arturus said, coming up on the other side of Flavius. 'Massive hunting and fighting dogs, trained solely to kill. Gaiseric keeps them leashed until the last moment, until their eyes are red and their mouths are foaming, and then he releases them along with the Alan warriors. When the howling turns to barking, that means they're coming.'

Flavius felt chilled to his core. Now he knew that the howling was a sound not of the desert, but of the northern forests, of a place where the dogs were really wolves and where those who had tamed them, the wolf-masters, came roaring with their charges out of the forest as one, bringing with them the darkness that had been sweeping over the western empire for more than fifty years now. He shut his eyes for a moment, trying to concentrate. *He must not lose his nerve.* He looked again, scanning the horizon, still seeing nothing. The howling had stopped, and had been replaced by a strange, unearthly silence, like the lull before a storm.

Arturus turned to him. 'What is your plan?'

Flavius took a deep breath. 'You'll have seen the catapults and the ditch with the naphtha pots beyond the watering hole. After the pyrotechnics it'll be a matter of archery and hand-to-hand combat. This ridge overlooks the road to the western gate of the city. It's the route that any attacker would try to force first. From our positions on higher ground we should be able to defend the defile long enough for any who still remain in Carthage and wish to flee to get to the harbour and embark on the last remaining galleys. When the time is right we will fall back to the city walls.'

Arturus looked back to the city walls. 'Gaiseric will let his men rape and pillage to satisfy their need, but he will spare the lives of the leading citizens and offer them generous terms. He intends to settle in Carthage, and their tax revenue is his future wealth. But he will spare nobody bearing arms.'

'You know much about Gaiseric,' Macrobius muttered.

'Gaiseric employs foreign mercenaries as his personal body-guard. They're safer for a king than his own men, as the loyalty of a mercenary is assured by gold. Before I took up the cassock, I was captain of his guard.'

Flavius saw Macrobius stiffen. 'I knew our trust in you was misplaced,' he growled, his hand back on his sword pommel.

Arturus put up his hand. 'That was ten years ago, after I left the northern field army. We were a small group of Britons who made up the *Cohortes Britannicus*, a *foederati* unit, but we had been ill-used by the *comes*, ordered to put down a peasant revolt in northern Gaul by massacring the population and burning the land. We deserted, yes, but we had no longer been fighting for Rome. Some of us returned to join the resistance in Britain, and others went to the barbarian kings as mercenaries. I was not yet ready to return, so sold my skills to the Vandal king. And have no fear. My cousin Prasutagus had come with me into Gaiseric's service, but the king decided that there should be no kinship loyalties among his guard and had him murdered. I may be a Christian, but I am still bound by the ancient *wergild* oath of the Iceni and am bound to avenge my cousin, in this world or the next. Gaiseric is no friend of mine.'

Macrobius grunted, his hand still on his sword. There was a commotion down the line, a rustling and a whispering among the men, and then a sentry came running up and spoke. 'There are people coming, centurion,' he panted. 'More refugees, visible from the left flank of the ridge. They seem desperate, running and stumbling, casting aside any belongings they have. It's as if something just out of sight is coming behind them, pushing them forward.'

'They won't make it,' Arturus said. 'We must gird ourselves. The enemy is nearly upon us.'

Flavius' head was swimming. He felt delirious, and then he had a sudden revelation. *He had heard that sound before.* A few months earlier after reading in Polybius of the ancient prophecy that Carthage would fall once again, he had travelled south from Rome to the Phlegraean Fields, on the way visiting the tomb, long neglected and overgrown, of the great Scipio Africanus, victor over Hannibal. He had wanted to visit the cave of the Sibyl, to see for himself the source of the prophecy. He had found the cave, making his way past the crosses and candles that filled the hearth of the long-dead priestesses of Apollo, and had stood in front of the yawning chasm, listening. It was said that the wizened blackened corpse of the Sibyl still hung in the inner recesses of the cave, and that if you listened you could hear her final exhalations. He had gone away disappointed, chastened, having only heard the westerly wind from the sea whistling and hissing through the rocks. Only now he realized what it really was. It had not been the sound of the sea at all. It had been the distant sound of dogs, howling and baying. The shade of the Sibyl had been warning him. *The prophecy would come true.*

He felt the cold sweat on his hands, and his heart began to pound. His mouth was dry, his breathing short. He tried to ignore the cavernous feeling in his stomach, the tremor in his hands, tried to convince himself that it was just exhaustion and the desert air and cold. Yet he knew that he was gripped by fear. He reached into the pouch on his belt and took out one of the gold coins he had used to pay the men the day before, trying to stop his hand shaking, peering at the image of the emperor: on the one side, stolid, square-faced, and on the other wearing old-fashioned legionary armour, bare-legged, breast-plated, one foot on a vanquished human-headed serpent and one hand holding up an orb with a cross. Flavius had planned to look at this coin in the moments before the battle, to remind himself of what he was fighting for – for the empire and the cross, for Rome. But all he could do was to clasp his hand around the coin to stop it from shaking, and look out and see the reality that was unfolding in front of him. He could see the refugees now, distant forms of people falling and staggering down the hillside, picking themselves up and trying to carry on, women and men dragging children along, all of them on their last legs after days of flight before a terror scarcely imaginable, baying and howling behind them. Flavius could hear the pounding of his heart in his ears. There was one difference between himself, a soldier of Christian Rome, and the legionaries who had gone before them, from the days before the amphitheatres had become holy places of pilgrimage and were still soaked with gladiators' blood. *He had never seen a person ripped to death by an animal before.*

Macrobius said something low, guttural, in the language that Flavius had heard him use before with several of the other soldiers from the Danube lands. He turned to him. 'What did you say?'

Macrobius looked grimly at the horizon, and then drew his sword. 'I said in the Vandal tongue what the wolf-master is telling his men now. *Unleash the dogs of war.*'

3

The dogs came terrifyingly, silently, a silence that Flavius knew
from his own hunting dogs was the silence of an animal intent
only on the kill, an animal that was past needing to terrorize its
prey. The first of the animals had overtaken the refugees
moments before, and now he could see dozens of them streaking
ahead of a rolling wave of Vandal warriors that he knew would
absorb the people trying to flee them as easily as a great tidal
wave engulfs all before it on its way inland. He and his *numerus*
were themselves part of that inexorability, a brittle line of defence
that stood no chance of halting the onslaught, but they would not
go down without a fight.

He forced himself to look away, turning around to make sure
that everything was ready. Half a mile behind them the walls of
Carthage were framed by the red glow of the rising sun, as if the
city were on fire already. He wondered whether anyone was
watching from the walls, or whether the sentries had fled to the
last remaining ships in the harbour. Beyond the hillocks five
hundred paces behind the trench he could just make out the
throwing arms of the five catapults, each one winched back by a
windlass against the torsion of the coiled rope that held the base
of the arm in the heavy frame. Under each arm hung a pouch
containing a clay ball filled with a combustible mixture, ready to
swing out once the artillerymen had struck the retaining pin with
a wooden mallet. He could see the men now, one for each
catapult, holding the burning tapers that they had lit from the last
residue of the cooking fire; on his command they would light
the fireballs and then the naphtha in the ditch in front of them.

They were staring at him now, waiting for his signal. All of the men in the trench were doing the same, their hands white-knuckled on their weapons, as if the entire *numerus* were wound tight like the catapults. He turned back to look over the parapet. The dogs were coming closer, no more than four hundred paces away, tearing ahead in their eagerness to reach their prey, a huge trail of dust rising behind them. Striding out of the dust he could see the first of the wolf-masters, the Alan warriors, immense men with furs on their shoulders, cracking the whips they used to drive the dogs forward, carrying the vicious nail-studded clubs that were their hallmark in battle. A torrent of Vandals seemed to cascade over the slope behind them, traversing the valley and running up the slope towards the trench, the dogs close enough now to be able to see their fangs and the red of their eyes. Flavius stared at the oncoming mass, gauging their speed and likely point of impact. *Something was wrong.* He turned to Macrobius. 'The fireballs are meant to fall on the mass of the enemy. The dogs will be upon us before the Vandals come within range.'

Macrobius held his sword at the ready. 'Then we will deal with the dogs as they come through,' he replied. 'Stick to your plan, tribune.' He turned and looked at his men. 'Steady,' he growled. '*Sagittarii*, tense your bows.'

The archers every fifth man along the line raised their bows and aimed, holding their position while Macrobius lifted his hand. Flavius glanced back at the artillerymen. He had told them only to loose on his command, and he hoped they would keep their nerve. They were men he had specially recruited into the *numerus* for the task, veterans from the frontier *limitanei* recommended by Macrobius who had sworn to draw their swords and stand their ground once the *onagers* had sprung.

The first of the Alaunt was only a stone's throw away now, a lunging form bigger than any wolf Flavius had ever seen, pounding its way up the slope towards them, its dark hair bristled and flecked with foam that was slavering out of its jaws. Flavius held his sword with two hands, ready to thrust into bellies, into necks, knowing that there would be little scope for swinging or slashing. He envied Arturus his *gladius*, and saw the Briton in his cassock further down the parapet close to the road along which he had sent his Nubians and his mule back towards the city. The dogs were nearly upon them, a line of great hulking beasts in a dust cloud that obscured everything that was coming behind. Macrobius tensed and then dropped his arm. '*Now!*' he bellowed.

Flavius was conscious of the whistling of arrows just as the leading dog reached the front of the parapet and hurled itself towards them. The arrow from the Sarmatian behind him sunk itself up to the feathers in the mouth of the beast, too late to stop the animal in its death throes from barrelling into the man and ripping out his throat, a snarling, shrieking tangle of limbs and gore that writhed and then fell still in the dust. Other dogs had fallen as they ran, skewered by arrows and tumbling to the ground, but some had come too quickly for the archers to reload and aim, throwing themselves on the men with their fangs laid bare. Macrobius fell back against the rear of the trench with his sword pommel jammed into the ground and caught a dog on its point, disembowelling it as it hurtled over him. Another knocked Flavius sideways and tore its claws into his forearm, leaving four streaks of red that quickly welled up with blood. It scrambled up the side of the trench and was gone, pounding past the artillerymen and the *onagers* towards the walls of Carthage, the new leader of a pack that was disengaging itself from the melee and following, as if the scent of Carthage was an even greater draw than the blood and gore around it.

Flavius dragged himself upright, his arm dripping red, and in a blur saw the heaving forms of the Alan wolf-masters coming next, followed by the Vandal horde no more than two hundred paces distant. *Now was the time.* He turned towards the artillery-men, raised his arm, feeling the blood spatter his face, and then dropped it. 'Let fly!' he yelled. The artillerymen dipped their tapers to light the fireballs and struck the retaining pins with

their wooden mallets. Slowly, gracefully, the arms sprang upwards, swinging their pouches in a wide arc until the arms hit the
blocking beams with a dull thud and the pouches released their
missiles. The catapults burst into flames as the fireballs flew forward, their clay cracking on impact, spewing out gobbets of fire.
The first one hit an Alan warrior full in the chest, igniting his furs
and hair in a jet of flame, and yet still he came, staggering and
pirouetting like a moving bonfire until he fell heavily into the
dust. The other balls crashed among the first line of Vandals,
creating a continuous wall of flame that the men tried desperately
to shake off, some falling and writhing in the dust, trying to put
out the fire, and others running forward blindly like human
torches, shrieking and dropping their weapons as the archers
behind Flavius tried to pick them off.

The Alans ahead of the fire stowed their whips and advanced
holding only their war clubs, terrifying weapons hewn from a
single limb of oak, embedded with iron spikes that glinted in the
sunlight. The nearest one charged directly towards Arturus, who
stood on the parapet with his hood down and his *gladius* held
ready. Flavius saw the artillerymen advance towards the ditch in
front of the catapults, their tapers ready to ignite the naphtha and
create a barrier of fire behind the surviving men of the *numerus*
to allow them to retreat. He was aware that arrows had begun to
whistle overhead from the Vandal ranks, some clattering harm-
lessly over the parapet and others finding their mark. Macrobius
turned to him, his chainmail dripping with entrails from the dog,
and together the two men turned and bellowed down either side
of the trench. *'Fall back! Fall back!'*

The order came too late for the men to the left of Flavius. An
Alan had appeared on the parapet, an immense man, his forearms
almost as thick as his club, and with a single swing he took off one
man's head and then swung the weapon back around into the
belly of another, the impaled head crushing against the man's
chainmail as the blow broke his back, causing a gush of blood and

innards to fall down his legs. The Alan moved down the trench, still swinging, the men desperately scrambling out of his way, the surviving archers turning and shooting at point-blank range into the man's chest and head, filling him with arrows until one through his forehead finally felled him, his body juddering to his knees and toppling forward among the carnage he had created around him.

Suddenly there was an Alan in front of Flavius, a vast shape silhouetted by the fire that was still raging along the Vandal line behind him. Flavius remembered what Arturus had told him in the moments before the battle, fulfilling his promise to tell them how to fight the Alans: *Do not fall back. Hold your ground and evade the first swing. Then, while his arms are high in the air and he is vulnerable, spring forward and thrust your sword into his heart.* The Alan roared, his teeth sharpened like those of his dogs, his yellow hair tied back and streaming behind him. But Flavius seemed to hear nothing, to see nothing, to be caught in a moment that seemed to expand infinitely, something he had heard about, but not believed, from those who had faced life or death like this in battle before. And then he was conscious of the rush of the club as it bore down on him, sweeping low to catch him by the legs. He leapt upwards as the club missed him and swung high up to the right, until the Alan was holding it above his head, the momentum tilting him back, his eyes wide open with rage as he realized his own vulnerability. Flavius imagined he could see the man's heart pounding under his heaving sternum and he thrust his blade in, driving it hard, feeling it crunch through his backbone and come out the other side. He held it there, every muscle in his body tensed, smelling the stink of sweat and adrenalin, feeling the heart flailing against the blade until it shuddered and stopped. The man coughed a torrent of blood and fell against him, the club dropping backwards and his arms hanging limp and lifeless.

Flavius heaved the body aside, put his foot on the chest and pulled out his sword. Macrobius had picked up the bow and quiver from the dead archer behind them and was shooting as fast as he could over the parapet. The Vandals had broken through the carnage caused by the fireballs and were seconds away now. Flavius looked left and right along the trench, seeing only corpses. Macrobius loosed the last of his arrows, grabbed his sword where he had driven it into the ground and pulled Flavius around. 'They are all dead or gone,' he bellowed. 'You have done your duty. Now we must join the survivors.' He dragged Flavius down into the trench and up the other side, towards the waiting artillerymen. As he did so Flavius saw that the Sarmatian lying closest to them was still alive, his mouth moving and his hand gesturing. Flavius dropped his sword and pulled him onto his back, but as he did so an arrow flew through the man's neck and head, spraying Flavius with blood and pitching them both forward. Macrobius wrenched them apart, the man's eyes now wide open in death, and together the two men stumbled over the ditch just as the artillerymen dropped their tapers into it and the naphtha erupted in a wall of flame.

Flavius halted for a moment, stooping down and panting hard, feeling the heat on his back, conscious of Macrobius and Arturus rounding up the artillerymen and pushing them forward, seeing other survivors from the *numerus* running ahead past the burning *onagers* over the open ground to the east. *Good. He would be the last man to leave.* He had upheld his honour, his word to his uncle Aetius a few weeks before in Rome, and had not abandoned his men. He stared at the blood dripping down his forearm, seeing his engorged veins, feeling his heart pounding. He had felt something else, not just pain and fear, but a huge sense of exaltation. He had killed a man in battle for the first time. In that moment he knew what the Greeks meant by *kharme*, battle lust, and why men yearned for it. *It felt good.*

Macrobius was in front of him, yelling. 'Come on, tribune. To the walls of Carthage. We must run for our lives.'

*

Half an hour later Flavius sat among his men just inside the east gate of the city wall, the great wooden doors having been opened for them by the squad of sentries from the garrison who had sworn to remain on duty until they were all safely inside. He had watched the sentries bar the gate and then retreat down the streets towards the harbour to join the other rear guard of the garrison, waiting on the quayside to be taken off by the last remaining galleys. The suburb around them seemed deserted, but Flavius knew that the people of Carthage were cowering inside their houses – those who had believed the assurances of the traitor Bonifatius that civilians who stayed would not be harmed nor would they have their property damaged, that city officials would be promised a place in the new administration under Gaiseric and his council of chieftains. It was not an assurance that had been extended to the *milites* of the garrison, nor one that would have been believed if it had. Their token display of resistance from the trench had inflicted enough casualties to stoke the Vandal's rage, extinguishing any slight chance of mercy that they might once have had. Their only chance of survival was to get out of Carthage, and to get out now.

Flavius lifted one of the skins that had been left for them by the sentries and let the water pour down his throat, swallowing great gulps and letting it splash over his face. He passed it back to the man who had handed it to him, and then looked around. Macrobius had given him the butcher's bill, but he could count well enough for himself. They had lost two more men during the retreat to the walls, one to a marauding Alaunt and the other to his wounds, collapsing dead as he was being helped along. Of the original *numerus* of eighty men, only sixteen survived. *Sixteen men.* Flavius had thought his command puny to begin with, but this was beyond a joke. And yet they were the remaining army of Africa, the last soldiers from the force that centuries ago had smashed its way up these slopes to claim Carthage as its own, and he was still their commander. Every one of them bore the scars of the onslaught, some of them gaping bite wounds from the Alaunt and others crushed and ripped flesh where they had endured blows from the clubs of the Alans; Flavius' own scars of battle, the four parallel gashes from the dog's claws along his forearm, were beginning to swell up and throb painfully.

The Sarmatian archer Apsachos rolled over, raised his right leg and peered at the shredded flesh of his calf. 'That was a dog's breakfast, sir, if you ask me.'

The man beside him guffawed, and then grimaced in pain, clutching a red patch that was seeping through the chainmail on his right side. 'You crack me up, Apsachos. If I wasn't holding my innards in, I'd give you a belly laugh.'

'Let 'em out, and let's see if you've really got guts. I didn't see you showing any back there.'

'That's because you were too busy waving your arse at the enemy as you were trying to escape, while I was taking on an Alan single-handed.'

'The only one I saw do that was your tribune, Flavius Aetius,' Macrobius said, squatting down among the men. 'But everyone showed guts here, as did our comrades who are now with God. And Apsachos, if you were as quick with the latrine-digging as you are with your quips, I'd get you the *corona civilis* with olive-leaf garlands.'

'Decorations for this action, centurion? A failed rear-guard stand in a failed campaign, Rome's finest running away with their tails between their legs after abandoning Carthage, the jewel of the empire? I think this is one that our beloved generals eating their grapes and saying their prayers in Ravenna and Milan would rather forget.'

Macrobius peeled back the mangled chainmail on his left arm, revealing a broken Vandal arrow deeply embedded in his shoulder. 'We've all got our decorations, Apsachos, decorations that will stay with us on our bodies to remind us of this day and our comrades who fell here. That's all that matters. The generals with their heads in the clouds and the bishops to lead them can go to hell. And now drink up that second skin that the guards left us. I can hear the Alaunt baying at the gates. If we don't go now, we'll be the dogs' lunch as well.'

4

Flavius helped the last wounded man up and supported him as they trudged east through Carthage towards the harbours, following the route that Arturus had taken ahead of them to find his Nubians and retrieve his saddlebag. The city would not withstand the Vandals for long; as soon as they realized that the walls were undefended they would use grappling hooks to scale them and then open the gates for the others to follow. Flavius could sense their presence outside, a vast, restless force surging against the city, waiting for their forward scouts to reconnoitre the walls and give the signal for the final assault. He tried to quicken the pace, and after twenty minutes they had put the eastern wall a good quarter of a mile behind them. Near the sea front they passed the vast structure of the imperial baths, breaking the line of the sea walls. Ahead of them lay the famous land-locked harbours, built seven hundred years before by the Punic Carthaginians against the threat of Roman naval attack, a threat that became real when Scipio Aemilianus landed his forces from the sea and razed the city to the ground. The harbours were in sight now, rebuilt at the time of Julius Caesar, and after another twenty minutes, during which they passed villas and tenement blocks, they came to the edge of the complex just before the eastern promontory where the city jutted out into the Mediterranean Sea.

The streets had been eerily quiet, almost devoid of people, but he could see a few dozen figures on the far side of the quay in front of the prow of a galley, the last ship afloat in the harbours. As they came closer he spotted Arturus in his cassock with the two Nubians and his mule, and beside them the white-bearded captain who had agreed to remain behind to pick up any survivors. Flavius hurried forward to the man, clapped his hand on his shoulder and spoke to him in Greek. 'We are only sixteen in number. There are no more. Thank you for waiting, *kyberbetes.*'

'No need to thank me, Flavius Aetius. Remember, I too was once a tribune in my youth, the commander of a *liburnian* in the Adriatic fleet, the *classis Adriaticus.* Even now as a civilian I would never leave behind fellow warriors of Rome. You and your men have *virtus,* unlike those members of the garrison who have already fled.'

'When can we board?'

'Very soon. We are loading the last of the silver and gold plate of the Bishop of Carthage. It is by express order of the emperor's *primicerius sacri cubiculi,* Heraclius.'

'That eunuch? The emperor's wet nurse?' Macrobius had joined them, and leaned over and spat. 'Better you truss him on board and then dump him out at sea.'

'Treasure before men,' another of the *numerus* grumbled. 'It's always been the way.'

The captain looked apologetically at Macrobius. 'You know the score, centurion. If I show up at Ostia with no treasure and only soldiers, Heraclius' Goth thugs will drag me off to the Mamertine Prison in Rome and flay me alive. If I show up with treasure *and* soldiers, all should be well.'

'Best for Heraclius that you show up with treasure but no soldiers,' Macrobius said. 'Then that snivelling toad might live another day. I've got time for Valentinian, but his eunuchs can go and piss in hell.'

Flavius looked at the captain. 'You have ten minutes, no more. The Vandals will have broken through and be here within the hour.'

'*Ave,* tribune.' The captain turned to where his crew were manhandling boxes and crates up the gangplank onto the galley, a wide-beamed single-decker with spaces for thirty oarsmen and the men of the *numerus*, if they could fit among the crates on the narrow deck that ran above the spine of the hull between the benches. The vessel was docked on the edge of the rectangular harbour opposite the eastern channel that led out to sea, their escape route. On the other side of the quay was the land-locked circular harbour, once home of the war galleys of the Carthaginians and then the headquarters of the Roman grain fleet. Drawn up against the edge of the harbour were the remains of four Roman war galleys, their bottoms staved in and their oars smashed. Flavius glanced at Arturus. 'At least once we're at sea the Vandals won't be following us in a hurry.'

Arturus tied up his saddlebag and then looked at the harbour. 'Don't count on it. There's a myth that because the Goths failed to cross the Bosporus at Constantinople after the Battle of Adrianople sixty years ago, the sea is the barbarians' Achilles' heel. But they were inexperienced in the ways of the Mediterranean then, and more intent on going west than east. When they reached the southern tip of Greece and then Italy in their great migration, it was not so much ignorance of the sea that prevented them from going further south as the fact that they could see no point in it; they wanted land, not to become pirates. Gaiseric is different. He understands that the sea is not a barrier but a route, that the Mediterranean is a battleground that any barbarian intent on Rome ignores at his peril. Among the mercenaries from Britain who stayed with Gaiseric after I left his service was a former artificer of the channel fleet, the *classis Britannica*, who knew how to build the flat-bottomed boats favoured by the sea peoples of the North-West. It was boats of that design that allowed Gaiseric to cross between the Pillars of Hercules, between Spain and Africa. And you can be sure that once he and his Vandals take the harbours of Carthage they will quickly assert themselves on the Mediterranean. Raiders on land will become raiders by sea. Remember, I know these barbarians. I have seen them with my own eyes, I have fought alongside them, in the mountains and plains of the north, in the forests, on the steppe-lands many *stades* to the east far beyond the reach of Rome.'

Flavius eyed him. 'You have travelled far, Arturus.'

'I have been to dark places.'

Arturus turned to the Nubians, delved into his cassock and gave each man a small pouch of coins, and then stroked the mule's nose, reaching up and whispering into its ear. He slapped its haunch and raised his hand in farewell as the mule trotted behind the two Nubians away from the harbour and towards the eastern gate of the city.

'Where will they go?' Flavius asked.

'Some place where men like them are not enslaved by men like us,' Arturus said. 'I have advised them to travel east beside the great desert to Egypt, and then south along the course of the river Nile to the kingdom of Aksum. It is the first Christian kingdom in the world, founded even before Constantine the Great had his revelation and converted the Roman Empire. If they reach Aksum safely, they may find sanctuary and freedom.'

'And you? Why do you not join them?'

Arturus heaved the saddlebag onto his shoulder. 'Because I swore an oath that I would take these works of Augustine to safety in Italy.'

'Are they for the libraries of Rome? There at least the monks of the *scriptoria* will preserve them as the word of God, and not deface and destroy them as they are doing to so many of the great works of the pagan past.'

'I will tell you once we are on the ship. We must go now.'

The captain of the galley beckoned them forward urgently. A fat cleric pushed ahead, a bishop to judge by his robes, dragging a sack that clunked with precious church metal in one hand and with the other pulling along a slave girl by her neck. She was tall, an African, but unusual, with curly black hair and bruised cheeks, and as she was hauled by she gave Flavius an unfathomable look. He had seen enough battered slave girls in his time to think he was immune to feeling any emotion, but the sight of this girl being dragged along by a sweaty cleric with his bag of loot repulsed him. He knew it was the last thing that should concern him now, and he tried to put it from his mind as Arturus mounted the gangplank and went on board. Flavius waited until the last of his men had followed, and then stepped up the plank after Macrobius. He thought for a moment, then turned and ran back past the sailor who was unlashing the plank from the quayside, squatted and pressed his hand against the old Punic stone of Carthage for the last time. As he looked down he saw something in a crack between the blocks, a corroded silver coin, and prised it out, seeing the head of a goddess on one side. He flipped it over, staring at it, and then shoved it into the pouch on his belt. He turned and ran back up the gangplank, jumping onto the galley deck just before the men began to haul the plank on board, then looked back to see only the discarded water skins and food peelings that were the last residue of the Roman army on the shores of North Africa.

The captain cast off and the galley edged away from the quayside, the oarsmen having sat down on the benches and flexed themselves in preparation for the task to come. Those few of the *numerus* who were still fit and able had taken a place alongside them at the oars, and the rest were sprawled along the central deck and in the bows. A Greek *iatros*, a physician who had been among the few civilians to leave with them, was already leaning over the first of them, his bronze scalpel poised to scrape away pulverized flesh and his sponge soaked with seawater to cleanse the wound. The girl with the curly hair stood up to help, but was pulled violently down by the bishop and made to massage his neck. The captain bellowed an order, and the first sweep of the oars took the galley out into the centre of the harbour and towards the narrow passage on the eastern side that led through the city wall to the open sea. The sounds of the conquerors were echoing across the city: yelled orders, the occasional word in a guttural language heard clear across the still morning air, the baying and barking of the dogs. The Romans had embarked with little time to spare, and Flavius knew that they would not be free until they had passed under the line of the city wall and out of range of any Vandal archers who might have reached the harbour gates in time.

The oars swept again, and the captain leaned on the steering oar to point the galley towards the passage. Flavius made his way among his men to the bows where Arturus was sitting, and knelt alongside. He was still running on adrenalin, and he felt jittery, his eyes darting everywhere looking for the enemy, as he turned and peered anxiously at the constriction ahead where he knew they would be most vulnerable. One of the men pointed back towards the acropolis of the city. 'You can see them now. On the platform.'

Flavius shaded his eyes and peered. The soldier was right. There was a stream of men along the edge of the massive masonry platform that rose above the city, the site of the old Punic temple to Ba'al Hammon and now a great basilican church. He could see one man standing apart, hands on his hips, staring out over the harbour and the sea, as if towards Rome itself. At that moment Flavius knew that he was looking at Gaiseric, that he was seeing a barbarian king for the first time. He felt a chill course through him, and he gripped the thwarts of the ship, staring hard, thinking no longer of the events of the last hours but instead of the months and years ahead, of the shape that men like Gaiseric would give to the empire that Flavius was sworn to defend.

'Now is the time to see Carthage burn,' the soldier muttered.

Arturus tightened the straps of his saddlebag to keep the contents dry, the first drops of backsplash from the oars having reached them. 'We may see fires, but they will be bonfires of victory, not fires of destruction,' he said. 'Just as the Christians in Rome converted basilicas to churches and the Colosseum to an altar to God, so Gaiseric and his chieftains will not destroy

Carthage but will convert the palaces and villas to their own mead halls. The great monuments of Rome will survive, but you should not be deluded. They will be mere skeletons, like the bleached bones of long-dead warriors on the battlefield, unless Rome regroups and reacts to the threat with force of arms far greater than anything that has been put against the barbarians yet.'

The captain barked an order, and the oarsmen pulled hard and then retracted their oars, holding them close to the gunwales as they slid into the gloom of the passageway. The sides were shadowy, indiscernible, the ancient blocks of masonry barely distinguishable from the living rock itself, while above them the towering form of the city walls was barely visible in the haze of sunlight. It was as if Carthage were already receding into history, ghostly, diaphanous, ready to be reclaimed by the silt and the marshland that had been there when the Phoenicians had pulled up their first galley on the shoreline, before Rome had even been born. Flavius turned to Arturus, remembering what he had just said. 'And what is it that we soldiers of Rome must do?'

Arturus himself seemed part of the shadowland, his beard and long hair caught in the strange semi-light of the passageway as he sat upright in the bows like some mythical king. He put his hand on his saddlebag and spoke quietly. 'I will answer by telling you what I intend to do with these books. As a boy in Britain before the arrival of the Saxons I was educated in Greek and Latin, and after my escape the soldiers placed me in a monastery in Gaul until I was old enough to join the army. I left when I was sixteen, but from the monks I had already learned of Augustine. After my years with the *foederati* and then as a mercenary to the barbarian kings I found much in his service that suited me. I had become sickened by killing, not hardened to it. The City of God seemed a better place than any city men could create. But then I saw how the weak men who ruled Rome began to see in the City of God an excuse for turning away from crisis, from the strategy and planning that were needed to counter the barbarian threat.'

'If the City of God is all that matters, why bother with earthly affairs?'

You have seen it for yourself, Flavius. Men – emperors – could use the teachings of Augustine as an excuse for living lives of indolence and pleasure. And then Augustine began to preach against free will, to claim that men could not influence their own destiny. The excuse was even stronger. If men's lives are pre-ordained, why bother debating strategy? After two years with Augustine in Hippo Regius I had begun to hear the call of my homeland, to remember the vow I had made as a boy to return to Britain and fight for my people. Word had come of a mounting resistance to the Saxon invaders in the hills and valleys of the West, of a resistance led by people and their elected captains. The teachings of Augustine no longer seemed to have a place in my vision of my destiny. I had become a secret heretic long before I left his service.'

'You determined to return to Britain.'

'That was my mission when you first saw me. The advance of the Vandals and the fall of Hippo Regius had released me from my obligation to Augustine, and coming to Carthage was the first leg on my trip home. I will fulfil my oath to Augustine. I will protect his work and take it to Italy, but not to Rome or Ravenna. I will take it to the monastery of Monte Cassino south of Neapolis, where I will entrust it to a monk of my own order among the brethren who will tell nobody and will keep it locked away in that mountain fastness.'

'Where it will gather dust, and not be read.'

'Where it will await a more contemplative age, an age when men can reflect on God and the path to Heaven without letting it interfere with the battle for a kingdom of men on earth.'

'And your order?'

Arturus paused. 'I cannot speak its name. We are outlawed

in Rome. It is an order that comes from my own people and believes that men can shape their own destiny. Battles are won by soldiers, not by priests. And it is kings who conduct the affairs of men on earth, not God.'

Macrobius came up from where he had been helping the Greek doctor and sat down heavily beside Arturus, 'I saw you slay two of the Alans and take on the first wave of Vandals. A fighting monk,' he said grudgingly. 'I grant you that, though whether or not your story holds any water I cannot judge.'

Arturus reached under his cassock and drew out his sword. Macrobius stiffened, and Arturus put his other hand on the centurion's shoulder, smiling. 'Fear not, my friend. It is just that I have noticed that your tribune Flavius Aetius is missing his sword. He dropped it trying to save a man, an action that in days past would have won him the *corona civilis*. Before that I saw him confront an Alan with that sword, struggling with its length. Mine will be better for him. It's shorter, designed for thrusting. May it serve you well, Flavius, as it did my legionary ancestors in Britain.'

He handed Flavius the *gladius*, its blade dull red with dried blood, the tip showing fresh dings and dents from the fight. Flavius turned it over in his hands, weighing it. 'And you?' he asked Arturus. 'Can a heretic British monk fight with his bare hands?'

Arturus folded back his cassock. 'I have fulfilled my vow of *wergild* for the murder of my cousin by Gaiseric. I have taken blood from his army, and the score is settled. A new sword will be forged for me in Britain, a sword for a new era, a new kingdom. But your kingdom remains the empire of Rome, and for you the sword of the legionaries still holds power. There will be war ahead.'

'Gaiseric will cross the Mediterranean.'

Arturus nodded. 'When he goes north from here and takes Sicily, the last breadbasket of Rome will be gone. With no handouts of grain, the people of Rome will run riot and the slaves will rise in revolt, just as they did when the Goths ravaged the city a generation ago. The navy of Rome must be prepared to take on this new threat. But there is worse to come, something we have spoken of before. All warriors of Rome must gird themselves against a new darkness on the horizon, a darkness sweeping in from the steppe-lands beyond the Danube, a new leader who has arisen from among the Huns. I clashed with him once, when the Gothic master I served took his bodyguard with him to their wooden citadel in a fold in the steppes to the east of the Danube. We fought in their duelling arena, and I won. But he was a youth then, the birth scars on his cheeks barely calloused over. He is now a man, toughened by war, ruthless and driven by ambition, his eye set on the western empire of Rome.'

'You speak of a son of Mundiuk,' Macrobius growled. 'They say he is named after the ancient sword of the Hun kings. They call him Attila.'

The galley slid silently under the city walls, the momentum from the last oar sweep still driving it forward, and then they were out in the blinding sunlight on the open ocean, the waves slapping against the bows and the full force of the north-easterly wind bearing down on them. The captain bellowed, the rowers extended their oars and the kettle drum in the stern began to resonate, the giant black-skinned drummer giving a beat each time the oars struck the water. The pace increased as they rounded the promontory and the captain heaved the steering oar to set course for Rome. A sheet of spray came over the bows and drenched them, a welcome cleansing after the dust of the city. Flavius used the water to wipe clean the blade of the *gladius*, sliding it into the empty scabbard beneath his cloak. As soon as he could he would take some olive oil from the ship's cook, to keep it from rusting.

He saw Arturus watching him, nodded and then braced himself as the galley began to rise and fall with the heave of the sea. He remembered the old coin he had found on the quayside and took it out of his pouch, holding it up to the sunlight. It was silver, but it had lost its glint, the metal covered by the patina of the ages. On the other side from the goddess he could just make out two horsemen and a small dog, and beneath them the single word **ROMA**. He remembered the freshly minted gold coins that he had distributed to the men of the *numerus* before the battle, the head of the emperor Valentinian on one side, stolid, thick-necked, and on the other side the emperor in armour with his foot on the snake holding the orb and the cross. He knew that the silver coin dated from ancient times, from the time of great victories and conquests, of generals like Scipio and Caesar whom they believed they could never emulate. Yet at this moment, with the adrenalin of battle still in his veins, the coin seemed spectral, like the walls they had just passed through, the colour sucked out of it, a thing of the past. He thought about what Arturus had said. If Rome were to survive as more than just a relic, she needed to plan ahead. Those coins of Valentinian seemed to say that, resplendent in gold, the images drawing on the strength of tradition but looking forward; here was an emperor in the venerated armour of the legionaries yet holding down a new enemy and raising the symbols of a new religion, of a new world order that could shape Rome for the future. He only hoped that the image of the emperor would not be belied by reality, something few could judge who had not been allowed into the emperor's increasingly remote inner court in the palaces of Ravenna and Milan.

The bishop was already being seasick over the stern of the galley, and the girl with the curly hair was watching him, her attention rapt, waiting to see what he would do with the coin. He thought for a moment, and then tossed the old silver coin far out to sea, back to join the detritus of history where it belonged. Now was the time for the soldiers of Rome to grasp their sword hilts and face a new enemy, not to wallow in the lost glories of the past. He stared at the girl, and then looked back at his men. His wound throbbed and he ached in every bone in his body, but the spray had invigorated him. He would take his place among the rowers as soon as the first man tired. It was going to be a long haul home.

PART TWO

ROME, ITALY

AD 449

5

Flavius looked on with bemused fascination as the Goth infantry advanced in blocks, forming a stationary line on the high ground while the cavalry ranged up on either side of them. It was a classic manoeuvre, straight out of the textbooks, something that commanders had been taught to do since the wars against Hannibal. It was also wrong, so badly wrong that Flavius began to despair that he would ever get this particular set of future generals to desist from nocturnal distractions and do their homework. He sighed, and watched the Roman forces deploy slightly more accurately on the opposing hill, the seven legions occupying the crest, the *lanciarii* and the *mattiarii*, the mace-armed infantry, in the centre, the *scutarii* shielded cavalry in reserve, the *sagittarii* dispersed along the front. He would give them a few more minutes to puzzle out how this evenly matched deployment could possibly end in anything other than a battle of attrition and then, not for the first time, he would attempt to fill the yawning gaps in knowledge that had clearly not been helped by time spent in the taverns and brothels around the forum the night before.

He stroked the four parallel white ridges on his right forearm, feeling the throb that came when the weather was hot or when he exercised, when the veins and arteries of his arm pulsed with blood and pressed against the hardened scar tissue. It had been nearly ten years since Carthage – two years of campaigning against the Ostrogoths in the north, two years of administration and training at the *comitatenses* headquarters outside Ravanna, and nearly six years now in Rome – but even so, the attack of the Alaunt war dogs that morning outside Carthage seemed as vivid as if it were yesterday, something he had relived for years afterwards in dreams that would leave him sitting stock upright in his bed, clutching his arm and bathed in sweat, unable to breathe or to scream. The nightmares were fewer now, but hearing a baying dog in the distance would still set him on edge, would send a trickle of sweat down his back. He looked again at the opposing armies. What he had experienced then could never be taught; it was something that those here today could only understand first-hand themselves when they too faced death in battle and when those who survived learned to live with the aftershock.

'Flavius Aetius.' Someone was shaking his arm. 'What do we do next?'

Flavius started, and stared at his cousin Quintus in the eyes. He suddenly remembered where he was, and turned back to the model on the table. 'I'm sorry. I was about fifteen hundred miles away, thinking of my own experience of battle.'

'Tell us about it,' one of the boys piped up. 'Were the Alans really as bad as all that? The only ones I've seen are farmers in Aquitaine, and they seem pretty tame to me.'

'Another time,' Flavius said, straightening himself up. 'We have twenty minutes until the lesson is over. Thorismud will talk you through the battle.'

The tall Goth nodded to him and took a wooden pointer from one of the boys. Thorismud had been Flavius' sparring partner in the days when they themselves had been students in the *schola* twelve years before. He was the eldest son and heir of the Visigoth king Theodoric, once an ally but for several years now an enemy of Rome, and he had come under a flag of truce from the Visigoth stronghold of Tolosa in Gaul to discuss terms with Flavius' uncle, the *magister militum* Aetius, seeking further grants of agricultural land and vineyards that Aetius had flatly turned down. Although the mission had been a failure, the terms of the truce allowed Thorismud and his retinue to stay a further day in Rome, and he had agreed to spend an hour sitting in on Flavius' class in the *schola* that afternoon.

'The Battle of Adrianople, near Constantinople, five days before the Ides of August, *Anno Domini 376*,' he began, his voice deep and his Latin only slightly accented. 'Who can tell me something about the conditions that day?'

His request was met by silence, and Flavius looked at the sixteen officer candidates ranged around the table. Half of them were direct-entry cadets, teenagers like Quintus who had passed the entrance examinations, and the other half were men of *optio* and centurion rank who had been recommended for a commission by their *limitanei* and *comitatenses* commanders, the oldest of them in their mid-thirties. The younger cadets were overawed by Thorismud, and some of the older ones were visibly apprehensive, men who may have faced the Visigoths in battle and be nursing memories as vivid and terrifying as those that Flavius had endured from fighting the Vandals and Alans before Carthage.

Flavius tapped his hand on the table. 'Well?'

Quintus cleared his throat. 'It was hot.'

'Good.' Thorismud slapped his pointer into his hand. 'Anything else?'

Quintus answered again, his voice quavering. 'And there was no water.'

'Very good.' Thorismud brought his pointer down hard on the table, cracking the end and shaking the blocks. 'That's what you don't learn in these games of war. Standing in this cool room, nursing your hangovers and wondering what pox you picked up from the whores along the Tiber last night, you can't be thinking like soldiers in battle, can you? Anyone with an aching head and bleary eyes can push blocks around a model and pretend they're generals. But being a good commander is not just about tactics. It's also about knowing what it's like to be a soldier: what it's like to feel exhausted, to feel hungry and thirsty, to feel disorientated, to feel let down by false expectations, to feel humiliated. If you don't understand that, you can push around those blocks until Jupiter comes back to rule in Rome, but you still won't win battles.'

Quintus pointed at the model, his hand shaking slightly. 'Before the battle, the Goths burnt the grass and crops, increasing the heat and reducing the visibility. It was already roastingly hot, sickeningly so. The emperor Valens marched his men for almost seven hours from the town of Adrianople towards the Goth encampment, arriving in early afternoon in the worst of the heat. At that time of year there were no streams and there was no other source of water. Men collapsed from dehydration even before the battle began, and others could barely move in their armour. That's as far as I got in Ammianus Marcellinus' account before the library shut,' he said, looking ruefully around.

'You mean before the taverns opened,' Thorismud said, glaring at him.

Another of the younger cadets suddenly pushed back his chair, lurched to a corner and threw up noisily, the smell filling the room. Flavius gritted his teeth, picked up his own pointer and pushed the line of red blocks around into a circle. 'It was like this,' he said. 'The Goths had formed a wagon laager, in effect a fortification protecting their women and children and possessions, with rings of infantry encircling it and their cavalry positioned nearby. The Romans arrived exhausted and dehydrated, as Quintus said, but believing that theirs was the stronger force. It seems possible that Valens lost control of his men; we'll never know, because he never made it out alive. My grandfather Gaudentius, who was at the battle on the Goth side, says that the Romans let passion rule, that on seeing the Goth army for the first time they remembered the devastation caused by the Goths to their land over the preceding years, and that they became enraged and charged without Valens' order. Others say that dehydration and exhaustion made them delirious, unable to think straight and make rational decisions. To me that's a good explanation of what happened next.'

He pushed the blue Roman blocks down the valley and up to the wagon laager. 'Leaving their vantage point on the adjacent hill, the Romans charged down the valley and up the slope towards the Goths, exhausting themselves even further in the process. Once there, they discovered that the laager was impregnable, and they were rebuffed every time they tried to attack it.' He pushed the blue blocks back into the valley, and then pulled the thin red blocks representing Goth cavalry down towards them, leaving the circle of red blocks unaltered. 'The Romans retreated in disarray, and as they did so the Goth cavalry charged down on them, followed by the infantry who by then knew they could safely leave the laager. Encumbered by their heavy chain armour and shields, the Romans were destroyed and the valley became a bloodbath. One estimate puts the number of Roman dead at twenty thousand, almost three-quarters of those who went into action that day.'

'The greatest battle of modern times,' Thorismud said. 'The worst-ever defeat for Roman arms. A humiliation for all who call themselves soldiers – and I speak as a Goth, like Flavius on his paternal barbarian side a grandson of one of the victors.'

'The Huns use wagon laagers,' one of the older men said, his face stony as he stared at Thorismud. 'I've seen it myself, in the far distance when the Huns advanced into Thrace. Instead of deploying their cavalry outside the laager like the Goths at Adrianople, they keep their mounted archers within the circle, launching them on the enemy lines when the time is right. It's said that the tactic was developed by Attila himself.'

At the mention of that name the atmosphere in the room changed, becoming tense, more focused, the pale faces of the younger cadets peering at Thorismud. 'What do you think our chances are against him?' Quintus said.

'In open battle? Nil, unless you learn the lessons of Adrianople.'

He glanced at Flavius, who turned to the class. 'You are

fortunate to have had Prince Thorismud instruct you. Now you will write me a ten-point summary of the main lessons to be learned from Adrianople. Those who pass will go straight to the exercise yard for this week's weapons demonstration with Macrobius, then they will go for a thorough cleansing in the Baths of Caracalla, entry fee courtesy of me, and then they will return here to prepare kit ready for infantry training on the Field of Mars. Those who fail will spend the entire evening with the monks in the Greek Library helping to rearrange the military history section. Wax tablets and pens are in the box under the table.'

Quintus quickly pulled out the box and distributed the contents, and everyone hunched over their task. Flavius got up and accompanied Thorismud to the rear door of the chamber, and spoke quietly, out of earshot of the table. 'I apologize for their state, my cousin Quintus especially. I could smell last night on his breath. He has the makings of a decent tribune, but if he fails his exam through carousing and drinking he brings dishonour on me, not just on himself.'

Thorismud coughed. 'He reminds me of someone I once knew.'

Flavius looked exaggeratedly serious. 'Who could you possibly mean?'

'Do you remember that drinking contest by the Tiber? A cup of each vintage from Falernian to Campanian, until one of us dropped.'

'I won.'

'Those fancy Roman drinks didn't suit my gut.'

Flavius put a hand on his shoulder. 'Until we meet again, Thorismud.'

'Fighting against each other, or as allies.'

'Do you think that's possible? That Rome and the Visigoths could be allies again?'

Thorismud stared at the ground. 'Black shadows are falling on the world. The threat from Attila is greater than anything we have ever faced before. We will only survive if new alliances are forged, if men who were previously enemies put aside their differences for the common good. Without that, we will be entering a dark age.'

'Save a place at your mead hall for me, Thorismud. We can do much together.'

'It is done. Now I must go.'

6

The door to the *schola* chamber opened and Macrobius appeared, legs apart and hands behind his back, his tunic freshly dyed red and the number of his old *limitanei numerus* still proudly displayed on his shoulders. Flavius glanced at the sundial visible outside the window on the side of Trajan's market. He had run over time, as usual. He let the cadets finish writing, collected the tablets and stood up. 'That's all for today. Next week it's barbarian culture.'

A groan came up from the front row. 'Not barbarian culture again, tribune. It's all woad and tree-hugging and shrieking.'

'Know your enemy, Marcus Duranius. And don't worry, you won't need to strain your eyes in the library over a book, trying to work out which way is up. For research you only need to talk to your friends. Half of you here have Goth ancestry.'

'When do we get back to battles?'

Flavius gave him a stern look. 'The following week you'll be receiving instructions in surveying and map-reading from Gnaeus Uago Alentius, a senior tribune of the *fabri*. He's a retired officer who taught in the *schola* for decades and he has agreed to come in and teach you as a special favour to me, so you're lucky. He's a Gepid on his father's side, with some Alan blood, so you can also question him about barbarian culture, Marcus Duranius. And he's a rock-hard disciplinarian, so watch your mouth. Now get downstairs, drink some water from the fountain and get ready for some interesting items from Macrobius' collection in the *palaestra*.'

'*Yes!*' Marcus Cato exclaimed, punching the air. 'The best part of the week.'

'Do we get to try them out?' Quintus asked.

'That's for the centurion to decide. Dismissed.'

The class quickly collected their things and filed out past Macrobius, who watched the last of them go and then turned to Flavius. 'You didn't tell them that this was your last day.'

'My appointment to Aetius' staff isn't yet confirmed. But I didn't want to leave with a flourish. After all, it's only been six years, and Uago was here for more than thirty.'

'It's an instructor's lot to see the departing class looking ahead, not back at you,' Macrobius said. 'The reward is in the quality of the officer corps you help to create.'

'How's the exercise ground been over the past weeks?'

'Some daintiness to begin with in this batch among the rich boys from Ravenna, but we soon ironed that out. Being in the same class as grizzled veterans from the frontiers does wonders for them.'

'*Corpora sano, mens sana*, centurion. I can see the effects of your training when they come into the classroom. Exhausted and battered, but sharper minds.'

'I'm looking forward to getting back to my own men.'

'Your appointment as centurion in Aetius' personal bodyguard should come through with mine. It means that the old *numerus* will all be together again, those of us who are still alive. You'll be at Aetius' disposal for any task he may give you, as will I.'

'That's the best an old veteran like me could hope for. And to serve Aetius directly will be a greater honour than any decoration.'

Flavius nodded, and put a hand on his shoulder. Macrobius was past the normal retirement age, having been in the army for more than thirty years, but he was as tough and sinewy as many men at the prime of their fitness. After Carthage, Flavius had tried to get him the *corona civica* for his courage in saving two of his men's lives in the battle against the Vandals, but because the defence of Carthage had been a failure he and all of the others recommended for awards had been passed over. Two years of hard campaigning against the Ostrogoths after that had added a fresh crop of scars to Macrobius' body, one of them a livid weal across his neck from a Saxon cleaver, and these were the only decorations that really mattered among soldiers. But Aetius had noticed them, and had rewarded the *numerus* as a whole by choosing them as his personal bodyguard, the greatest honour that could be bestowed on a unit. With the *numerus* removed from the front line, Flavius had accepted a position as instructor in battle tactics at the *schola militarum* in Rome, bringing Macrobius along with him to fill a vacant post in the physical training department. Over the six years since then they had seen off three classes of newly commissioned tribunes, young men still in their teens along with veterans promoted from the ranks, men who were bolstering the front-line *limitanei* and *comitatenses* units against the growing threat from the steppe-lands beyond the upper reaches of the river Danube to the east.

Macrobius jerked his head back towards the *schola* entrance. 'There's someone here to see you.'

Flavius stared towards the guardroom by the street, and his heart sank. 'Tell me it's not Livia Vipsania,' he muttered. 'If it's her again, we need to beat a hasty retreat out the back.'

'This time you're lucky. It's an old friend.'

Flavius breathed a sigh of relief. Livia Vipsania was the very persistent mother of one of a number of girls who had been pushed in front of him as possible candidates for marriage. As a nephew of *magister militum* Aetius, the most powerful man in the western empire after Valentinian himself, Flavius was considered a prime catch, even though he had given away most of his in-heritance as handouts to the men of his *numerus* so he was worth little more than his salary as a middle-ranking tribune, and he only lived in modest officer's quarters in the barracks overlooking the Circus Maximus. He already had a girlfriend, a woman called Una, the former slave he had seen being abused and beaten by the bishop on the galley from Carthage; after narrowly avoiding murdering the bishop following a particularly savage beating, he had been persuaded by Macrobius to offer all his remaining gold for the girl, a payment that the bishop had all too readily accepted. Flavius had offered to do all he could to return Una to her own people, but she had elected to stay with him. The last thing he wanted now was to be sucked into the world of dynastic marriages and upper-class etiquette in Ravenna and Rome, at a time when the gathering war clouds over the empire made any domestic ambitions seem not just irrelevant, but irresponsible.

They made their way into the vestibule, where a man who had been sitting in the shadows got up, threw back the hood of his cloak and embraced Flavius, who led him quickly back into the classroom out of earshot. Flavius nodded at Macrobius, who pulled the door shut behind him and stood guard, the shadows of his feet remaining visible through the crack at the bottom. Flavius turned to the newcomer. 'Arturus!' he exclaimed, holding the man by the shoulders. 'I thought you were supposed to be in Parthia. I hadn't expected to see you for months.'

Arturus slumped on a chair, taking the cup of water that Flavius passed to him. It was not the first time that he had seen Arturus looking the worse for wear after returning from an intelligence mission for Aetius, but this time he looked older, the first wisps of grey in his beard and hair, the skin of his face deeply tanned and cracked around his eyes. He looked thin, almost emaciated. 'You need food,' Flavius said, looking at his friend with concern. 'Come with me to my quarters, and Una will rustle something up.'

Arturus shook his head. 'Later, I promise. There are more urgent things now.'

'What happened?'

Arturus leaned forward. 'I travelled east from Persepolis to Ctesiphon, disguised as a wine merchant. At Ctesiphon I spent four months in a dungeon for daring to ask whether I could sell my wares to the emperor's agents, as a way of getting into the palace. One of those months I spent staked out in the desert sun every day. Even the best intelligence agent can put a foot wrong, and now I know that nobody in the Sassanid empire even mentions the word palace, let alone the name of the emperor. But after being released and recovering, I took some of my wine from where I had stored it to my captors, who admired its quality and passed on the word to the palace. The short of it is that I was invited into the domestic quarters and then the royal dining chamber, where, after being plied with my own wine to test it for poison, I spent a day and a night serving it at a great imperial feast, listening to everything I could. The good news is that a small family wine concern in Hispania Tarraconensis is about to get a surprise order and become very rich indeed. The bad news I've just conveyed to Aetius.'

'Which is?'

Arturus gave him a grim look. 'The Sassanids will not countenance an alliance with either the eastern or the western Roman Empire against Attila. The Huns are their enemy, but they prefer to meet them on their own terms in their own territory, on desert ground with which their troops are familiar and where they believe that a Roman ally inexperienced in those conditions would only be an impediment. They believe that they can contain any attack from Attila in the bottleneck of the old Parthian frontier to the north, between the Black Sea and the Caspian Sea south of the Caucasus Mountains. They also believe that Attila has no intentions on Ctesiphon and that his eye is firmly set on the West, so that any attack on Parthia would only be play, stoking up his warriors and whetting their appetite for the real war of conquest he has planned against the West. Judging by all of the other evidence that Aetius' agents have gathered, I think the Sassanids are right.'

'So how does this affect Aetius' plans?'

'If an alliance with the Sassanids is out of the question, the only other way of making up sufficient numbers to confront Attila will be to turn to Theodoric and the Visigoths.'

'His son Thorismud was just here. He left before you arrived.'

'I managed to collar him on the street as I came in. He knows who I am, as he once saw me when he was a boy and I was a mercenary in Gaeseric's service, visiting the Visigoth court. He told me he will not go to Aetius directly, but he will bring up the matter with his father in Tolosa at their council of war.'

'You must not let word of this leak out. Valentinian's eunuch Heraclius knows how much the Visigoths detest him, and he will do anything to sabotage plans of an alliance between Rome and the Visigoths, even if the consequences doom the western empire.'

'Heraclius is the main reason why Aetius no longer brings Valentinian into his confidence on intelligence matters,' Arturus said. 'The emperor's predilection for eunuchs, as with Theodosius in the East, is turning him into little more than a figurehead, leaving the *magister militum* holding the real reins of power, but also creating a dangerous vacuum that Heraclius and the eunuchs in the East could fill. Thorismud understands this, and before the council meets he will only bring up the question of an alliance privately with his father, Theodoric.'

Flavius pursed his lips, and shook his head. 'I know my uncle well, and I also know Theodoric, a distant kinsman of my Goth grandfather who I met when Thorismud took me to the Visigoth court when were together at the *schola*. They are both men of reason, but they are also warriors who would be reluctant to stand down. The winds of war from the East will have to be strong indeed to sway them from their animosity.'

'That's why I've come here and why I am telling you this.' Arturus reached into his tunic and pulled out a wooden tube containing a scroll. 'That's confirmation of your appointment as a special tribune in Aetius' service, and of Macrobius as a centurion in his bodyguard. You now answer directly to Aetius. He has another plan, and it involves both of you.'

Flavius felt a frisson of excitement. 'Tell me what I have to do.'

'First, we need to go tomorrow morning to see your old instructor Uago, to look at some maps. After that, we need to play it by ear. Valentinian and his retinue are in town, and Heraclius' agents will finger any officer who doesn't go to the palace to pay their respects. If we have to go to the court it should be no more than a distraction from our true purpose, which should see us leave the city by next sundown, on a mission from which we might not return.'

Arturus stood up and shrugged off his cloak, revealing the tunic and insignia of a tribune of the *foederati*, the wolf emblem of the *numerus Britannorum* attached to his shoulder. Flavius put his hand on his shoulder. 'Aetius has reinstated your commission. It's been long overdue.'

Arturus slung the cloak over his shoulder. 'It's no more than a smokescreen. I'm less conspicuous walking around Rome in this uniform than I am in the cloak of a spy.'

Flavius went to the door, opened it and looked at Macrobius. 'When you finish with the cadets in the *palaestra*, go to Una and ask her to lay out my weapons and equipment. Then go to your quarters and do the same.'

Macrobius stared at him, his eyes gleaming. 'I knew something was afoot! Arturus has never before come to the *schola* so openly to find you.'

'I'll know more tomorrow. Meet me at my quarters at midday.'

'*Ave*, tribune.'

'And Macrobius.'

'Tribune?'

'Do you have anyone to say goodbye to?'

'Only the girls in the taverns down by the Tiber. They humour an old veteran like me, one who Rome has never paid enough to start a family. Who is barely paid enough for a visit to the tavern.'

Flavius grinned and slapped him on the shoulder. 'Well, you'd better go there this evening. I have to say my own goodbyes, too. We may be out of Rome by tomorrow evening.'

'*Ave*, tribune, with pleasure. But before that, to the *palaestra*.'

7

Half an hour later Flavius stood outside the classroom on the balcony overlooking the *palaestra*, a rectangular courtyard surrounded by colonnades and spread with sand to soak up the blood. It was only twelve years since he and Thorismud had fought each other to exhaustion here, wrestling and sword-fighting and practising with every barbarian weapon they could lay their hands on, and yet now Flavius was overseeing his last class himself. It was in the *palaestra* and on the Field of Mars outside the city that the instructors made their final choice of those suitable for commissioning as tribunes, weeding out cadets with any traits that they knew would earn them the disrespect of their men in the field. Hesitation, even fear, could be forgiven, especially among the younger candidates; arrogance and blink-ered thinking could not. This might be his last day in the *schola*, but Flavius knew that it should be no different from the rest, that he was going to have to try to forget Una and Arturus and focus a keen eye instead on the dozen or so officer-cadets whom Macrobius would soon be leading out onto the sand.

He glanced beyond the *palaestra* at the upper drums of the great marble column that rose from the Forum of Trajan beyond, at the bronze statue of the revered emperor himself who seemed to stare down directly at him. Here, within the four walls of the *schola*, he felt cocooned from the corruption and sleaze of the court of Valentinian outside, as if that gaze from on high were bathing the courtyard in the purity of its vision. Sometimes he felt that if he were to stare at the statue for long enough he would be drawn back in time, that he would be able to go down and open the doors to the street outside and join the throng of legionaries who were depicted on the column, marching in step with them through roaring crowds to lay their booty at the foot of the emperor before following him to yet more conquests and victories beyond the frontiers. It was a vision of Rome that had sustained him as a boy growing up among these monuments, and one that could still seduce him, despite everything he now knew about the hollowness of imperial power and the darkness ahead that seemed to offer little chance of a triumphant return to the glories of the past.

He was jolted back to the present as four slaves appeared on the *palaestra* ground carrying a wooden trestle table, followed by Macrobius with a wrapped bundle of weapons which he rolled out on the table top. This afternoon's practical was to be their final class on the weapons of their enemies. Last week it had been the throwing nets of the Suebi, said to have been based on those used by the *velationes* in the days of the gladiators, something that not even Macrobius could master; today he would be on firmer ground with the weapons of the Huns. From here they would go for three months' intensive training on the Field of Mars, leading infantry and cavalry *numeri* in mock battles, learning the basics of artillery and field engineering from the catapult men and the *fabri*, and finishing with the route marches and endurance tests that would determine the final selection. In the class that morning Flavius had been less harsh than he might have been following their obvious indulgence in the taverns the night before, remembering his own last night of freedom before the drill centurions of the Field of Mars bawled their orders and locked them inside for the duration.

They came trooping out now, a dozen boys and veteran cadets, and formed a loose semi-circle in front of Macrobius, squinting and shading their eyes against the sun. Macrobius glanced up at Flavius, who nodded, and then he glared at the class. 'Welcome to the daylight. This should roast the last of the wine out of you. Who can tell me about the Huns?'

There was silence for a moment, and then Quintus put his hand up and stepped forward. 'They live east of the Danube and north of the Maeotic Lake, near the Frozen Ocean, and they are a race savage beyond parallel.'

He paused, and Macrobius stared at him. 'Well? Go on.'

Quintus cleared his throat. 'They are of great size, but low-legged, like shaggy two-legged beasts. At the moment of their birth they are slashed across the cheeks three times, giving them scars for life and meaning the men can't grow beards. They roam wild about the grasslands, sleeping under the stars or in rude tents, and on campaign they live in wagons like the Goths.'

Marcus Cato put his hand up as well. 'And they eat the half-raw flesh of any animal, merely warming it up by placing it between their own thighs as they ride or on the backs of their horses,' he said, adding enthusiastically, 'and they wear round caps with ear flaps, and leggings of calf-hide, and tunics made from the skins of small mice intricately sewn together, and armour made of small bronze plates knitted into their tunics, said to have been copied from the warriors of the land of Thina itself. And they cover themselves in blue woad.'

'No, you idiot,' Quintus scoffed, turning to him. 'That's the Agathyrsi.'

Macrobius narrowed his eyes at them. 'Some of this sounds familiar. What have you two been reading?'

'It was yesterday afternoon, in the Latin Library,' Quintus replied.

'When you were supposed to be researching the Battle of Adrianople.'

'I found this volume by Ammianus Marcellinus, *Res Gestae*, "Things I have done", written in the time of our grandfathers,' Quintus said. 'It was the coolest book, way more interesting than those books on Adrianople. No disrespect, but the Greeks who wrote them didn't seem to know much about battle, whereas Ammianus was the real deal. *And* he wrote in Latin.'

Macrobius grunted. 'Ammianus was a real soldier, I'll give you that, unlike the so-called historians of our time, monks and pen-pushers who've never raised a sword in anger in their lives.'

'He wrote that he was in the *protectores domestici*,' Quintus said. 'It was a unit modelled on the old Praetorian Guard, for protecting the emperor.'

'That was early on in his career, a ceremonial posting for rich boys like half you lot. But then he went on to do some real soldiering, campaigning in Gaul and Persia under the emperors Constantius and Julian. He became the right-hand man of *magister militum* Ursicinus, the greatest general of modern times until Aetius. My own grandfather fought alongside Ursicanus' son Potentias at Adrianople,' Macrobius said gruffly, 'standing astride his body after he had been felled and dragging it back to the Roman lines, an act that would have won him the *corona civica* had any officer been alive to see it. Ursicinus and Ammianus were both dismissed from the army after the Persians took Amida in Asia Minor. It was an impossible place to defend, but the emperor needed someone to blame, so he cashiered his best general and his most able lieutenant. Typical.' He glared again at the two boys. 'Well? What else does Ammianus say?'

Quintus cleared his throat again. 'I didn't have time to get any further on the Huns, but I did see where he said that no wild beasts are more deadly to humans than Christians are to each other.'

Macrobius glanced up at Flavius on the balcony, and then leaned forward with a hand on one knee, his voice lowered. 'In this man's army, whatever god, whatever idol gets you through the night, whatever steels you before a battle, is yours to worship, no questions asked. But outside the four walls of this *schola*, be on your guard. Repeat anything like you've just said, and you'll be in trouble. I'm amazed the monks who run the libraries haven't spotted it and put Ammianus on the scrap pile. The bishop of Rome now thinks he's God himself, and has spies everywhere.'

Quintius nodded thoughtfully, and then put his hand up again, his face flushed with excitement. 'Ammianus also says that beyond the land of the Huns is the tribe of the Geloni, who flay the enemies they've slain in battle and make clothes out of the skin for themselves and their horses.'

'I've heard that,' another of the boys said. 'My old riding master had been taught by a Scythian horseman who'd actually seen it. He said the Geloni prefer to flay a man before he's dead, because then the skin is still alive and when you put it on it clings to you like a glove, and fits perfectly. Saves paying for a tailor, doesn't it?'

'That's sick,' another of the boys said.

Marcus Cato stood forward, his eyes gleaming. 'Quintus, do you remember that last passage from Ammianus that you read out to me in the library? About the anthropophagi and the Amazons?' He turned to the group. 'The anthropophagi live beyond the Geloni near the land called Thina, and they eat only human flesh. The Amazons, well, we all know about them from the Taverna Amazonica down by the Tiber, where the whores dress up as Amazons. They fight naked except for a loincloth, and are always hungry for men. They give a special discount for cadets from the *schola*.'

The other boy who had spoken sneered at him. 'You mean they give *you* a special discount, Marcus Cato, because you always finish your business before they even have a chance to touch you. You wouldn't know how to pleasure a she-goat, let alone a woman.'

'I'd have a crack at real-life Amazons any day,' another said assertively. 'If they're hungry for man flesh, I'll show them what a real Roman is made of.'

'Real Roman, or real Goth?' another said. 'You should remember your lineage, Julius Acer. And last I heard, real Goths only get it up when they're chasing a retreating army of bare-arsed eunuchs.'

'Watch what you say,' an older *optio* growled. 'Half of us here are Goths and combat veterans, and we know what it's like to spill blood on the field. If you want a demonstration, you can bare your arse to us on the Field of Mars after the *schola*. That is, if you're not too busy being chased by Amazons.'

'Enough,' Macrobius bellowed, barely suppressing a smile. 'Save it for the exercise ground. As for flesh-eaters and skin-flayers, I can't vouch for that. But I can vouch for Amazons. And you wouldn't be taking a crack at them, Julius Acer, they'd be taking a crack at you.' He turned and carefully picked up an object from the table, a blackened, congealed mass that looked like a coil of long-dead snakes. 'Anyone recognize this?'

Quintus stepped forward, peering. 'It's a whip. A very old whip.'

'Good.' Macrobius stood with his legs apart, showing the object around so the others could see. 'It is said that this war whip was carried by a Scythian princess who fought alongside Scipio Aemilianus at the siege of Carthage, and that her use of it broke the will of the Carthaginian Sacred Band. For almost six hundred years it passed down through the generations of the Scipio family, and now it's one of the prized possessions of the *schola* armoury. The princess had ridden with the Berber tribesmen in the desert, and had learned from them how to embed razor-sharp slivers of obsidian near the tip of the whip, as you can see here. She left it with Scipio when she returned to her people, but she took the idea with her and ever afterwards the warriors of her tribe have been armed with steel-tipped whips. She never married, but her son, said to have been fathered by a Gaulish prince who had also been with Scipio at Carthage, became the first great warrior king of the people who were to call themselves the Huns, the ancestor of Mundiuk and Attila.'

The cadets stared silently at the whip, their banter forgotten. 'So these will be used against us in battle?' Quintus said, reaching over and touching one of the obsidian blades, drawing a drop of blood.

'I myself have only seen them at a distance, when a Hun unit joined the flank of the Ostrogoth line before Aquileia, the first action of my *numerus* after we returned from Carthage,' Macrobius said, puffing his chest out. 'All we could see was a silvery shimmer above the heads of our soldiers caused by the polished steel blades reflecting in the sun, but it was enough to put the fear of God into some of the *foederati* among our line who had seen the Huns ravage their homelands. Those closer to the action said that while the front rank of the Huns engaged our troops with swords, the next rank used whips to draw forward our men in the second row, lassoing them around the neck and dragging them into the melee, throwing our front line off balance. The Huns then leapt forward and finished them off with the sword, except for those, that is, who had already had their throats cut or been decapitated by the blades on the whips.'

'Can the whips be parried?' Marcus Cato asked, his voice wavering.

Macrobius snorted. 'They come as fast as a scorpion's tail, too fast to see. All you can do is pray to whichever god tickles your fancy that you are not the one chosen, and try to press forward to within thrusting range. But they are skilled at using the whips at close range too, cracking them high in the air so that the tip coils round viciously at neck level, slicing into our soldiers even when they are on top of them.'

He picked up the second weapon on the table, a bow, and held it out to show the cadets. 'Some of you may rue the day that you first saw one of these. This is a Hun bow, taken from a Goth by the men of my *numerus* in a skirmish in the northern forests of Gaul eight years ago. It's composite, made from three different elements laminated together. The inner surface is a wood said to come from a stunted tree of the steppes, and the outer surface a wood the barbarians call *iwa* or *yew* and we call *baccata*, a strong and flexible evergreen. In between these is a continuous length of ivory said to come from the tusks of long-dead elephants of gigantic proportions found by the Huns along the edge of the Frozen Lake to the north. Because only the Huns know the source of the tusks, it's impossible for our *fabri* to replicate the laminate. These three elements give the bow its incredible strength.'

To make his point he placed the bow between the ground and the edge of the table and then leapt on it, an action that would have snapped a normal Roman bow but that left him bouncing off and the bow intact. Marcus Cato stooped over and picked it up, handing it back. 'Why the strange shape?' he asked, pointing at the asymmetry of the bow, the upper recurve larger than the lower and the grip placed below the centre and at an angle.

Macrobius straightened up and took the bow. 'It allows you to shoot an arrow at a greater initial velocity than you can with our bows, if you have the strength to hold the grip at that angle and take the strain it puts on the wrist and forearm. Our archers find these bows almost impossible to use without months of practice. Our bows have the edge over Hun bows in their maximum range, as it makes them better suited to lobbing arrows high and dropping them into an enemy formation, but the Hun arrow with its heavily weighted iron tip flies faster and on a level trajectory for a greater distance, perfectly suited to the Hun mounted archers who ride to within fifty paces before loosing at their enemy.'

He picked up another bow, a more orthodox shape bearing the numerical mark of one of the *sagittarii* units stationed in the city, strung an arrow and aimed at a post that the slaves had placed in the centre of the *palaestra* with a thick slab of wood attached to it about head height as a target. He pulled back as far as he could and then released, the arrow flying forward and embedding itself in the board up to the end of the tip. He put it down, picked up the Hun bow and another arrow, this one shorter, strung it and clenched his teeth as he pulled back, the muscles and veins in his arms taut with the effort. With a grunt he loosed the arrow and it shot forward, just hitting the corner of the target but driving right through it up to the feathers, the wood split and the arrow quivering on the far side.

He put the bow down, rubbed his right bicep and turned to the cadets, his face set like stone. 'I'll tell you what else Ammianus Marcellinus had to say about the Huns. He said they charge at huge speed, on horseback or on foot, bellowing and ululating and making a throat chant to terrorize their enemy, who fall back in disarray; they are then broken into smaller clusters by the Hun cavalry, who ride round and round each cluster in turn, finishing them off with their arrows. Even against an unbroken line their foot archers and infantry inflict terrific casualties with bone- and iron-tipped arrows, and with lassos. At close quarters they fight on horseback and on foot with the sword, not shying away from using their hands and even their teeth to finish off those who have survived the onslaught. Ammianus, a veteran of war against the Gauls and the Goths and the Persians, said that of the barbarians he had encountered, the Huns were the most terrible of all warriors.'

He paused, eyeing the group. 'Do you know why I know Ammianus' account by heart?'

Quintus put up his hand. 'Because he was a soldier. Because he knew what he was talking about.'

Macrobius gave them a grim look. 'That's part of it. But there's something else. I myself have seen Huns in battle, but only at a distance. I know Ammianus by heart because we have no other eyewitness accounts, because no Roman alive has stood before a Hun onslaught and survived. Think about that.'

They all looked sombre, and then Quintus pointed to the last weapon on the table. 'Is that a Hun sword, centurion? Can we see it?'

Macrobius picked up the sword, holding it by the hilt and the flat of the blade. 'This is our final weapon of the day, and equally fearsome in the right hands. You will see that it comes from the same tradition as our swords, a long, straight blade of cavalry fashion, of the type that the Roman army chose for standard issue over the *gladius* as it has a longer blade more suited to mounted action. Below the diamond-shaped guard you can see how the edges of the blade begin parallel, but then slowly converge to the point, making the blade heavier near the hilt and strangely balanced, but suited to thrusting as well as slashing. It is said that the steel of the blade is tempered in such a way that it makes it stronger than our blades, using a secret technique brought from the East that our smiths cannot replicate. As a result it holds its edge longer than ours, and can be sharpened to the fineness of those slivers of obsidian embedded in the whip. It will cut through leather and slice through flesh more easily than ours, but is a more difficult sword to master, with the balance closer to the hilt and therefore requiring more dexterity and strength to deliver a powerful blow.'

He handed the sword to Quintus, who felt its heft and eyed the blade, the others crowding around to look. Macrobius pulled out the sword he was wearing, a standard-issue Roman blade about half a foot shorter than the Hun sword, and gave it to Marcus Cato. 'You two get to demonstrate. It's your reward for doing your homework. Remember, use the flat of the blade.'

Quintus grinned at his friend, and the two walked into the centre of the *palaestra* in front of the target pole and squared off. They began by gently clashing blades and parrying, slowly circling each other. 'Come on,' yelled the boy who had been bantering with Marcus Cato. 'Put some elbow into it.' Marcus Cato gave him an annoyed look, spun round under the Hun blade and whacked Quintus hard on the buttocks, making him stagger sideways under the weight of his sword. 'So much for Hun weapons!' the boy guffawed. 'If the weighting's all wrong, what's the point of having harder steel and sharper blades?'

Quintus picked himself up, grimaced exaggeratedly and grinned, and then they squared off again, slowly circling each other. Suddenly he swung his sword at Marcus Cato's midriff, pulling it back at the last moment as Marcus Cato raised his sword to parry the blow. Seeing Quintus' swing fail, Marcus Cato raised his sword behind his head to deliver his own blow, but instead of recovering, Quintus had let the momentum of the swing bring him round again, turning nearly full circle on the spot. Too late, Marcus Cato realized that Quintus' initial swing had been a feint, designed to make him raise his guard and expose his midriff, and too late Quintus realized that his sword had righted itself and was now swinging at Marcus Cato edge-on. In the split second of his realization he tried to pull the blade back again, but the momentum this time was too great. The blade sliced through Marcus Cato's tunic and halfway through his torso, cutting so quickly that for the first second there was barely a trickle of blood from the wound.

There was a gasp from the others and then a horrified silence as Quintus pulled the blade out. Marcus Cato staggered back, his arms falling to his sides, letting the sword drop. He stared at Quintus uncomprehendingly, and then he toppled sideways like a falling statue, his head hitting the ground with a thud and his eyes glazed open, his mouth drooling. With a slurp his bowels fell out of the gaping wound in his side, a slithering mass in lurid colours, exposing his severed backbone. He convulsed violently, his arms juddering and his mouth foaming. A terrible sigh emerged from him as the blood gushed out over the sand, and then he was still.

Quintus dropped the sword and put his hands over his face, shaking and moaning softly. Macrobius immediately marched over to him, picked up the sword, wiped the blood on Quintus' tunic, pulled down one hand and thrust the hilt back into it. Quintus continued sobbing, almost doubling over, and Macrobius slapped him hard on the face, making him reel back with the sword dragging behind him. Macrobius pulled him up by the collar and pointed at the body. 'You see that?' he snarled, looking around. 'I'm talking to all of you. That's called *death*. If you're going to use a sword, you'd better get used to it. Now, we will make our salutations. Marcus Cato Claudius, you have helped to make a better soldier of Quintus Aetius Gaudentius Secundus, who now will always have you with him when he goes into battle, will have the honour of your name to uphold as well. Marcus Cato Claudius, *salve atque vale*. Now, all of you are due for your induction in the Field of Mars this evening. Make a bad impression by arriving teary-eyed, and then for the next three months you'll wish you were where Marcus Cato is now. I want to see you with all your kit lined up in full marching order outside the front entrance of the *schola* in half an hour. And that goes for you too, Quintus Aetius. Go now.'

Two of the others, veteran cadets, went on either side of Quintus and walked him away out of sight under the balcony, followed by the rest. Macrobius picked up his own sword, gathered the weapons in the leather roll and walked off towards the armoury on the far side of the *palaestra*. The slaves who had brought in the table then reappeared with a cart and a sack of sand, wheeling it towards the body. They emptied the sand in a pile, heaved the body onto the cart and then used a shovel to scoop up the innards, pouring them into the sack and throwing it on top of the body. They spread the sand around, leaving it for a minute to sop up the blood before shovelling it on top of the body, finishing by sprinkling a fresh layer of sand on the ground and raking it out with another tool. Two of them wheeled the cart away while the other two carried off the table. A moment later one of them dashed back out and pulled up the target pole with the split wood and the arrows, running with it out of sight. The scene was as it had been before Macrobius had arrived, as if stagehands had removed the props in a theatre after a play, the statue of Trajan still presiding from his column and the only evidence of what had happened the hint of a stain in the sand.

Flavius had looked on dispassionately. His mind had strayed to Una once the sword-play had begun, and it had taken him a few moments to register the accident. He remembered his own first shocks as a young man, watching as men of his *numerus* were ripped apart by the dogs before Carthage, feeling stunned by his own first kill. Quintus had suffered the cruellest of blows, killing his best friend in practice combat, but Macrobius had been right to respond as he did, and Flavius would not be seeking his cousin out. Either Quintus would go to pieces, another reject from the *schola*, or the experience would make a man of him, would toughen him up, his ability to ride it through strengthened by a drive to uphold the honour of his family, of Flavius himself, who he knew had been watching, of their uncle Aetius, of a Rome imbued with glory and honour and military virtue that they all desperately hoped to rebuild. He glanced up at the statue of Trajan again and turned back to the door. It was time to go.

8

That night Flavius lay with Una on the sands beside the mouth of the river Tiber, watching the moonlight dance across the ruffled surface of the Tyrrhenian Sea. They had ridden down from Rome that afternoon on Flavius' horse, through the dilapidated town of Ostia and past the canal that led to the octagonal harbour of Portus, and now they were on the great stretch of sand near Antium that extended south as far as the eye could see. Fewer ships came up the Tiber now than in the days of Flavius' youth, the fall of Carthage having cut off the trade in African grain and oil, and the last vessel of the day had left hours ago, their solitude since then broken only by a few fishermen who had come and cast their nets during the early evening but who had left as soon as darkness set in.

Flavius propped himself up on one elbow as he took some grapes from the food they had brought with them and drank from a flagon of wine, and watched Una as she lay with her eyes closed stretched out on the blanket beside him. She was long-limbed, taller than he was, with high cheekbones and tightly curled black hair, and even among the people of Rome, used to slaves and soldiers from all quarters of the world, she raised eyebrows as she passed through the streets and the markets, more beautiful in Flavius' eyes than any of the pasty-looking girls from noble families who were endlessly paraded in front of him as suitable prospects for marriage.

Una was not like the black-skinned slaves he had seen sold as exotica in the markets of Rome, slaves said to have come from far-off lands to the south of the great African desert, nor like the Nubians and Berbers who had thronged into Carthage in the city's final days; instead she was from an African land to the east where the river Nile rose in the highlands overlooking the Erythraean Sea, a place that she called Ethiopia. She had told him that on the high plateaus of her homeland the girls would run between villages carrying messages and news, effortlessly covering thirty or more miles in a day, further even than a day's route march for a soldier, and that when they came down from the thin air of the uplands to the plains and the desert below they could run even further and faster. He had seen it for himself on the many occasions he had brought her from Rome to run on these sands, and she had done so again this evening, Flavius cantering and galloping alongside her while she covered miles and miles, her breathing barely quickened and her legs seeming to float above the sand. Afterwards they had made love and swum in the sea, and her skin still glistened with the water that left the taste of salt on Flavius' lips, a cleansing taste that for a few precious hours made the machinations of Rome and the venality of the emperor and his court seem a distant irrelevance.

She opened her eyes and sat upright, pulling up her robe against the first chill of the night, and stared out to sea, saying nothing. Flavius drew himself alongside her, dragging over the flagon and taking another draught, feeling the warmth of the wine in his belly. 'What are you thinking?' he said, wiping his lips and passing her the flagon.

She took it, raised it to her lips and then put it down again. 'I was thinking about Quodvultdeus, the Bishop of Carthage.'

'Why think about that monster in this place? He nearly beat you to death on the ship back from Carthage. If Macrobius hadn't held me back, I would have killed him with my bare hands.'

She was silent for a moment, and then spoke quietly. 'You must remember what I'd been through. After the slavers kidnapped me from my village in Ethiopia I spent two years working for a Nubian whoremaster, caged up with other girls in wagons that travelled from oasis to oasis waiting to service the men of the camel caravans when they came in. I had already learned of Christianity from the followers of the monk Frumentius who had first brought the new religion from Alexandria to my people, and it became my salvation; knowing of the suffering of Jesus and the two thieves on the crosses gave me the strength to carry on. When Bishop Quodvultdeus rode by one day, pointing to me and two of the other girls, giving the whoremaster a purse of gold, I thought that Christ himself had answered my prayers, and I fell down on my knees and worshipped him. Later, when he led us in prayer, entrancing us all with his messianic eyes and deep voice, he used to say that we were the holy innocents, that those who would abuse us and vent their fury on us were really paying us homage, as Herod did when he wreaked his fury on the Christ child. It was only much later, after far too long under his spell, that I realized he was no messenger from Christ but a venal and cruel man who had bought us to satisfy his own desires, when he wasn't occupied chasing boys around the cloisters in Carthage.'

'Quodvultdeus, "What God Wants",' Flavius muttered, flinging a stone into the surf. 'If a man like that thinks he's what God wants, then we're better off without a Church.'

'I never lost my faith,' Una continued, 'because the Christianity taught in my land is not the Christianity of Rome. I never saw Quodvultdeus as an intermediary to God, just as one who seemed in my fevered imagination to have been sent by God to bring my deliverance. Once I saw through him I saw the truth of the Church he represented, a hollow vessel created by men to satisfy their own ambitions and cravings, as far from God as he is from the courts of the emperors.'

Flavius pursed his lips, looking out to sea. 'The last I heard, Quodvultdeus had set himself up as the Bishop of Rome's special inquisitor in Neapolis, leading a squad of thugs house by house to root out so-called heretics who don't believe that the Bishop is already up there sitting in judgement alongside Christ himself.'

Una shuddered, clutching her robe closer around her. 'That's only two days' ride from here. The closer he gets, the more I want to leave. I'm conspicuous enough in Rome as it is, but the methods he uses to extract confessions will lead to someone pointing the finger at me.'

Flavius peered at her. 'You often go out quietly in the night, and don't return until dawn. I've never asked questions, but I've guessed.'

Una reached out and put a hand on his arm, squeezing it, and then drew back under her robe. 'You may as well know now. We meet in the catacombs, under Rome and along the Appian Way. There are secret places, known only to a few.'

Flavius stared at her intently. 'Have you met Pelagius?'

'We never know the names of those who lead us in prayer, or see their faces. It's too dangerous for them. It's been that way for almost four hundred years, since the time soon after the crucifixion when the Apostles came to Neapolis and Pompeii, worshipping in secret among the sulphur pits of the Phlegraean Fields before spreading to Rome when the first catacombs were being dug. We are an underground Christianity, always in hiding, persecuted now under the Church of Rome just as we were in pagan times.'

'What will you do?'

She reached into the folds of her robe and pulled out the golden cross on a necklace that she had removed when she went running, an elaborate latticework of geometric patterns with a square at the base that she had told him represented the Ark of the Covenant. She held it up, the moonlight shining through the lattice, and then turned to him. 'What do you know of the kingdom of Aksum?'

Flavius hesitated, then said, 'It's the place Arturus told his two Nubian slaves to find when he sent them away before the fall of Carthage. He said it would offer them safe haven, and freedom from slavery.'

She lowered the cross and looked out at the horizon. 'Aksum borders my own land to the north, occupying the valleys and hills that lead down to the Erythraean Sea. It's the first nation you reach when you travel south from Egypt. Its capital city has great granite columns, taller even than the column of Trajan, and tombs and houses dug from the living rock, built by an ancient civilization that some believe was one of the lost tribes of Israel, those who brought the Ark of the Covenant with them. Since the time of Constantine the Great when the monk Gregorius converted the Aksumite king Ezana to Christianity the kingdom has grown ever stronger, spreading its influence north to Egypt, south to the Horn of Africa and east across the narrows to Arabia, to the land of the Sabaeans. It controls the Erythraean Sea trade from India to Egypt, but its real strength lies in its Christianity. It is the word as taught by Jesus, spread from person to person, from village to village. There are no priests in Aksum, no bishops. All are welcome, whatever their faith, Jews, pagans, the Arabs with their desert religion, as long as they follow a path of peace.'

'Do you wish to return, Una?' Flavius said.

She held the cross with one hand and grasped his with the other. 'You know I can bear you no children. The whoremaster and his wife saw to that. And ahead of us now can only be long absences, campaigns and battles, and then one day you won't return. Everyone in Rome knows what the future holds. Mothers are doting on their sons, knowing they will soon be drawn away to war. At night the stands of the Circus Maximus next to our quarters are full of lovers not willing to wait any longer for marriage. Fathers of military age who fear conscription are taking their children around the monuments of Rome, teaching them everything they know while they still have time. And it's not only the men whose lives may be foreshortened. If darkness falls on the city of Rome itself, if Attila arrives, if the Vandals sweep up from the sea, then all of our lives are at risk. There is more and more talk of the biblical apocalypse, of a coming doomsday, spread by the monks of Arles and now taken up by others who have descended on the city in droves, real monks and charlatans, persuading people to give up all of their gold and silver in return for a special prayer to the Lord.'

'The army will prevail,' Flavius said, emotion in his voice. 'We *will* defeat Attila.'

Una shook her head and looked at him, gripping his hand hard. 'It makes no difference for us. I've made up my mind.' She was crying, but there was a fervour in her eyes he had never seen before. She wiped them, and carried on. 'I listen when you talk, you and Arturus and the other officers who share your views, followers of your uncle Aetius. Just as you wish to break away from the emperor and take the war yourselves to the barbarians at the frontiers, so we wish to wrest Christianity from the hold of the Church and take it to places beyond the empire, beyond the reach of the priests and the bishops. Some will go north, Pelagius himself, to try to establish a new Christian foothold in Britain. But others among us are planning to go south to Aksum. Already monks of the East who have turned from the Church in Constantinople are going there, and they will soon be followed by others from the West. There are some who believe Aksum is the promised land, that it could become the kingdom of Heaven on earth.'

'Do you feel that God is calling you?' Flavius said, his voice wavering.

'All I know is that I was able to bring the words of Jesus to the other girls enslaved with me in the desert, and it gave them hope. If I can do the same to the distant people in the mountains of my own land, then I will have found purpose in life. And I want to run again, not along these sands that lead only south to Neapolis and persecution or north to war, but between the villages of my home in the Ethiopian highlands, bringing messages only of peace. I have had enough of Rome and her wars.'

She turned and drew something else out of the folds of her

robe, handing it to him. It was a small stone, black and polished smooth, suspended from a thin leather thong that had been threaded through a hole in the centre. 'I found this piece of jet outside my village when I was a child, and have worn it smooth by handling it. Take it, and remember me.'

Behind them Flavius' horse whinnied and stomped, moving down from the grassy knoll in the dunes where they had left it grazing while they went swimming. Flavius picked up the nosebag he had prepared and got up to feed it, stroking its nose and whispering into its ear, and then slapping it on its haunches as it cantered over to the river for a drink. He felt suddenly alone, standing behind Una as she stared out to the horizon, watching his horse dip its head into the waters where the Tiber flowed into the sea. He had expected to be the one breaking the news to her of his imminent departure, but instead she had turned the tables on him. He had felt thrown by it, confused, unable to reply. Yet standing here, poised between her and the restless horse, he knew where his future lay. The free will preached by Pelagius and his followers was all very well, but in a world on the verge of imploding, the lives of men were as constrained as those of the gladiators of old in the Colosseum. He was as locked into war as Una was into her vision of peace.

He heard a distant noise, a drumbeat, and stared out to sea. Beneath the light of the moon a galley came into view, a single-banked *liburnian*, one of the patrols they had seen leave the mouth of the Tiber shortly after they had arrived. Even here on the beach under the stars the sense of peace was an illusion. For months now Gaiseric's Vandal navy from Carthage had been raiding and pillaging its way along the coast, using the Roman ships that he had seen abandoned in the harbour of Carthage before its fall. Arturus had been right in his prediction that day: the warriors of the forest had become warriors of the desert, and now of the sea. Gaiseric had not been content to rest on his laurels at Carthage but had taken his men on the only route of campaign open from there, out onto the Mediterranean. All of the strategists in Rome knew it was only a matter of time before raiding and pillaging became a seaborne assault. The Roman navy was too weak to confront Gaiseric in a full-scale naval battle, so the only hope was a victory for the army, not against the Vandals but against the Huns, a victory that would allow troops to redeploy along this shore to counter an invasion. Yet even that strategy was riddled with uncertainty: any victory against Attila was likely to be one of attrition, leaving the Roman army too weak to redeploy effectively. Everything was on a knife-edge. All that seemed certain was that one day soon these beaches, like the shore before Troy, would run red with blood, that those left to defend Rome would make the invaders pay a dear price among the dunes and hollows of this shore.

The horse returned and kicked at the sand. Una got up and Flavius quickly rolled the blanket, leaving the grapes and the empty flagon in the sand. He leapt on the horse, reining it in as it reared into the air, whinnying and stomping again, and then he put out a hand, pulling Una up behind him. She held him tight, her breasts warm against his back, and they rode hard for Rome.

9

Early the following morning Flavius led Arturus out of the *schola*, over the exercise yard and onto the street in front of the emperor Trajan's great column, its white marble drums soaring a hundred feet into the air between the Greek and Latin libraries. As a boy, between lessons with his teacher Dionysius, Flavius had spent hours staring from the upper floors of the libraries at the column, scrutinizing each scene on the spiral frieze until it was etched in his memory: scenes of war and conquest, of weapons and fortifications and river crossings, of defeated barbarians and victorious Romans, of the emperor himself commanding his men from the front and leading them on. He saw the inscription at the base of the column, the place where the ashes of the emperor lay in a casket of Dacian gold, and read the first line: SENATVS POPVLVSQVE ROMANVS, remembering the rest by heart: *The Senate and the people of Rome give this to the emperor Caesar, son of the divine Nerva, Nerva Trajanus Augustus Germanicus Dacicus, Pontifex Maximus, in his seventeenth year in the office of Tribune, having been acclaimed six times as imperator, six times consul, pater patriae.*

He looked up and saw a scene featuring the vanquished King Decebalus and another of the Romans crossing the river Danube, the image that had most fired his imagination as a boy, and he felt the excitement course through him. He could hardly believe that he would soon be going to the same place, that he and Macrobius and Arturus would be crossing the river where the legionaries had gone three hundred and fifty years before, treading where his revered hero Trajan has taken his army on a war of conquest that would reach the limits of Parthia and see the Roman Empire expand to its greatest extent ever.

They left the column behind and climbed up a winding road on the north side of Trajan's forum into the adjoining market complex, a huge brick structure that had been converted under Aetius' orders into the Rome headquarters of the *fabri*, the corps of military engineers. They passed several buxom slave girls carrying baskets behind an overweight cleric and flashing smiles at them, and he thought of Una, wondering when he was going to see her again. Just before leaving the *schola* he had called Macrobius back and asked him to tell Una to leave, to take her belongings to his sister's house in Cosa up the coast and await his return. It was just a niggle, but he had a sudden feeling that it was not worth taking chances, that if Heraclius was on to Arturus then he might also have agents who had seen the two of them together, who might be following them now. He had little else to lose in this world, but if anything happened to Una he knew he would have to exact vengeance on those who had perpetrated it, something that could start a terrible bloodbath that might bring down all of those around him and destroy Aetius' plans. Not knowing when he might see her again was a small price to pay for avoiding that, though it was one he knew he was going find hard to bear in the days and weeks ahead.

After passing inspection by the guards Flavius and Arturus went along a corridor and through a door into a hall almost as large as a law court, the wide windows letting in sunlight that lit up a row of tables in the centre. Around the walls below the windows were pinned-up charts and maps, one of them a continuous scroll that extended over two walls, and at the tables several dozen men were copying maps and annotating illustrations on large sheets of vellum and papyrus.

One of the men saw them, waved and quickly made his way over – a white-bearded man in late middle age wearing the insignia of a senior *fabri* tribune. He slapped Flavius on the shoulder and immediately doubled over in pain, his hand on his back. 'It doesn't get any better,' he exclaimed, letting the two men ease him onto a seat. 'Too much time hunched over maps, not enough fresh air. It's far too long since I saw active service.'

'When was that?' Arturus said.

'Flavius can tell you. No decorations, no glory. But it taught me a thing or two about soldiering, something I tried to pass on in my years teaching the boys in the *schola*.'

'Go on, Uago,' Flavius said. 'Arturus was given his commission as a *foederati* tribune in the field, so he never had the benefit of the *schola* and your experience.'

Uago stared into the middle distance, his brows furrowed. 'It was during the Berber rebellion in the fifteenth year of Honorius' reign, nearly forty years ago now. I'd been among the first batch of tribunes to graduate from the *schola*, set up only the year before in the wake of Alaric's sack of Rome. My first job with the *fabri* had been to help clear the rubble created by the Goths on the Capitoline Hill, when they had tried to pull down the ruins of the old temple. After that I volunteered for frontier service, and was posted as second-in-command of a *fabri numerus* on the edge of the desert in Mauretania Tingitana. The *limitanei* garrison had been depleted to make up numbers in the Africa *comitatenses*, and when the rebellion started we were remustered as infantry *milites*. It was hard campaigning, with many men falling to disease and exhaustion, and there were no battles, only brief violent skirmishes and chasing shadows in the dark. Towards the end we reverted to our role as *fabri* and were used to make roads, improve fortifications and dig wells, much more to my liking than hunting down rebels and burning villages. I discovered a fascination for survey and mapmaking, and that's been my calling ever since.'

'Forty years is a long time to be in the army,' Arturus said.

'Aetius dug me out of retirement when he wanted a detailed new map to be made showing Attila's conquests. He gave me free rein to call in the best cartographers from Alexandria and Babylon, and I've had the copyists in my *scriptoria* working day and night to get the map ready to dispatch to the *comitatenses* and *limitanei* commanders.'

'That's what we've come to see,' Arturus said. 'Specifically, Illyrica and the river Danube, and the lands leading east to the Maeotic Lake.'

Uago got up, took the walking stick that one of the *fabri* had discreetly handed him, and peered at Arturus intently. 'An unusual destination for a British *foederati* commander,' he said. 'I am right about your origin, am I not? In my spare time I make a special study of lexicography and etymology, especially barbarian personal names.'

'I am from the tribe of the Brigantes, from the line of Boudica, though my maternal grandmother was the Roman descendant of a legionary,' Arturus replied. 'My name is an ancient British patronymic meaning bear-king, from the time when bears roamed the forests of my land.'

'I thought as much,' Uago said, looking pleased. 'I'd like to tap into your knowledge of British names. Over the years I've done the same with soldiers who have come here to consult my maps from all corners of the empire. Meanwhile, to your request.' He pointed his stick at the scroll on the wall. 'This is the *Tabula Cursorum*, an illustrated representation of the *cursus publicus*, the official road network of the empire. It was made by the monks of Arles under Honorius. Really it's not a map at all, but a visual representation of a series of itineraries, and as an image it's full of distortions, pointless embellishments and anachronisms, the kind of things that monks enjoy but most annoying for a cartographer like me. Here, from the bottom up, you can see southern Italy, the Adriatic Sea and the Dalmatian coast, with the mountains surrounding the river Danube schematically represented further inland. But I believe this will only partly suit your purpose. It will give you the distances and staging posts for the first part of a journey, from Ravenna or Rome along the roads and across the sea to a port such as Spoleto, but there is nothing depicted beyond the official roads. The *tabula* is designed for official travel and the postal service, not for those intent on covert missions beyond the frontiers.'

'You assume much about our purpose,' Arturus said.

Uago looked around, making sure they were out of earshot of the others. 'I know what it means when one of Aetius' special tribunes, a man usually with a commission in the *foederati*, comes looking for maps of regions beyond the frontiers,' he said quietly. 'But I will provide all you need with no questions asked. I may be stuck in this room while you and the others are out in the field, but my maps provide the intelligence hub of the empire, and my loyalty to Aetius is unswerving. He was once my star pupil in the *schola*, and I now am his servant.'

'Show us the new map,' Flavius said.

Uago backed away from the wall and pointed up at a mottled vellum sheet above the *tabula*, at a map depicted on it. 'That one you'll be familiar with, Flavius, the representation of the known world based on the *Geographia* of Ptolemy that I always had in my classroom in the *schola*. Arturus, you will of course identify your home land of Britannia to the left, with a representation of Wales and the western peninsula containing the tin lands, the place where Aetius tells me that most of the fighting is taking place between the Britons and the Saxons. As a visual representation of the world it is far more satisfactory than the *tabula*, but it lacks the precise measurements between known points, with their orientations, that would allow it to be used as an accurate tool for navigators and travellers. What we really needed was a marriage between the two, between the Ptolemaic map and the itinerary as represented in the *tabula*. That's what my *fabri* have been trying to perfect over the last months, and I believe we now have it.'

He led them to the tables, and for the first time Flavius saw the maps that the men had been copying out. In the centre was a large map, close to the Ptolemaic representation but covered with a latticework of triangular shapes; the men around it were making reduced copies using measuring tools, and others were reproducing sections of it in more detail. Uago walked along the line and stopped beside one of the men, who put down his stylus and moved out of the way. 'Here's what you want,' he said. 'You can see the river Danube running inland parallel to the Dalmatian coast, through the gorge known as the Iron Gates and then east towards the Black Sea. Upstream from the Iron Gates it flows from its source past the great steppe-lands of Scythia, the Hun heartland.'

'The Hun world has always been difficult to define, and that's one of its strengths, strategically speaking,' Arturus said. 'The borders are porous and ill-defined, really just broad swathes of grassland where few, if any, people live, and even to the west the river Danube is as much a crossing point as a boundary. I don't think Attila cares very much about borders, and that's a huge difference from the Roman strategy. Attila has a concept of homeland, and has his citadel, but the Hun empire is wherever he decides to do battle, and consequently it can change from one month to the next.'

Uago nodded. 'It's a cartographer's nightmare. We like our boundaries and provinces. With the Huns, you can only put broad arrows on maps, slashing across all of those fixed points and delimiting lines that we hold so dear.'

Flavius put his fingers on the map, measuring distances. 'According to the scale, the distance from the Iron Gates to the beginning of the steppes is about three thousand *stades* – say one hundred and thirty miles,' he said. 'That would normally be a route march of a week, but we'd have to do it by river, on the Danube.'

'Against the current,' Uago added. 'But if you're lucky you might have a southerly wind and sail against the flow, as boatmen do on the Nile in Egypt.'

Arturus stared at the map. 'Can we have a copy of this?'

'You can take this one.' He unpinned and rolled up the vellum, checking first to make sure that the ink was dry. 'Show it to nobody else, and return it here in person when you have finished with it. Soon, if Aetius approves it, this new world map will be common currency, but until then it's gold dust in the hands of a hostile strategist who might have his eyes set on conquest.'

'Understood,' Arturus said, tucking the map inside his tunic. 'And now we must go.'

Uago led them towards the door, and then stopped and stood for a moment in obvious pain, leaning on his stick. 'If you do get there,' he said, 'you couldn't bring back a Hun or two, could you? My own Goth dialect from my father's side is close to Scythian, but I'm having the devil of a time making a concordance with the Hun vocabulary. To hear it from the horse's mouth, so to speak, would help, though it really is the most impossible language, you know. I've been thinking of creating a universal language to get over these troubles. If everyone spoke in the same tongue then perhaps we'd have fewer wars. Another project, if Aetius ever lets me go.'

Flavius grinned and held the older man's shoulder. 'We'll see what we can do.'

Arturus gripped Uago's hand. 'Before we go, I'm curious. What was it that you told the young tribune candidates based on your field experience?'

Uago paused. 'I may not have been in any battles, but I've been around long enough to know that the glories of war are transient. I've seen generations of young men I've taught go off to war, high-spirited young bloods when they set out, too often pale shadows when they return, if they return at all. As soon as one generation passes through the charnel house of battle the next one is raring to go. I told them what I learned in the desert, that war is not about glory but is about hard slog and persever-ance, about looking out for your comrades. The memory of that is greater for me than any regret I might have over missed laurels and decorations, mere transient glories.'

Arturus nodded. 'Wise advice, tribune. *Salve*, until next time.'

He and Flavius began to walk off, but Uago called after them. 'One last thing.'

Flavius turned around. 'What is it?'

'I was meaning to ask. During your jaunt in Carthage, you didn't happen to pick up any of the leaves that the Berbers call *khat*, did you? I acquired something of a taste for it when I was in Mauretania. It might help to ease the pain in my back.'

'My centurion Macrobius had some, but that's long gone. We had to leave Africa in something of a hurry.'

'Pity. Perhaps I'll have to go there myself.'

'There'd be the small matter of a Vandal army to deal with, and a not entirely sympathetic warlord called Gaiseric.'

Uago gestured back into the room, a twinkle in his eye. 'You remember what I said about my men all those years ago in Mauretania? They were soldiers first, *fabri* second. My men here are of the same stock. I think a *numerus* of *fabri* could handle a small barbarian annoyance like Gaiseric.'

Flavius grinned and waved. '*Salve*, tribune.'

They made their way out of the building and onto the street below, the column of Trajan rearing up again in front of them. 'Rome needs more soldiers like Uago,' Arturus said.

'The *fabri* officers are a rare breed, my uncle Aetius says,' Flavius replied. 'Devoted to their work, meticulous, with a keen eye for detail, and loyally quiet about the failings of their superiors. When he fields a *comitatenses* army he always has a *fabri* tribune as his senior staff officer.'

'He's going to need to recruit the best he can for the war that lies ahead.'

'Where are we going now?'

'We will pay our respects to Valentinian. After that, we're going to a secret place where you will learn of our plan. By tomorrow evening, all going well, you and Macrobius and I will be heading east, about to embark on the most perilous mission that any of us has ever undertaken.'

Flavius stared ahead, his mind racing, conscious of passing the old Senate House and beginning to climb the steps towards the imperial palace. It had been almost eight years since he had last been on campaign, time usefully spent instructing at the *schola*, but he was itching to be in the field again. He began to think of everything he would need to do before leaving, of people to see and equipment to organize, of the old *gladius* that Arturus had given him after the retreat from Carthage, the blade to be sharpened and oiled. He felt his breathing quicken, and his heart pound.

He could hardly wait.

10

Flavius stood to attention with his back against the wall among a long line of other officers, from the *magister* of the Rome *comitatenses* to the left near the imperial throne to the most junior tribunes to the right, men newly commissioned from the *schola* who had not yet been assigned a unit. The line was mirrored on the opposite wall by officers of the *foederati*, among them Arturus, inconspicuous alongside Goths, Suebi, Saxons and other *foederati* who now made up more than half of the Roman officer corps, not counting those in the regular army like Flavius himself, who had barbarian blood in their veins. It was an image of modern Rome and her army that would have seemed inconceivable at the time when Trajan's Column was made, when the distinction between Roman and barbarian had been cut so clearly into stone; yet it was also an army arrayed more strongly than ever before against another barbarian force from beyond the frontiers, a threat that would have been understood all too well by Trajan and the other Caesars who had first taken Rome into the forests and steppes of the North.

A pair of trumpets sounded, blaring from the entrance hall, and those in the line who had been rustling and restless became silent. They were all dressed in their finest tunics, resplendent with insignia of rank and service decorations, yet by order of the eunuch Heraclius they were without sword belts or weapons, a reasonable precaution against assassination, yet somehow also deliberately demeaning, as if Heraclius were projecting his own emasculation on men he regarded with almost total contempt. The great *velarium* that covered the roof flapped in the breeze, and Flavius saw the awning tighten where the sailors who managed it were ratcheting up the retaining ropes from outside. They were within the old private hippodrome of the imperial palace on the Palatine, a space that had once been open to the heavens but was now concealed beneath the awning; at the far end, the imperial box that had once overlooked the Circus Maximus, the place where the Emperor could be seen by almost the entire population of Rome, was now walled over so that it had become yet another inward-looking throne room, a place where the emperor could preside over a world that was almost completely artificial and divorced from the people he was meant to rule. Despite his years in Ravenna and Rome and his proximity to Aetius, Flavius himself had never seen the emperor in the flesh before; realizing this only served to enhance the otherworldliness of this place, as if they were all part of a stage set in which those who were to parade in front of them were mere actors whose personas would fall away as soon as they walked out of sight.

The first in the procession appeared, the Bishop of Rome, having just been awarded draconian powers by the emperor Valentinian, his decrees now carrying supreme authority as the word of God, with no others allowed. He was a corpulent man, carrying the imperial orb and crozier, his fingers crammed with gold rings and his jewel-encrusted robe held off the ground by a dozen small boys, an image about as far removed from Jesus of Nazareth as Flavius could imagine. Behind him came a cluster of Valentinian's Egyptian catamites, slim young men naked except for loincloths, their dark skin glistening with oil, and then fifty of his ferocious Suebi bodyguard forming a square around the imperial retinue. Within the square Flavius could see the emperor himself, instantly recognizable from the image on his coins, holding his hands up high, with on either side two elaborately coiffured women whom Flavius knew must be his sister Honoria and his wife Eudoxia.

Flavius may never have seen Valentinian in the flesh before, but ten years after gazing at the image of the emperor on those gold *solidi* in front of the walls of Carthage, he knew he had been right to have his doubts. Superficially Valentinian looked the part, his face square-jawed like the soldier-emperors of the past, but Flavius knew that it was no more than a façade, the face of an emperor who had never once led his army into battle or reviewed them on the parade ground; even the legionary armour he appeared to be wearing was a sham, the breastplate made of puffed-out golden cloth and the chainmail from woven strands of shimmering silk. Like the bishop, his eyes and those of the two ladies were looking upwards, not even glancing at the lines of officers, a seemingly devotional act that Flavius knew in truth represented a sense of their own divine status, an emperor and his sycophants as divorced from God as they were from their own people.

Bringing up the rear, surrounded by boys throwing flower petals, came the eunuch Heraclius, grossly corpulent, taller even than the Goths, the rolling fat of his chin and stomach wobbling as he went forward, skipping and gesticulating as if he were delighting in a garden, gasping and clapping his hands and singing snatches of verse in his high-pitched voice. It was a spectacle beyond farce, repulsive to a soldier's eyes, and yet this was not a man with eyes that were aloof like the others – his shifted constantly, staring, absorbing what he saw, catching Flavius' eyes in a split second that unnerved him, the piggy black orbs inscrutable and frightening. In that moment Flavius understood what scared even Aetius about the eunuchs – the ability that their singularity gave them to operate outside normal parameters, with motivations that were unfamiliar and disarming to those trying to undermine their power.

Flavius thought of another ancient monument that had fascinated him as a boy – the arch of the emperor Titus on the south side of the forum. There, the sculpted reliefs showed scenes of triumph, of great treasures held aloft by Roman soldiers as they processed forward, armed and exuberant, the people of Rome crowding around and cheering them, the emperor standing tall and visible. If today's procession of catamites and eunuchs was the modern equivalent of the triumphal processions of old, then Rome truly had gone to the dogs, and the time when the barbarians among the officer ranks rose up and swept away this grotesque spectacle could not come too soon.

The trumpets blared again, and the Suebi guards began jostling the officers out of the hippodrome. The once-in-a-lifetime encounter with the emperor for whom they had fought and bled was over. Flavius walked a discreet distance behind Arturus, watching the other officers stream away outside the palace towards the barracks and the Field of Mars, and then he caught up with him on the stairs leading down to the old forum. Macrobius was waiting at the bottom, his cloak on and carrying two army-issue backpacks. As Flavius approached he handed him his belt and *gladius*. 'I sharpened and oiled it myself,' he said. 'You wouldn't have had time.'

Flavius buckled the belt on, staring at Macrobius. 'I was expecting to see you at my quarters.'

Macrobius took him aside, speaking quietly. 'I asked Una to bring your gear to me on her way out of the city. It was fortunate, because when I went to your quarters they had been ransacked.'

Flavias stared at him, aghast. '*Ransacked*. How?'

Arturus swivelled around, checking for anyone following them, pulling up the hood of his cloak. 'It was only a matter of time before Heraclius' agents were on to us. We need to get to our rendezvous, fast.'

'There's worse news,' Macrobius said. 'Uago has disappeared. Four men were waiting outside the *fabri* headquarters this evening, and they pounced on him and took him away hooded and gagged. The captain of the guard at the headquarters is a friend of mine and saw everything, but was powerless to intervene. The men wore the purple capes of the emperor's bodyguard.'

'That means Heraclius,' Arturus said. 'And it means we won't be seeing Uago again.'

'But he knows nothing,' Flavius said, a cold feeling in the pit of his stomach. 'He shouldn't pay with his life for our visit to his map room.'

'If he knows nothing, then he can tell nothing,' Arturus said grimly. 'Put him from your mind. The best thing we can do for him is to carry on with our mission.'

'We need to know what that is.'

'Follow me. It's dark enough now that we won't be conspicuous. It's time we received our orders.'

As they stole away into the night Flavius thought again about the procession he had just witnessed. He had been repelled by what he saw, and was sickened to have been standing so close to one who had probably just ordered the execution of his revered teacher and friend Uago. But above all it was the hollow image of the emperor that troubled him. At the time of the Caesars, despite all the corruption and the venality, the boorishness of Nero and the insanity of Caligula, there had always been men of the imperial purple ready to lead Rome to war, and warrior emperors such as Trajan whom any of the officers in that hall today would have yearned to follow into battle. But with Honorius and then Valentinian that seemed a thing of the past. Flavius now understood more than ever why Arturus and so many other officers held his uncle Aetius in such high regard, a man who seemed to stand, as Julius Caesar had, at the end of the Republic, both of them seeking to return Rome to the honour and virtue of the past. And just as it had been for Julius Caesar five hundred years ago, that return now could only be to a republic. The imperial experiment had seen its glory days, its moments of supreme triumph when the idea of an emperor seemed unassailable, but it had run its course and was now sinking bloated into a mire of its own creation. If Flavius were to return from this mission, and if Rome herself had not by then been conquered by a barbarian king, by Attila himself, he would no longer fight in the name of the emperor, but in the name of Rome as the founding fathers of the Republic saw it, a Rome where a man like Aetius would find his greatest fulfilment in serving the people and the state.

They had passed through the Aurelian Walls and now marched quickly along the worn stones of the Appian Way, the tombs of Rome's greatest *gens* looming around them. Flavius recognized the entrance to the Tomb of the Scipios, a place he had visited in his youth to pay respects to another of his heroes, the conqueror of Carthage, Scipio Aemilianus Africanus. Arturus took them off the road to the left, hurrying past the perimeter of the Circus Maxentius and then through a complex of baths and around another corner, pausing to look back and see whether they were being followed. He pointed to a low entrance in a wall – an old sewer or an abandoned aqueduct channel – then ducked and led them down it, pausing about ten paces in and lighting a tallow candle with a flint and steel. 'These are the catacombs of Zakarias,' he said. 'This is a secret entrance used at the time when Christians were being persecuted, but abandoned after the emperor Constantine's conversion when the catacombs became public. The section beneath us has been unused for centuries, cut off from the rest, and is a meeting place for Aetius and his agents. There are about five miles of passages and tunnels, and thousands of bodies. Watch your heads, and follow me closely.'

He sat on the edge of a hole in the wall and slid in, dropping softly to the floor below. Flavius followed, and then Macrobius, pulling their bags down with him. The passage ahead had been crudely cut out of the rock, providing just enough room for one person to get through bent almost double, and Flavius was grateful that Arturus' candle only hinted at the claustrophobic dimensions of the place. He had been expecting the sickly sweet smell of decay, the odour he was used to from the drainage holes in stone sarcophagi, but here it was just musty and cloying, the last body having putrefied and decayed generations before. Almost immediately they began to pass niches and alcoves in the walls, some of them filled with shrouded human forms and others with stacks of bones where families had reused the same *cubicula* for centuries. They turned a corner and came across the first sign of early Christianity, a plastered-over alcove with the painted words PRISCILLA IN PACE and a Chi-Rho symbol, and then they entered a wider chamber with an altar and a crude wall-painting of Christ with thorns and the two thieves being crucified on the hill of Calvary. Flavius thought of those who had worshipped here, some perhaps apostles of Jesus himself, and then he thought of the dripping opulence of the bishop he had just seen in the palace, a world away from the simplicity and austerity of the early followers of Christ.

They turned another corner, past a blackened shrivelled corpse whose arm had fallen out of its niche, and then carried on through a sinuous passage where another source of light was visible ahead. Arturus snuffed out his candle, and then they were there, standing in a widened chamber lit by oil lamps, in front of a man in a cassock sitting on a chair with a book. He had long hair and a beard like Arturus, but it was almost completely white, and as he looked up and smiled, Flavius saw that he too had the blue eyes and high cheekbones of the Britons. He stood awkwardly, his tall frame bent under the low ceiling, and clasped hands with Arturus, who turned to Flavius. 'This is Pelagius, my superior in the intelligence service.' He gestured into the shadows beside Pelagius, where another figure could be seen. 'And this man you know.'

The second man was wearing a hood, but on a military cape rather than a cassock, and as he stood out of the shadows and threw it back Flavius saw that it was his uncle, Flavius Aetius Gaudentius, *magister militum* of the western empire, the most powerful man in the known world other than Attila the Hun. He tried to stand to attention, saluting his uncle, and then turned back to Pelagius. 'I didn't know you worked for Aetius.'

Pelagius sat down again and looked at him. 'You will know me for my heretical writings against Augustine and the Church in Rome. Unlike Augustine, I believe that we are able to make choices of our own free will, that battles, for example, are not preordained in some grand divine plan, but that their outcome depends on the free decision-making of individuals. Mine is not a bellicose Christianity, but it provides a better creed for the soldier than the Augustinian version, which makes the soldier out to be nothing more than an agent of a higher purpose.'

'I have not seen your writings,' Flavius said. 'They are banned in Rome, by order of the Bishop. But I have heard much about you from Arturus.'

'I take my beliefs from what you see around you here, from the reality of early Christianity, from what attracted my people to the teaching of Jesus when Christianity first reached the shores of Britain more than four hundred years ago. I am a Christian monk, but I come from a long line of druids, the spiritual leaders of the Britons, and I have another, older name that I will revert to when Arturus and I leave the service of Rome to lead our people against the Saxons.' He smiled at Arturus, reaching out and holding his arm, and then looked deadly serious. 'Meanwhile, there are more pressing matters to hand. I have also worked for Aetius for more than fifteen years now; it was I who first brought Arturus to his attention. Aetius first came to me in secret because he shared my beliefs, and after that I agreed to use my network of contacts among my followers in the monks and monasteries of Gaul to provide him with intelligence. I believed in his cause then, and I still do now, more strongly than ever.'

Flavius stared in astonishment at his uncle. 'You are a follower of Pelagius? That carries an immediate death sentence.'

'You will have seen the Bishop of Rome today,' Aetius said, his voice measured and precise. 'Could you follow such a man?'

Pelagius leaned forward. 'When the emperor falls, the new Rome will have no bishops, no priests. The people will be encouraged to reach out to God without mediation, without fear.'

'*When the emperor falls,*' Flavius repeated, his voice almost a whisper. 'Is that what this is all about? Are you planning a coup?'

Aetius gave him a grim look. 'Nothing can happen until Attila is destroyed. For now, all of our attention is focused on that goal. That is why you and Macrobius are here. Less than an hour from now you will have embarked on a mission that could change the course of history.'

Flavius squatted down. 'Tell us what we have to do.'

Arturus pulled out from his tunic the map that he had taken from Uago and handed it to Aetius, who knelt down and unrolled it on the floor. 'Has Uago told you anything?' Aetius asked.

'What do you mean?' Flavius said.

'He's one of our circle. For years he has been my eyes and ears in the city of Rome, the main reason he stayed teaching in the *schola* for so long. I've kept his role secret even from Arturus, for Uago's own protection.'

Flavius glanced at Arturus. 'Then we have some bad news. He was taken by four imperial guards this afternoon.'

Aetius stared at the ground, and Flavius saw his lips flicker almost imperceptibly. 'Then you must move quickly. The purpose of your journey is only known to those of us in this room, but Uago knew your destination. He will attempt suicide if he thinks there's a risk of him being forced to talk, but Heraclius' torturers are brutal and ingenious, and they have a eunuch's fascination with male anatomy to guide them. We cannot risk Heraclius' agents already being on the route, ready to waylay you.' He pursed his lips and then pointed at the map. 'You will go disguised as monks. Pelagius has cassocks for you here. You will travel up the river Danube, and from there make your way to the Hun capital, using Arturus' insider knowledge and contacts to get what we want. Once you have it, you will return to Rome and leave it at this spot, where it will be taken and concealed by Pelagius until it is needed, until the long-awaited battle is nigh.'

Flavius leaned forward. 'What is it?'

Aetius paused, staring at him intently. 'We've tried to build up our strength against Attila. I've worked on the *comitatenses*, improving recruitment and training, bringing in the best officers and centurions such as you and Macrobius to train a new generation of tribunes, keeping you in Rome when I know you must have been itching for active service. And we have tried to forge alliances. Pelagius has worked among the monks of Gaul to influence the Visigoths in our favour. Arturus has just returned from an arduous undercover trip to the Sassanid court. But neither has yet given us the results we want, and we need more, some other way of combating Attila's power.'

He nodded at Pelagius, who leaned forward. 'Every time a new Hun prince is born, a great sword is revealed as if by magic and used to slash the marks of a warrior on his face, to see if he can bear the pain. Those who pass the test become the next king, and the sword becomes their most powerful symbol of status, a rallying point in battle. Without it, the power of the king would be weakened, and battle might be swayed in favour of the enemy.'

Flavis stared in astonishment at his uncle. 'You want us to steal the sword of Attila.'

Arturus looked at him. 'It can be done.'

Macrobius, who had been standing behind listening, heaved his two bags back up on his shoulder. 'When do we leave?'

'You leave now,' Aetius said. 'Arturus has gold for the journey, and knows the route.'

Flavius stood before his uncle. 'I will not fail you.'

Aetius took his hand. '*Salve atque vale*, Flavius Aetius Gaudentius.'

Pelagius put his hand on the book in front of him. 'Godspeed to you all.'

PART THREE

THE RIVER DANUBE

AD 449

11

Ten days later Flavius sat with Arturus and Macrobius in a boat on the middle reaches of the river Danube, the sail billowing and the paddles they had used to strike out from shore now stowed away. It had been an arduous if uneventful journey from Ravenna, first across the plain of the river Po to the lagoon port of Veneto, then by ship down the Adriatic to the site of the palace of the emperor Diocletian at Spalatum, from there by stages east across the rugged foothills and mountains of Illyricum, and finally on horseback and then on foot as they traversed the high passes and carried on towards the course of the great river, reaching its western bank and the furthest extent of Roman territory the evening before. As they were monks travelling towards barbarian lands no questions had been asked about the purpose of their journey, and the weapons concealed beneath their cassocks had gone unnoticed by fellow travellers and the owners of the inns where they had stayed on the way. Others had come this way in a trickle from the western empire, some lured by the riches to be had in the Danube river trade, others seeking escape and anonymity in the borderlands of the empire, others genuine monks looking to convert the pagans beyond the frontiers, but only they were intent on the perilous journey up the river and across the steppes to the court of Attila the Hun.

Macrobius was at the tiller in the stern, his hair tonsured like a monk and his face uncharacteristically clean-shaven, a crude wooden cross hanging from his neck over the front of his cassock. He had grown up along the Illyrian shore and had taken charge of navigating the boat, having first inspected it with the hoary old fisherman who had sold it to them. The man had wagged his finger when they had told him they were intending to go upstream, shaking his head and listing the dangers, but no questions were asked after Flavius had produced a generous handful of gold *solidi*. The boat reeked of fish and its scuppers were plastered with the distinctive palm-sized scales of the sturgeon that was the main catch on the river, but it was a flat-bottomed type familiar to Macrobius, with a shallow keel and ample room for the three men and their shoulder bags. Crucially, it had a retractable mast and a square sail, large enough for them to make headway against the current using the south-easterly wind that had begun to blow that morning.

Flavius stared back at the river bank. They had just passed between the crumbling concrete piers of a great bridge built by the Caesars to cross the Danube, the wooden roadway that had once been held up by the arches long gone and the piers themselves buffeted and damaged by the floodwaters of the river. On either side was a *castrum*, the one on the far side abandoned long ago, but the nearer one garrisoned within living memory, its walls built in sections of brick alternating with courses of flat tile that Arturus said he had seen in the Roman ruins of Britain. Before taking to the boat, they had spent the night in the fort – an eerie experience among the detritus of men who could have been from their own unit, *limitanei* who had been ordered to abandon the fort early in Valentinian's reign and who had been absorbed into the mobile *comitatenses* army.

This had once been a frontier of the Roman Empire, but the concept of frontier had changed radically since the time when emperors such as Trajan had pushed forward against barbarian resistance and established a border that needed to be manned and defended, in this case along the natural boundary of a great river. Now, the barbarian threat was greater, but it was concentrated far away in the forests and steppe-lands to the north; there, great armies could be marshalled to strike deep into the Roman Empire, to east or to west. Even the most strongly defended frontier would stand no chance against such a force, and it made more sense to withdraw the remaining frontier troops and absorb them into the *comitatenses*, armies that could meet the barbarians head to head on battlegrounds that might be deep within the boundaries of the empire, places to which the barbarians could be drawn to increase their exhaustion and make foraging more difficult, among a hostile population. The decisive battle would no longer be spread out along the frontiers, but instead would take place hundreds of miles within the empire, in Gaul and in Italy itself. Flavius remembered the policy being drummed into the tribune candidates at the *schola militarum*, and yet seeing these ruins today had made him wonder. Despite the strategic sense of withdrawal, the abandoned forts were a sorry sight and represented the one inevitable drawback of the policy: it removed the visible display of Roman troops and Roman might from barbarian eyes, meaning that for many soldiers of both sides, their first view of the enemy, their first chance to size him up, came in the few seconds of headlong charge as the opposing armies joined in battle.

Ahead of them on both sides the rocky ground rose to jagged cliffs as the river narrowed into a gorge, the beginnings of many miles of virtually impenetrable upland terrain that divided the final Roman outposts from the steppe-lands beyond. The wind had picked up as the gorge constricted, and Macrobius brailed up the sail to half-size in order to slow them down and make it possible to navigate around any of the submerged rocks that the fishermen had warned them lay in the passage ahead. Arturus came up to the bows beside Flavius, his grey hood still over his head, and together the two men scanned the water for any signs of danger. It was opaque, but without the milky hue of glacial meltwater that Flavius had seen in the Alps; here, the waters were darker, a deep brown, a colour that Arturus said he had seen in the tributaries that fed the Danube from the peaty uplands of the North. It was a forbidding sight, and impossible to tell the depth of the water or whether there were any submerged rocks. As the wind began to funnel and echo from the cliff walls, Flavius had a sense of the foreboding that had led many before them to turn back at this point and let the current return them to safer lands in the South.

Macrobius gestured at the cliff face on the west shore, brailed up the sail completely and swung the tiller so that they came alongside, holding the boat off from the rock with a paddle. An eroded inscription came into view, set within a recessed plaque that had been carved into the living rock:

IMP.CAESAR.DIVI.NERVAE.F
NERVA.TRAIANVS.AVG.GERM
PONTIF.MAXIMUS.TRIB.POT.IIII
PATER.PATRIAE.COS.III
MONTIBVS.EXCISIS.ANCONIBVS
SVBLATIS.VIAM.FECIT

Flavius held up his hand and Macrobius steered closer so that the letters loomed above them. 'It's old, from the time of the Caesars,' Flavius said. 'When I was a boy in Rome my teacher Dionysius taught me how to read these inscriptions.' He paused, scanning the lines, before translating it for the others. '*Emperor Caesar, son of the divine Nerva, Nerva Trajan Augustus Germanicus, Pontifex Maximus, Tribune for the fourth time, Father of Rome, Consul for the third time, by excavating mountains and using wooden beams has made this road.*' He looked back at the ruined arches of the bridge still visible behind them. 'That's the work of the emperor Trajan, from almost four hundred and fifty years ago, during his campaign against the Dacians,' he said. 'This records the completion of the military road, and must mark the furthest point up the river reached by Roman forces, then or since.'

'Take a look ahead,' Macrobius said, pointing high above them.

Flavius followed his gaze, and gaped in astonishment. Where the gorge reached its narrowest point just beyond the inscription, the cliffs towered higher than before, constricting the passage until the river was no more than two hundred paces wide. But instead of the craggy cliff face they had seen before the rock had been carved into two enormous human figures, facing each other across the gorge with their heads almost out of sight high above. On one side the figure was Roman, wearing the breastplate of the legions and with the cropped hair of the Caesars, and on the other side a barbarian king, with long, flowing hair and a beard; both held swords point-down in front of them, the Roman a *gladius* like Flavius' own, and the other a longer sword similar to those of the Goths and the Huns. It was as if the two figures had walked forward towards each other, a Roman emperor and a barbarian king, but had been turned to stone just before they had made contact, doomed to stand before each other for eternity like ancient giants frozen by the gods on the cusp of combat.

'It's Trajan and Decebalus, the Dacian king,' Flavius said. 'Roman and barbarian, neither victor nor vanquished.'

'They call these the Iron Gates,' Arturus said. 'Here the rule of Rome ends and the lawless land before the empire of Attila begins.'

'You have been here before, Arturus?' Macrobius said, unbrailing the sail and steering the boat out again. 'You seem to speak with first-hand knowledge.'

'I only know about this place from intelligence reports,' explained Arturus. 'Before we left Ravenna I spoke to everyone I could who had been this way before. When I went to Attila's court as a mercenary in Gaiseric's bodyguard it was through the mountains of the North, east from the Alps and over the upper reaches of the Danube.'

'What is our next stop?' Macrobius asked.

Arturus pointed down the gorge. 'The island of Adekaleh, perhaps a full day's journey ahead if this wind keeps up, beyond a place where the river widens again. The island is a free port, an emporium where traders arrive from all over the known world, inhabited by a race of merchants who are said to have been there for hundreds of years. From Adekaleh the Huns get the silk from Thina which has become the fashion for their women, as well as green peridot from the Red Sea which they favour for their jewels. With the gold that has been pouring into Attila's coffers from Theodosius in tribute, the Huns can get anything they choose. But it's a place outside any jurisdiction, ruled only by the merchants themselves who employ mercenaries to police the rules of fair trade. Sometimes the mercenaries take over, and there have been decades, whole generations, when it has been the most dangerous place on earth, where enormous profits could be made but the life expectancy for anyone with gold in their pockets could be measured in days, if not hours. Traders arrived, did their business and got out as fast as possible.'

'And us?' Macrobius said, leaning on the tiller. 'Why are we going to this hellhole?'

'To do precisely that,' Arturus replied. 'To get there, to do our business and to get out. But our business is with one who has hidden himself away there, one who can tell us the best route to the Hun capital and give us the latest intelligence on Attila.'

'Tell us about him,' Flavius asked.

'His name is Priscus of Panium. He's from Constantinople, and he was an emissary to Attila.'

'Not another eunuch, I hope,' Macrobius grumbled.

Arturus shook his head. 'Theodosius made that mistake before. He sent eunuchs, and never heard from them again. Both Theodosius and Valentinian are so out of touch that they don't realize how it looks from outside. Eunuchs may be good at flattery and keeping ledger books, but they are not going to impress the world's most powerful warlord. Soon after that experience, Attila decided to attack Constantinople.'

'So this Priscus is some kind of diplomat?' Macrobius said.

'He was,' Arturus said. 'He's in limbo now, hiding away in this place, apparently writing a history of the Huns.'

'You seem to know a lot of people in limbo, Arturus,' Macrobius said. 'Pelagius hiding away in the catacombs of Rome, Priscus in this godforsaken place.'

'When you've lived the life I have, a deserter from the Roman army in Gaul, a renegade mercenary with a price on my head from half the barbarian chieftains of the North, you learn about the hidden world that's around us, the places where fugitives and outcasts can live unnoticed and unmolested.'

'If you've got that price on your head, how does is make sense for you to be heading to the court of Attila?'

Arturus paused. 'Because it's one of those hidden places. If you're a eunuch, forget it. But if you're a scholar like Priscus with knowledge that interests Attila, or if you're a soldier who can demonstrate his prowess in combat, then few questions are asked. Attila knows that nobody seeks his court who is not a risk-taker, that those who are not emissaries or traders are likely to be renegades and fugitives, escaping problems elsewhere rather than coming as spies or assassins. And it's a seductive place, a hidden kingdom that seems outside the orbit of normal existence, dangerous but alluring. Go there and fall under the spell of Attila and his daughters, and you won't want to leave.'

Macrobius stared at him. 'And his daughters. What do you mean?'

'Erecan and Eslas and Erdaca. Attila has sons, but it's his daughters who have inherited the martial strength passed down from Attila's father, Mundiuk. Eslas and Erdaca have been married off to Ostrogoth princes, but Erecan remains in the court. It was she who I fought in unarmed combat when I went to the court of Attila twelve years ago, when she was a teenager and I had arrived in the service of Gaiseric.'

Macrobius narrowed his eyes at Arturus. 'Is there something you're not telling us?'

'What do you mean?'

'Are you really here to visit your old girlfriend? Is that what this is all about?'

Arturus turned and gave Macrobius a steely look. 'I volunteered for this trip partly because of Erecan, but not for the reason you might think. She's proud of her Hun heritage, but there's no love lost between her and Attila. Erecan's mother was a Scythian slave girl, a servant of Attila's main wife, but the baby was brought into the household and raised as a legitimate daughter of Attila and his queen. From an early age Erecan knew the truth, told to her in secret by her real mother and indisputable because they share the same eyes and face, and Erecan looks nothing like Attila's Hun queen. When Erecan went to Attila afterwards and told him that she knew, he became enraged and had her mother executed. Erecan has hated Attila ever since, and has nursed a desire for vengeance – and among the Huns such desire is stronger than it is among any other barbarian race I have encountered. I told Aetius the story and he thought I might persuade her to help in our cause.'

Macrobius coughed. 'Which might just see the two of you engaged in unarmed combat again?'

Arturus gave him a wan smile. 'You have a soldier's imagination, Macrobius. But there's another personal reason for me. If Attila is left unchecked he will roll across the western empire and reach the northern coast of Gaul. He may not yet have the ability to cross the sea himself, but he will soon absorb by alliance and threat the Saxons and Angles and Jutes who have been raiding Britain, and use their seagoing craft and skills to bring his army to the shores of my country. To many in Rome and Ravenna my land means a place of cold and damp and homesickness, but all the Huns know of it is tin and copper and iron and gold, a place where their smiths could forge a thousand swords of Attila. By doing all that I can now to sabotage Attila's power base, I am fighting for the future of my people.'

'Tell us more about Priscus,' Flavius said.

Arturus paused again. 'Two years ago, after Theodosius sent the eunuchs to negotiate, and after they were murdered, Attila launched his attack on Constantinople, the attack that put the fear of God into Valentinian in Ravenna and made Aetius realize the threat that Attila also posed to the western empire. At the last minute Attila ordered his army to withdraw, after he was put off by the walls of Constantinople and the fact that his army had no capacity for siege warfare or long-term supply, and he returned to his lair in the steppes. But Theodosius in Constantinople was shaken by the speed and ferocity of the Huns' assault, as they had swept away all of the Roman forces fielded against them, and he decided to send out renewed offers of negotiation and concession.'

'You mean bribes of gold,' Flavius said.

Arturus nodded. 'The eastern emperors had gone down that slippery slope a long time before, even in the time of Mundiuk, and the Huns now expect payouts as a matter of course. The war with Attila is bleeding the coffers of Constantinople dry faster than her manpower is being depleted, and if Valentinian isn't careful the same thing will happen in the West. It's the main reason why Aetius wants us to undermine Attila's power as soon as we can, before Valentinian decides to send wagonloads of gold from Ravenna.'

'Aetius can predict the cost of appeasement too well,' Flavius said. 'We can give away land in Gaul and Spain as concessions to the Visigoths and Alans, and that's worked in our favour by pacifying and civilizing them, making allies out of enemies, but giving away gold is another matter. Do so, and you have nothing left to pay the army with. The problem of backlogged army pay is bad enough as it is.'

'What pay?' Macrobius grumbled. 'I haven't seen a *solidus* of official army pay for more than ten years.'

Arturus gave him another steely look. 'Well, if we get into Attila's strongroom you'll be able to feast your eyes on more gold than you've ever dreamed of before, all of it gold that should have been in the pay packets of your comrades in the eastern Roman army.'

'Will you tell Priscus our purpose?' Flavius said.

Arturus stared out over the river. 'Theodosius entrusted the embassy to Maximinus, a cavalry tribune in the eastern *comitatenses* who I got to know after we captured him when I was in Gaiseric's service and I secretly helped him to escape. Priscus was his childhood friend and he went with the embassy as an adviser and scholar, as someone like Maximinus whom Attila might respect. They were allowed into Attila's court, but word reached Maximinus of subterfuge among the eunuchs in Constantinople, of a plan being hatched to paint their purpose as espionage rather than diplomacy, and he decided to cut short their mission before Attila got wind of the plot. Maximinus returned to Constantinople determined to root out and bring in front of Theodosius those responsible for working against him, but Priscus was fearful for his life and decided to stay on the island of Adekaleh until the conspirators were dealt with.'

'Has Maximinus been successful?' Flavius asked.

Arturus pursed his lips. 'He has learned, as Aetius has, about the hold that the eunuchs have over the emperors. The plot had been a result of power play between two of the eunuchs who were jostling for position as controller of the imperial household, with one of them concocting the story of espionage and blaming it on the other in order to turn Theodosius against him. The plot worked and Theodosius had the innocent eunuch executed, but when Maximinus tried to expose the true perpetrator to the emperor he was stonewalled, earning him the enmity of the emperor in the process. Maximinus has only made his position and that of Priscus even more precarious; he himself has now survived numerous assassination attempts and Priscus has been left helpless against anyone sent by the eunuch who might discover his hideaway on the island. The machinations of the eunuchs in Constantinople make Heraclius seem like an amateur, though he and his cronies in Ravenna are doubtless watching and learning.'

'And you somehow know the location of Priscus.'

'When Aetius told me of his plan for us to go to the court of Attila I sent word to Maximinus, who sent word back telling me where to find Priscus and also forewarning him of our arrival. I have never met Priscus before. We will need to play it by ear. But their mission to the Hun court was only a few months ago, and he knows Attila's state of mind. Priscus may be the best source of intelligence we have.'

Flavius looked behind them. The sail had filled again and was driving the boat into the current, the wake giving the illusion of speed. As they edged forward he felt more than ever that their quest was a battle against the odds, an enticing adventure that had become a daunting challenge in a world far removed from his own experience, a world where law and morality, even the rule of God, were nothing but concepts to be discarded at a whim. He could still see the Iron Gates, the two colossal statues confronting each other across the narrow void. There was a time when all encounters between Roman and barbarian seemed fated to end that way, in a permanent stand-off, when Rome had pushed her frontiers to their maximum extent and Trajan and Hadrian had begun to build them in stone. But that was a time long past, and the frontiers were fluid again, the barbarians no longer a threat to be excluded but part of Rome herself, a symbiosis that Flavius knew was at the heart of his own being. And yet for each tribe that was absorbed, each chiefdom that was mollified and settled, there seemed to be a further threat that loomed behind, and it was one that now gathered strength somewhere ahead of them in the land of the Huns.

He narrowed his eyes at the statues, their forms now nearly lost in the haze. Maybe the Caesars had been right, and the only viable strategy was to drive forward and create a permanent frontier. But perhaps the best of them, emperors such as Trajan, also knew that the strategy had an inherent weakness, that it would provide no defence against a force that might one day coalesce with greater power than Rome could counter and come hurtling towards the frontiers, smashing its way through as if the walls and forts were made of matchwood. Flavius watched the Iron Gates recede and disappear, and then turned back to the bows. There was no changing the past, or turning back on this river. He needed to focus now on the challenges ahead. The evening and night on the river were still in front of them, hours when they were going to confront the dangers that the old fisherman had told them about, the whirlpools and cataracts and gorges, before they came to the lake and the island of Adekaleh. He nodded back at Macrobius on the tiller, picked up a paddle from the scuppers and shifted to one side of the central thwart, Arturus doing the same on the other side, and without a word they both began to paddle hard.

12

Soon after dawn the following morning they slid out between the last of the rocks at the end of the gorge, using a backwater eddy along the cliff face to avoid the current in the centre of the channel that had made their progress so difficult during the night. They had snatched a few hours' sleep in the early hours, having pulled up in a bay and tied up to a rock, but otherwise the going had been relentless, with each of them taking a turn at the tiller while the other two battled against the current, always looking out for the treacherous submerged rocks that showed up stark white in the moonlight. The wind had steadily died down during the night, adding to their travails, and for the last hour before dawn it was the paddles alone that had propelled them forward, inch by agonizing inch, until they were at last out of the narrows and in a wider channel where the current was less powerful. By skirting the shore of the great lake that now lay ahead they had been able to avoid the current completely, and with the sun up and the first brush of breeze in the air the sail had begun to flap and fill again, allowing them to lie back and rest for the first time in hours.

Macrobius took a deep swig from a water skin that they had filled from a spring that flowed out into the bay at the point where they had pulled up, and then ripped off a hunk of bread and cheese from the food supply in his bag. 'I think I can see the shape of the island ahead, due north, about a mile away across the lake,' he said, munching noisily. 'To get there we'll have to cross the current again, but with this breeze behind us we could make it within an hour.'

Flavius and Arturus lay stripped to the waist on the thwarts beside the paddles, their bodies covered with the scars of battles long past. Arturus raised himself, took a swig of water from the proffered skin and shaded his eyes, looking north. 'One of my informers told me that the island is always shrouded in a kind of fog, making it seem cut off from the world completely. I think you're right, Macrobius. I can see it too.' He jostled Flavius, who was half-asleep on the thwarts. 'Time to put our cassocks on again. Even an order of self-flagellating monks wouldn't have the collection of scars we've got, and to be seen like this would be something of a giveaway. We need to keep up the disguise and suffer the heat until we make contact with the first Hun outpost, when we would do best to divest ourselves of anything Christian and reveal ourselves for who we really are.'

Flavius reluctantly pulled on the heavy cassock and swung around on the thwarts, taking the skin from Arturus and drinking deeply. Macrobius steered away from shore and towards the bank of fog, helped along by Flavius and Arturus paddling where the pull of the current was more discernible, and then letting the sail take them into the northern part of the lake. As they approached they could see the curious play of the wind that kept the island shrouded in fog, a consequence of its location, nestled against the cliffs, and the continuing gorge of the river beyond – the high ground caused the southerly wind to swirl back on itself and push the following breeze high into the air, in turn causing the water in front of the island to appear unruffled and the morning mist to remain over it, hanging beneath the wind like a miasma well after the rest of the lake had cleared.

The sail flapped as the breeze rose above them and Macrobius brailed it up, swinging the yard so that it was perpendicular to the boat and unstopping and shipping the mast. He took the tiller again, and Flavius and Arturus slowly paddled forward into the fog, the mist swirling around them until they could see only a few paces ahead. They began to hear sounds, distant knocking and hammering, the rise and fall of human voices. A line of evenly spaced wooden posts appeared out of the gloom, evidently there as waymarkers for approaching boats and indicating that the lake was becoming shallower. The smell of rotting fish and human ordure began to rise off the water, sure signs of habitation nearby, and then another smell assailed them, a sickly sweet odour that they knew too well from the aftermath of battle. It was Macrobius who first spotted the source, pointing to the posts coming into view out of the mist ahead. 'We've got company,' he said.

Flavius peered, and then he could see it clearly – a post with a cross-beam and the blackened form of a human corpse suspended from it, the ribcage bared and holes in the abdomen where birds had pecked it clean. Further on there was another, and then another, dozens of them in varying stages of decomposition, some no more than torsos with the heads and parts of the legs missing. Flavius nearly retched as they slid by, trying to breathe as little as possible. Macrobius pointed up at the last one in the row. 'Looks as if our disguise won't keep us safe here either.' The corpse wore the shredded but unmistakable remains of a monk's cassock, with a wooden cross on a leather band wound around one skeletal hand. Arturus took away the sleeve he had been holding against his mouth and curled his nose in distaste. 'As monks we won't have people pestering us for our wares or assuming we're carrying hidden gold. But nobody's safe here. Every moment we're on that island we'll be one step away from a knife in the back; put a foot wrong and you'll be out here in this execution ground. We're going to have to be careful.'

To their right the piles of a wooden quay appeared, and then the mist parted to reveal a dockside filled with small boats like their own and men heaving goods up ladders and tossing them from boat to shore. They veered away from the execution ground, leaving the terrible smell in their wake, and slowly made their way between the boats until they found space for a berth, Flavius and Arturus raising their paddles while Macrobius turned the tiller and let the boat glide in. A boy in filthy rags appeared from nowhere, leapt on board, took the painter from its coiled position in the bows and tied it to a post on the quay, holding the boat tight while Arturus and Flavius jumped ashore. Macrobius picked up one of their bags to heave it up, but Arturus halted him. 'Best to pay the boy to watch over them,' he said quietly. 'Anything brought ashore will be assumed to be trade goods, and will be searched and taxed. If they do that, they're likely to search us as well, and if they find our weapons we've had it. If we're questioned, we say there's a small monastery at the far end of the island and we're stopping on our voyage north to pay our respects, and then will be on our way.'

Macrobius grunted, laid a blanket over the bags and leapt ashore, narrowly missing jamming the tip of the scabbard under his cassock into the post. Arturus took out a gold coin and showed it to the boy, who shook his head, and then he added another, eliciting the same response, until he produced a fifth coin, at which the boy snatched them and ran up the quay to a huge Goth mercenary who had been standing with crossed arms watching their arrival. He inspected the coins, bit into one to test its purity, took them and gave the boy one in return. When Arturus saw that their payment had been accepted he quickly led the other two up the quay and onto a stone revetment, the place where goods were offloaded and where trading took place. Goth mercenaries were everywhere, policing every transaction, each one accompanied by a boy who collected money and scurried between the bales and amphorae and barrels that filled every available space, with traders of all nationalities weighing goods on scales and using volume measurements that had been carved into marble tables on the quayside.

It all seemed orderly, but there was none of the hustle and bustle of a normal market; to Flavius, the absence of shouting and theatricality was unnerving, as if this were a place governed by threat and fear rather than by the normal rules of commerce. As if to underline the tension, there was a sudden bellow from one of the tables and the Goth policing the transaction hooked his arm around a trader's neck and yanked him up by the throat, dragging him shrieking and gesticulating towards a metal cage at the far end of the quay facing the execution ground; the boy who had been standing beside the Goth picked up the gold coins that had spilled from the trader's hands and handed them over to the Goth when he returned, the two of them resuming their positions in front of the table and the traders elsewhere carrying on as if nothing had happened.

Arturus pulled his hood close over his head and led them towards the mass of tightly packed buildings that covered the island beyond the trading area, most of them constructed from crudely hewn timbers with river mud used to plaster over the walls at street level, keeping out the sewage that ran down ruts in the alleys between the buildings. Arturus held up his hand to halt them as a cart trundled by, stacked with wine amphorae cushioned in straw and bundles of other goods. Flavius peered out from under his hood, and then quickly dropped his head and kept his eyes averted, a tremor in his heart. In front of the boys pulling the cart had been two heavy-set men in black cloaks and segmented armour, their foreheads sloped and their hair bound tightly behind their heads, three parallel scars running down each cheek. Flavius knew that he had just seen his first Hun warriors, close enough to kill or be killed. It brought home the reality of their mission as never before, and as he shuffled forward he felt his breath shorten and a metallic taste in his mouth, the signs of apprehension and excitement that he had only ever experienced before in the lead-up to battle.

On the edge of the square a prostitute leered out of an upstairs window, the first woman he had seen on the island; she exposed her breasts before being pulled back inside by one of the Goths who were up there with her. Arturus led the way as they plunged into an alley and followed its winding course up a series of terraces and embankments, the rickety upper storeys of buildings crowding in around them. Macrobius suppressed a curse as he narrowly missed being drenched by a bucketful of slops from an upper-floor balcony, its reeking contents joining the filth that lay in pools and gutters on the alley floor. Arturus paused at a cross-roads and then veered left and took a sharp right, taking them down a covered section like a tunnel and then through a succession of small courtyards. Eyes were watching them from the darkness, under hoods and in the recesses of doorways, and Flavius felt uneasy and vulnerable, his hand on the hilt of his sword under his cassock. Here they could be murdered and robbed and nobody would ever know what had happened to them, their bodies pulled off into a dark alley and pushed out into the river.

Arturus stopped for a moment, cocked his head as if listening, and then carried on. 'There's someone following us,' he said in a low voice. 'Keep on walking as if nothing is wrong. When I move to conceal myself, do the same behind me.'

They passed a dilapidated shrine to the Holy Mother, paused in front of it and crossed themselves with a due show of devotion before carrying on. The alley ahead was blocked by a throng of people around a fish-seller, all of them bidding for a great sturgeon laid out on the cobbles in front, so Arturus led Flavius and Macrobius down a parallel street towards another quay beside the river, partly shrouded in mist. He turned right, then ducked behind a pillar and flattened himself against a wall, gesturing for the other two to do the same. All that Flavius could hear was the dripping of condensation from the roof gables onto the street, and the lap of the current against the stones of the quayside. Suddenly Arturus darted out and pulled a figure back against the wall, one arm locked around his throat and his other hand over his mouth. It was a small, nondescript man, swarthy and bearded like many of the boatmen Flavius had seen in the port, possibly a Thracian from the lower Danube. Arturus twisted the man's head up and spoke close to his ear, in Greek. 'Who do you work for?'

The man tried to say something, but Arturus kept his hand clamped over his mouth. He twisted his head more sharply, and the man made a strangulated noise, his eyes wide with fear and his nose dripping blood. 'I said, *who do you work for?*' He took his hand from the man's mouth, and he gasped and spluttered, coughing and retching. Arturus clamped his hand down again and the man made a noise like a squealing pig, the blood from his nose splattered over the wall as he tried to breathe. Arturus released his hand again and held him higher, his arm still held like a vice around the man's neck. 'I won't ask again,' he snarled.

'An Illyrian named Segestus,' the man said through gritted teeth, his Greek heavily accented, his voice hoarse and tight. 'He paid me to look out for three westerners dressed as monks who'd be arriving on the island. I was supposed to follow you and find out who you were meeting, and then report his location to another.'

Arturus twisted hard, and the man gasped in pain. 'Who?' he demanded.

'I don't know his name,' the man said, spitting blood. 'One of the Goths who controls this place. Let me go, and that's the last you'll see of me.'

Arturus put his hand again over the man's mouth, twisted hard and held him suspended just above the ground. Flavius heard the crack as his neck broke, and then saw him go limp. Arturus carried the body to the water's edge, slipped it in and pushed it out into the current, watching it disappear into the mist as he washed his hands. He shook off the water, stood up and returned to them. 'Segestus is one of Heraclius' agents,' he said, wiping his hands on his cassock. 'The man they're after is Priscus of Panium. Ever since the embassy to Attila, the eunuchs in Theodosius' court have wanted him dead. Even though it was their emperor Theodosius who sent him to Attila, the eunuchs don't like the fact that Priscus gained Attila's confidence, and they especially don't like the fact that he's writing a history of the Huns, something that might paint their own machinations in a bad light.'

'But Heraclius is Valentinian's eunuch,' Flavius said.

'We've known for a long time that Heraclius is in the pay of the eastern eunuchs. He's their eyes and ears in the western court, and is able to influence Valentinian to comply with their wishes. Aetius has tried to warn the emperor, but to little avail. All we can do is limit the damage by keeping the emperor ignorant of much that goes on, thus reducing the chances of Heraclius overhearing anything of strategic importance. Valentinian had the makings of a capable emperor, but as long as Heraclius is there it suits us that Valentinian spends his life aloof from the real world in the palace in Ravenna, where his relationship with that odious creature can do least harm.'

'And yet somehow he found out that we were planning to meet Priscus.'

'He has spies everywhere, probably even among Aetius' trusted staff,' Arturus said grimly. 'He knows that we're on to him and that we've tried to limit his access to important information, so he's redoubled his efforts with his own circle of spies. It's a constant battle, a game of cat and mouse.'

'Do you think he knows our true purpose?'

'He knew that we were heading to this place to find Priscus, and he must have guessed that we intended to carry on to the court of Attila. Whether he knows about the sword is anyone's guess. We need to be on our guard.'

They went under another arch and then into a courtyard from which there was no exit, only a series of low doorways into the buildings. There was nobody to be seen, only a pair of emaciated cats fighting over a fish skeleton, and rats scurrying along the sides of the walls. Arturus glanced back the way they had come, looking out for anyone else who might be following. 'Wait under the arch. I was told to go to the furthest court to the north, and then to enter the second doorway from the left. I'll call you when I've found him.'

It began drizzling, and Flavius looked up at the grey cloud that seemed to have settled into the mist, blinking the water from his eyes. 'Let's hope he's there. If he's not, we're not waiting. We need to be out of here by sundown.'

Twenty minutes later Arturus reappeared in the doorway, his hood up and his face in shadows, and beckoned them over. Flavius and Macrobius followed him under a low doorway, down a narrow flight of steps and along a passageway barely wide enough to squeeze through. At the end a chute led down to the water's edge, a foetid smell rising from a muddy mass at the bottom. Arturus opened a creaking wooden door to the left, led them through a dark passage and opened another door into a dimly lit chamber. In the far corner a spluttering oil lamp revealed a man hunched over a mass of papers on a table. He looked up, took off his polished-crystal spectacles and peered at Flavius and Macrobius, his eyes watery but sharp. 'Well?' he said in Greek, looking at Arturus. 'Should I speak in Latin or in Greek?'

'Flavius put a hand on Macrobius' shoulder. 'Latin, for the benefit of my Illyrian friend here, masquerading as a monk.'

'So I see,' the man said, switching languages and eyeing them up and down. 'If Arturus is anything to go by, you would both be fighting monks too?'

'Flavius Aetius Gaudentius, special tribune in the service of my uncle, *magister militum* Flavius Aetius. This is the centurion of my old *limitanei numerus*, Macrobius.'

'Ah, the *limitanei*,' the man said. 'They are much missed around these parts. Better troops for my money than the *comitatenses*, who never stay in the same place for more than ten minutes and never get to know the local people and their customs, and anyway are based too far behind the lines.'

Macrobius grunted. 'I'm with you there.'

'You must be Priscus of Panium,' Flavius said. 'I salute you for undertaking your embassy to Attila.'

'Not the general view in Constantinople, I fear,' Priscus said, getting up. 'For reasons that are beyond the grasp of a mere scholar, I seem to be on the hit list of most of Theodosius' eunuchs, hence my self-imprisonment in this hole.' He was extremely tall and very ill-looking, and Flavius saw him totter as he sniffed the air. 'I apologize for the smell. All of the sewage from this rotten carcass of a town goes straight into the river, of course, and gets swept downstream by the current, but they forget that there are little backwaters and creeks by the quays where it accumulates, especially the solid variety. But I can hardly call the city *urinatores* to clean it up, can I, or try to do it myself and risk one of the thugs who infest this island jumping on me.'

'Arturus disposed of one of them,' Flavius said.

'So he tells me, and for that I'm grateful, but they're like rats. Get rid of one, and ten take their place.' He coughed violently, his whole frame racked with convulsions, and then he sat down again, wheezing and trying to recover himself. Flavius could see that he was little older than he was, but he had the sunken cheeks and sparse hair of a much older man. 'I'd offer you water, but I have to draw it from the river out of my back window only a few paces from that mess at the bottom of the chute. But what I can give you,' he said, uncorking a small pot and spilling out wine into three cups beside his bench, 'is some vintage Judaean. My house slave from Panium is a Dacian who has been able to pass himself off as a trader, and he has used my depleting supply of gold to tap into the food and wine brought here for trade from civilized parts of the world. It's the only thing that keeps me alive.'

They took the wine and drank it down, replacing the cups and then sitting on wooden stools in front of the table. 'We don't have much time,' Flavius said. 'We want to set out before sunset.'

'Very wise,' Priscus said. 'Your boat will mysteriously disappear into the night otherwise, and you probably will as well.'

Flavius pointed at the sheaves of paper on the table. 'Your history of the Huns?' he asked. 'Arturus mentioned it.'

'I'm writing it as a codex. I can't get decent scroll any more, in papyrus or in vellum. It's a history of the Huns from earliest times to the present day, including an account of my visit to Attila. If I'm to get nothing for my efforts other than death threats from people who were supposed to be on my side, then I thought I could at least write an account for posterity.'

'It's the present day that concerns us, not posterity,' Flavius said, leaning forward with one hand on his knee. 'What do you know of Attila's intentions?'

Priscus picked up the metal stylus that was lying on the table and placed it in an open inkpot. He stared at what he had been writing, and then looked at Flavius intently. 'I can tell you this much. Attila intends to march east on Parthia, skirting the northern Black Sea and dropping down past the Caucasus mountains and over the plains of Anatolia to the headwaters of the Euphrates. But that's really a sideshow, to keep his warriors exercised. His eyes are on Rome.'

'On Rome?' Flavius said. 'Not Constantinople?'

Priscus shook his head. 'He knows that he can defeat Theodosius' army in the field, but he does not have the ability to maintain a siege or to launch the seaborne assault that would be necessary to take the city. The land walls of Constantinople can be defended by the city garrison, especially if the field army is withdrawn to reinforce them, and as long as the sea lanes through the Bosporus and the Dardanelles are kept open Constantinople could survive almost indefinitely even if the rest of the eastern empire disintegrates. But the city of Rome is another matter. Attila knows what the Goths managed forty years ago, when Alaric smashed his way through and set up his standard in the old Capitoline Temple above the Roman Forum. The city may have been replaced by Ravenna as imperial capital in the West, but the sack of Rome was still a huge blow to Roman prestige and set other barbarian chieftains around the frontiers hungry with ambition. Attila's father Mundiuk was one of them, and he passed his ambition on to his son.'

'It was a wake-up call,' Flavius said. 'After the Goths got bored and left, the walls of Rome were strengthened, the garrison was reorganized and the *schola militarum* was set up for officer training, building on the lessons learned.'

'I'm no military strategist, but if the *schola* in Rome is anything like the one in Constantinople, you'll have been taught how many men are required to defend a city wall, right? My friend Maximinus tried to explain it to me once when we walked the walls of Constantinople. The walls built by the emperor Aurelian around Rome are impressive enough, but at nearly twelve miles in extent they are impossible to defend properly without a garrison far larger than Rome could ever sustain. Attila knows this, and he knows that if he marched his army on Rome he would be likely to take the city. He has his eyes above all on the abandoned palace of the Palatine. The city of Rome may be a backwater now, but under Attila it would become the capital of a new Roman Empire, one ruled by a Hun dynasty.'

'Do you know the size of his army? Are there any alliances?'

Priscus pursed his lips. 'As Maximinus and I were making our hasty farewells, two other emissaries arrived, one from the Ostrogoth king Valamer and the other from the Gepids, ruled by Ardaric. There were other indications of alliances being forged, including the marriage of two of Attila's daughters to Goth princes. Maximinus reckoned that in alliance with Alaric and Valamer, Attila could field an army of fifty thousand men.'

'*Fifty thousand men!*' Flavius repeated, shaking his head and turning to Arturus. 'The only way Aetius could match that number would be in alliance with the Visigoths.'

'You mean with Theodoric?' Priscus said. 'With his sworn enemy?'

Flavius thought hard. 'The eastern and western Goths have

grown apart, with the Ostrogoths scorning the Visigoths for settling down in Gaul and Spain and becoming Romanized, and the Visigoths in turn despising the Ostrogoths as barbarians. There are blood feuds between the two that Aetius could play on to get the Visigoths on board, though he would want those set aside if the Visigoths were to be treated as allies alongside the *comitatenses*. Blood feuds do not make for good battle discipline; they lead men off on missions of their own to find some hated rival.'

'Aetius would need to persuade Theodoric that he would have no future if he joined with Attila,' Arturus said. 'If that alliance were to be forged, the Visigoths would soon be subsumed by the Ostrogoths and Valamer would become the dominant Goth chieftain. But on the other hand, if Theodoric were to be persuaded to join Aetius, then he would need to be convinced that a Roman alliance with his forces would produce an army equal to Attila's, of fifty thousand men or more, enough to give even chances of a victory.'

'It would be a tall order,' Flavius murmured. 'But there are enough mercenaries and renegades with military training floating around the western provinces for Aetius to be able to rustle up *foederati* units to bolster the *comitatenses*, boosting the size of the force he can show Theodoric. If anyone can do it, Aetius can.'

'Provided that he sees the sense of an alliance with Theodoric,' Priscus said.

'The future of the western empire is at stake,' Flavius said. 'And they may be sworn enemies, but the two men speak the same language. There are advantages to my uncle's Goth ancestry.'

'They'll have no choice,' Priscus said. 'One of Attila's daughters, Erecan, the one remaining in his court, came in secret to our camp on our last night and told Maximinus of her father's plan. She said that Attila intended to destroy Milan and Ravenna and to march on Rome, but before that he would meet Aetius in one final apocalyptic showdown, in the greatest and bloodiest battle ever fought. She said he called it the mother of all battles.'

'*The mother of all battles,*' Flavius repeated, trying to absorb the enormity of it, and then turned again to Arturus. 'We need to get word back to Aetius as soon as possible after we've reached the court of Attila. Aetius needs to begin marshalling his forces now.'

Priscus leaned forward, his skin pale and diaphanous in the lamplight. 'Whatever you hope to achieve there, you should know that what lies ahead, what lies beyond this island, is not for the faint-hearted,' he said, his voice hushed and tremulous. 'Everything we learned from the time of Trajan and the Dacian Wars is true, of another world out there, of witchcraft and shamans and human sacrifice, of shrieking eagles and wolves that howl in the night. You will see sights that will shock you, but you must keep your nerve. Those who do make it as far as the borders of the Hun kingdom have passed their first test, and may be allowed into the court of the great king.'

Arturus stared back, his eyes intense. 'We are prepared, Priscus. And now we have one last request.'

'What is it?'

'Tell us what you know about the sword of Attila.'

13

Flavius sat in the bows of the boat staring ahead into the mist, his cassock now used as bedding and the tribune's insignia on his shoulders gleaming in the dull light. It had been an arduous three-day voyage since departing from the island, a place they had been all too happy to leave, through gorges and rapids and whirlpools, always against the current of the great river. But for the last day the rocky shoreline had steadily dropped in height until the banks now were no higher than the boat's mast, and they had begun to feel that they were through the worst of it. They had been lucky with the wind, always strong enough to fill the sail and push them at a slow walking pace against the current, but every so often that morning there had been a chill brush from the north-east, a hint of the harsh winds that they knew swept across the steppe-lands of their destination. Priscus had told them that they would feel it as they approached the rock that marked their turning point in the river, the entrance to a tributary that would lead them to a landing stage where their river journey would end and the final leg of their trip through the flat open grasslands would begin.

Flavius thought about what Priscus had told them of the sword of Attila. It had been forged long ago in the days of the ancestors of Mundiuk, before the time of Trajan and Decebalus and the Dacian Wars, before the Romans had even tried to penetrate the northern lands of the barbarians. It was said that the smiths had come down the silk route from a mysterious island in the sea beyond Thina, a place where swords were made so sharp that to touch a blade was to lose a finger. The men with narrow eyes had set up their forge in a dark dell in the steppes, in one of the places at the bottom of an eroded stream bank where the

Huns lived protected from the sweeping winds above, venturing out only to hunt and trade and go to war. There, for months on end, they had tempered and annealed the steel, making a blade that was immensely strong and yet ductile, adding to the iron a rare electrum that made the blade shine with a radiant lustre even in the dull light of the North. The chieftain who had ordered the sword made, a distant ancestor of Mundiuk, had given the smiths a stone that his own ancestors had seen fall from the sky on the ice sheets of their northern hunting grounds, a stone that attracted iron to it; they had made it the pommel of the sword. The smiths were still there now, burned and buried in the dell with their forge, killed by the chieftain with the very sword they had made him in order to prevent them from selling their skills to others who might stand against the power that now shone from his hands.

Attila's daughter Erecan had told Priscus that at the future king's birth, Attila's father Mundiuk had placed the sword in a bonfire, and that when he used it to cut the marks on the baby's face and he had not cried Mundiuk knew he had beheld the future king, one whom he named after the ancient name for the sword itself. And then by tradition the shaman who had read the auguries had taken the sword and buried it in a secret place, arranging for the boy to find it when he came of age as a warrior. Since then Attila had used the sword at the birthing ceremonies of his own children, of Erecan herself, and had raised it in battle, at all other times storing it in a strongroom in his citadel along with his gold and the booty of war waged to east and west as he had grown stronger and his ambition for conquest had become all-encompassing.

And yet Erecan had also said that Attila himself was not swayed by the shamans, that he did not believe that the sword itself had magical properties; like Aetius, who scorned the monks for wishing to bring the forces of Rome under the sign of Christ, Attila was too good a general to allow mysticism and religion to influence his judgement except where he could see its effect on the morale of his men. Attila knew that the power of the sword came not from the gods but from the genius of the smiths, from those able to create a weapon that shone over the field of battle, and that their skill was not some divine gift but the result of generations of them having crafted weapons for the warriors across the expanse of the known world who were able to call on their expertise.

A rock suddenly loomed ahead, a stark white sentinel on the bank of the river, and in front of it Flavius could see the mist swirling over the entrance to a tributary that joined the river from the east. He put his hand up and Macrobius swung the tiller, then quickly furled the sail and lowered the mast for the final leg of their journey. The dense coniferous forest of the gorge had gone, and all they could see now was stark grassland and a few small trees. The tributary narrowed to little more than a stream, and as Flavius' paddle struck the bottom he knew that their destination could not be far ahead. Minutes later he saw a gravelly foreshore with two boats pulled up on it, and Macrobius turned the tiller until the bow grounded into the gravel. Flavius leapt out, followed by Arturus and then Macrobius, who reached in and tossed their bags out before pulling the boat up as far as he could and tying the painter around a wooden frame in front of the other two vessels. He stripped off his cassock, stuffed it in his bag, slung the bag on his back and then peered over the stream, his hands on his hips. 'Well, what now?' he said.

'That's what,' Arturus said, nodding up the slope. The other two followed his gaze, walking forward and then stopping abruptly in the same instant. A line of Hun horsemen was standing above the bank, the riders helmeted with their cloaks thrown back but their weapons still sheathed. They wore armour and garb that Flavius recognized as typically Hun: a blue woollen undercoat and light brown trousers, leather boots and a leather flapped cap, a conical helmet and the distinctive Hun body armour, a vest of segments of iron sewn into closely fitting flexible armour covering the torso and shoulders. Two of the men carried Hun bows, recurved composite bows made of horn, wood and sinew laminated together, two of them had war axes and all of them wore long swords in sheaths buckled to their waists. Unlike the Goths and the Alans, they were relatively short men, stocky and muscular, typical in their facial appearance of men from the windswept steppe-lands and tundra plains extending from the Hun heartland in the Danube watershed to as far east as men from the West had gone, to Thina and beyond.

One of the riders cantered down to the gravel, coming to a halt about ten paces away, the horse stomping and snorting and being calmed by the rider, who Flavius could see was a woman. She wore the same armour as the rest but her head was bare and her long hair was tied tightly back, and she bore the birth scars of a warrior on her cheeks. She stared at them haughtily, lingering on Arturus, whose face was still concealed under his hood, and then cantered back to the men, speaking to them in the guttural language of the Huns.

'That's Erecan,' Arturus said quietly, his face still down. 'Like Attila, she speaks Latin fluently, having been educated by scholars brought from Constantinople for the purpose. She was the only one of Attila's children to pass the birth ceremony, so she's been brought up as a warrior princess.'

Erecan returned to face them, and Flavius stepped forward, bowing his head slightly. 'I am Flavius Aetius Gaudentius, tribune, nephew of *magister militum* Aetius and special envoy to the court of Attila of the emperor Valentinian, and this is my centurion Macrobius.'

'Do you serve Valentinian or Aetius?' she said, swinging her horse around, her voice sonorous and resonating. 'I hear that Valentinian is only served by eunuchs.'

'Valentinian is my emperor, and Aetius my general.'

The horse snorted and she pulled its neck around, facing Arturus. 'And who is this?'

Arturus pulled back his hood and threw off his cassock, revealing his long hair and beard and the tunic and sword belt of a *foederati* commander. 'I am Arturus of the Britons, former tribune of the *foederati Britannorum* of the *comitatenses* of the North.'

She stared at him, and then leaned over and spat. 'I do not know this man.' She reined her horse hard to the right and galloped back up to the others, Arturus remaining stock-still. 'Hold your ground,' he said quietly. 'This is just theatre.'

'Just theatre?' Macrobius exclaimed. 'How well did you know this woman?'

'I was her bondsman.'

'Meaning?'

'She was my wife. In a manner of speaking.'

'*Your wife*. So it was a bit more than unarmed combat.'

'A bit more.'

Macrobius turned and peered at him. 'When you left this place twelve years ago, did you say a proper goodbye to her?'

'There wasn't time. Quiet now. She's returning.' Erecan halted her horse again in front of the three men but this time she leapt off and walked towards Arturus. She stood in front of him and stared him in the eye, the birth scars on her cheeks livid, then took out a knife and held it under his chin. 'Explain yourself,' she demanded. 'It was not like a future king to run away with your tail between your legs.'

'A future king?' Macrobius exclaimed, staring again at Arturus.

'He used to tell me his dreams,' Erecan said, the knife still at his throat. 'About how one day he would return to his native Britain and rally the people against the Saxons, and create a kingdom that would be a worthy successor to Roman rule. After he left me without a word, I decided that it had all been hot air, that he was just another one of the renegades who come this way with delusions of grandeur. Most of them we kill, and I thought I should have done so with Arturus. Now could be the time.'

'I came to your father's court twelve years ago as captain of Gaiseric's bodyguard,' Arturus said. 'Already my cousin in the bodyguard had been murdered, and I was bent on vengeance. On the day that I left, one of the bodyguard, a Saxon with no love for a Briton like me, told Gaiseric that I knew he was responsible and was planning revenge. Once I heard that, I knew I had to leave immediately or risk being knifed in my sleep. You were out hunting on the steppe and I couldn't wait.'

She brushed the knife down his beard. 'Well? Did you get your vengeance?'

Arturus gestured at Flavius. 'Thanks to my friends here, two years after leaving you I was able to stand my ground before the walls of Carthage and face Gaiseric's army, sword in hand. Before the day was out I had accounted for two of his Alan bodyguard and six Vandal warriors, as well as an Alaunt war dog. The price of *wergild* for my cousin was easily paid, and vengeance was satisfied.'

'And after that?'

'My commission in the *foederati* was restored, and I have been fighting for Rome ever since.'

'Fighting, or spying?'

Arturus lowered his voice. 'Erecan, we need to talk. Out of earshot.'

She sheathed her blade and led them back a few paces towards the boat. 'None of my Huns knows Latin. Their loyalty is to me, and not to my father. You can speak openly.'

'It was no coincidence that it was you who came to meet us, was it?'

'You're lucky that I was back from hunting, and that it was not my father's older brother Bleda who met you. He was passed over for the kingship at his birthing ceremony, but he has made up for it by being the most savage of my father's henchmen. It was he who took away the eunuchs who came from Constantinople and butchered them like the fattened pigs that they are, with his own hands. If Priscus and Maximinus had not left when they did, they would have suffered the same fate.'

'So you knew we were coming.'

'By chance the Huns who arrived from the island ahead of you were in my service, providing wine and food for my retinue. One of them saw you when they passed you in the town and recognized you from twelve years ago, despite the beard and the cassock.'

'Then you will know that we have met Priscus of Panium.'

'It's an open secret that he's hiding somewhere on the island. My father liked him, admired his scholarship, and the two spent hours discussing the geography of the outer reaches of the world, my father telling him much that was new about the ice cap to the north where the Huns have gone on expeditions to hunt whales and the great tusked seals. But my father has a mercurial temper, and would have ordered Priscus executed if he had caught wind of the machinations in Constantinople. He detests intrigue, and rates men only as scholars or as warriors. Priscus is beleaguered from both sides, and there is little I can do for him.'

'He told us everything, Erecan. He told us of your nocturnal visit, and what you told him and Maximinus about Attila's plans. You remember me telling you of my dreams for Britain, but I remember you telling me of your hatred for your father after he murdered your mother, and your desire for vengeance.'

'It remains undimmed. It is with me night and day. I will have it in this world, or in the next.'

'Then there's something I must tell you. Something that Flavius and Macrobius know only in part, though they may have guessed the truth. Fifteen years ago when I deserted my *foederati numerus* it was not just because of my distaste for what we'd been ordered to do – to mop up and exact retribution after a peasant revolt in northern Gaul. When I voiced my discontent I was brought before Aetius, who'd heard about my background and recruited me into his newly formed intelligence service. Everything I've done since then, joining Gaiseric's bodyguard and coming to the Hun court, gaining Augustine's confidence and becoming his secretary, our mission here today, all of it has been in the service of Aetius. And there's nothing Aetius desires more than the destruction of Attila.'

'Then you are my bondsman again, Arturus. But this time there will be no more unannounced departures. When there is a need to go, we go together.'

'Agreed.'

'We have horses for you. As we ride you can tell me exactly what you are plotting.'

For the next few hours the group wended their way ever further into the steppe-land, passing the two Huns and the traders they had encountered on the island, seeing how they had lashed their amphorae on the sides of donkeys and put the barrels and parcels into a cart that was being pulled along slowly by a pair of bullocks. Erecan had stopped, smashed the top off an amphora and filled a wineskin for her men, pouring the remainder into another skin and passing it to Macrobius. He had drunk his fill, and then passed it to Arturus and Flavius, who did the same. It was a Gaulish vintage that Flavius had recognized from the amphora stamp as Lugdenese, made close to the hunting estate that had been given to his grandfather Gaudentius when the Romans had decided to settle the Visigoths in the old province of Gaul. Wine had been made there since earliest times and had been drunk by Gaulish chieftains before Germanic warriors had acquired a taste for it, and now it seemed fitting that it should be drunk by the next wave of those beyond the frontiers who had found some of what Rome had to offer intoxicating.

Flavius had tossed the wineskin back into the bullock cart and resumed his place beside Macrobius as they trotted forward, enjoying the warmth in his belly but momentarily regretting not wearing his cassock as a sharp blast of wind hit them from the steppes. The path dropped out of the wind into a gully, and Arturus dropped back too, the three of them now riding side by side behind the Huns. Macrobius turned to him. 'Nice one with the *wergild* story, by the way, Arturus. That might have saved our skin.'

Arturus gave him a rueful look. 'If you want to get out of a scrape with Huns, tell them you were seeking vengeance. That goes straight to their soul, and they'll forgive you just about anything.'

'So,' Flavius said. 'Arturus, future King of the Britons?'

'The word *king* was Erecan's, not mine,' Arturus replied. 'For now, I'm no more than a special agent of the *magister militum*; I'm just a man who exists in the shadowlands of history and might well leave no trace of his passing.'

'But it could be otherwise.'

Arturus reined up his horse as they waited to go over a wooden bridge. 'If we succeed in our mission here, you and Macrobius can return to soldiering, as men whom Aetius might value highly for the first-hand knowledge you will get here of Attila and the Huns. But for me it's different. Already Heraclius is on to me, and soon enough he'll know the extent of my intelligence activities for Aetius. He might try to woo me into his own fold, but I would never serve a eunuch. This will be my last mission for Aetius. I plan to return west from here to my own people, and use the skills I've learned in the service of Rome to lead the resistance against the Saxons.'

'If any of us survives whatever lies ahead of us in this place,' Macrobius said.

The last of the Hun horses clattered over the bridge, and they moved forward. Ahead lay a deepening cut in the folds of the steppe, an old river channel that had eroded into a ravine. An eagle flew high above them, dark and menacing, flapping against a wind that they could barely feel down below the level of the plain. A well-trodden path beside the stream in the centre led them along a sinuous route, left and then right. Flavius could see how the ravine could easily be defended by archers and catapult men ranged on the slopes above, the turns of the ravine breaking up an attacking army into sections of a few hundred infantry or cavalry who could be dealt with before the next section attempted to force their way through. After about a mile the ravine widened, large areas of well-watered land now abutting the stream on either side, some of it cultivated in patches of green, with people visibly hoeing and picking. They turned a corner, carried on for another quarter of a mile and came to a huge earthen vallum that stretched across the entire ravine from one side to the other, a wooden palisade with crenellations and low towers running along the top. The gate in front of them swung open and Erecan led them inside, the Hun horsemen now encircling the three men in a tighter formation as they carried on forward.

As Flavius looked up an astonishing sight met his eyes. Ahead of them lay a vast wooden citadel, rising almost to the height of the surrounding cliffs, but far enough away to be out of arrow or ballista range. In the foreground were numerous butts for archery practice, and to the right a track the size of the hippodrome in Rome where groups of galloping horsemen were kicking up great clouds of dust. Tented encampments lay everywhere, round huts of hide with wisps of smoke issuing from holes in the centre of their roofs, horses tethered nearby and the smell of cooked meat wafting over the road. Flavius could see that Priscus was right, that this was the encampment of an army numbering in the tens of thousands, with many more men presumably in outlying encampments and on the steppes ready to heed the call to arms when it came.

It was the sight of the citadel itself that most riveted Flavius. A palisade surrounded it, enclosing an area at least as great as the Palatine Hill and the Old Forum in Rome. In the centre was a fortress-like structure rising above the plain, surrounded by tiers of buildings in a tightly packed mass that descended to the valley floor; in overall appearance it was as if one of the circular huts of the encampments had been recreated on a grand scale. The palisade had been built from huge trunks of cedar of a size that Flavius had only seen in the forests surrounding the gorge of the Danube near the Iron Gates; to cut and transport such timbers would have been a prodigious feat, one presumably carried out by the Danube woodsmen themselves under contract to the Huns. In a land where wood was scarce and trees were stunted, the Huns' own tradition of woodcraft was seen in the walls of the interior buildings, all built from short planks of varying breadths seamlessly mortised together, giving the flush appearance of ships' hulls that, as a boy, Flavius had watched being constructed shell first in the building yards of Portus near Rome. The weakness of the citadel was its vulnerability to fire, but the chances of an attacker getting close enough with the right artillery seemed remote indeed; the Hun strategy was one of offence, fighting wars hundreds of miles from their homeland, striking out from a base with little in its location or resources to attract an attacker intent on loot or conquest.

At the gate into the palisade Erecan leapt off her horse, dismissed her warriors and watched them canter off to an encampment nearby. Earlier, she and Arturus had fallen back from the group, talking intently, and Flavius had known that she was being told of their plan to find and take the sword. The men got off their own horses, handing the reins to waiting boys, and followed Erecan inside, past the gate guards and up a wide stairway that led to the central part of the citadel. When they were out of earshot of the guards and had reached another entranceway, Erecan stopped and turned to Flavius. 'Arturus is your manservant, your armourer. He'll go down this passageway and await my return, and then he and I will go to the strongroom. First I will take you to the audience chamber. My father will only have a short time for you, as he is intending to ride on Parthia tonight. But he respects Aetius as a general, and he'll listen to what you have to say.'

'I'll decide what that is when I see him,' Flavius said.

'Don't offer him concessions of land, as Rome did to the Visigoths and the Alans. Attila will regard that as a sign of weakness. And offers of gold he is used to from the eunuchs of Constantinople. You don't want to remind him of eunuchs. He despises them, and then he will despise you.'

'No eunuchs,' Macrobius said gruffly, hand on his sword pommel. 'At least that's one thought I share in common with Attila.'

'And take your hand off your sword. You'll be allowed to wear your weapons into the audience chamber, as any man who willingly lets others take his sword from him is regarded as a weakling. But to touch them will be to invite instant death.'

'This sounds like it's going to be a bundle of laughs,' Macrobius grumbled.

Flavius glanced at him. 'It'll be one to tell your grandchildren.'

'Children would be a good start. Coming here isn't exactly going to increase my chances of that. Most soldiers my age are veterans with a nice plot of land and a wife, and sons already in the army.'

'Wait until you see the gold,' Erecan said. 'Then you'll be pleased you came.'

'Now you're talking.'

'When you've had your audience, I'll take you to the strong-room,' she went on. 'Once there, we will need to work out our best route of escape.'

'That sounds like a plan.'

'And one last thing. Watch out for Bleda. He's loyal to his brother, but embittered after years of resentment at not having been selected for the kingship. He hates me because he took my slave mother for his own after I was born and Attila then decided to kill her, and he blames me for that. He would happily find an excuse to destroy me.'

'Do you have anyone you can rely on?'

'My two closest bodyguards, Optilla and Thrastilla. They've been my guards since my birth. They will come with us.'

'All right. Let's move,' Flavius said.

Arturus and Macrobius disappeared down the passageway to the left, and Erecan led Flavius up the stairs and into a wide chamber with wooden colonnades around the walls, and with the floor and the wall spaces between the columns covered with over-lapping carpets, brightly coloured and tightly woven. It reminded Flavius of the interior of Berber tents he had seen in Africa before the fall of Carthage, the dwellings of another people more at home with a nomadic than a sedentary lifestyle; to the Huns, even a citadel as impressive as this one would have none of the permanence or meaning of Rome or Constantinople, and would only be seen as a temporary capital while their king marshalled his forces for his final apocalyptic thrust westwards.

Erecan pushed her way through two more sets of doors, and then pulled a final set inwards, standing aside while Flavius made his way forward. He was inside another colonnaded chamber, but instead of being enclosed, this one was open to the elements, a large circular aperture in the roof drawing out wisps of smoke from a smouldering fire in a stone hearth below. On either side of the entrance were two huge Goth mercenaries, both carrying axes, and beyond the hearth Flavius could see a Hun warrior, presumably Bleda, his hair streaked with grey, cross-armed and glaring at them, the birth scars on his cheeks livid in the firelight.

The doors slammed shut behind him, and Flavius took another step forward. Beside the Hun warrior he could see another figure, seated on a wooden throne, slouched to one side, with his moustache and sloped forehead clearly visible. He too bore the birth scars on his cheeks, and he was drinking from a golden tankard and eating meat off a bone, and staring across the hearth at him.

Flavius had reached his destination.

It was Attila.

14

Flavius stood in front of the hearth in the audience chamber, trying to keep his posture relaxed as Attila and his brother stared at him. 'My name is Flavius Aetius Gaudentius, tribune of the Roman army, nephew of Aetius of the same name, *magister militum* of the western armies. I come before you on his behalf.' Bleda leaned over and spoke close to Attila's ear in the guttural language of the Huns, his body tense and his fists balled. Attila replied to him and Bleda swung away, his face contorted with rage, pacing behind the throne. 'My brother wishes to kill you on the spot,' Attila said, his voice deep and sonorous. 'He thinks that an envoy who does not represent an emperor is not an envoy at all, and is an insult to the court of the Huns.'

Flavius had already decided how to play it with Attila. There would be no talk of concessions, no offers of gold. They would talk as men and as soldiers, not as negotiators. 'I come representing Aetius because he is the only general on earth who is a worthy opponent to Attila. Valentinian is a weakling, served by eunuchs. I would not dishonour myself by agreeing to represent such a man. You can tell this to your brother Bleda, warrior to warrior.'

'My brother understands every word you say. We were as well schooled in Latin and Greek by scholars brought here by my father as any of the Goth princes who were sent to Rome.' He took a mouthful of meat, chewed and swallowed it, tossed the bone into the hearth and contemplated Flavius, wiping his hands on his tunic. 'We don't like eunuchs either. Bleda especially doesn't like them. Any he finds he uses for pig-sticking practice in the field.' He glanced up at Bleda, who grunted, his face slightly less ferocious. Attila turned again to Flavius. 'So, what do you want?'

'I bring you a gift.' Flavius began to open a satchel that was hanging from his side, having previously been stored inside his backpack, but he was immediately pounced on by one of the Goth guards, who twisted his arm painfully behind his back and put a knife to his throat. Attila watched in amusement and then waved his hand, the Goth releasing him. 'My bodyguards are touchy about weapons,' Attila said. 'The last three Hun kings were assassinated in this very chamber, including my father, Mundiuk.'

'It's not a weapon,' Flavius said, nursing his arm. 'It's a book.'

Attila grunted, his interest piqued, and waved his arm again. The Goth backed off and Flavius unwrapped the package in the satchel. It was a small leather-bound codex with vellum pages, a gift from Uago on his passing out from the *schola* twelve years earlier. Along with the *gladius*, it had been his most prized possession among the belongings that Una had taken from his quarters and left with Macrobius, and with nowhere else to store it, he had decided to bring it along to annotate during their voyage. Their conversation with Priscus on the island about Attila's interest in geography had prompted the idea that it might be a suitable gift, a way of keeping Attila occupied while the others were attempting to enter the strongroom. He walked forward, bowed slightly and passed it over. 'It's a pocket-book compilation of maps of the known world, based on Ptolemy but incorporating later additions, including a more detailed image of Britannia, for example. I thought you might use it to trace your conquests.'

Attila took the volume, opening it carefully and turning the pages. 'But not, I see, incorporating the latest work carried out by the cartographic department of the *fabri* in Rome.'

'You know I'm unable to bring you that. But this was based on the latest intelligence when it was created by that same department at the time I was a candidate in the *schola*, twelve years ago.'

Attila opened a page and stared at it intently, tracing his finger over the map and then shaking his head. 'Ptolemy got the land to the north-east of the Danube all wrong, and the mistakes have been repeated on maps ever since. The Maeotic Lake is further east, and the great ice sheets much further north. I myself have not seen them, but Bleda and my father as young men went to the edge of the ice and encountered a race of hunters who live in snow huts, bringing back walrus ivory. One day I should like to go north too.'

'There is much of the world still to conquer.'

'To conquer or to explore. We Huns are not people who claim ownership over land. These steppes belong to the eagle and the wolf, the northern ice sheets to the great white bear.'

'That's what makes you so dangerous,' Flavius replied, calculating his response. 'The Romans conquer to occupy territory, building frontiers and forts, expending manpower and resources on it. For the Huns, to conquer means to go to battle. All of your manpower and all of your resources are put into one cataclysmic clash with an enemy. It is why Attila has become the most feared name across the world.'

Attila looked at him shrewdly, his legs apart and one hand on his knee. 'So, Flavius Aetius Gaudentius, nephew of *magister militum* Aetius. Why have you really come here?'

Flavius stared him in the eye. 'I have come here on behalf of Aetius to challenge you to battle.'

'To challenge me to battle.' Attila wiped his nose and glanced at Bleda. 'That's a new one. I don't recall any of the eunuchs offering me that as a concession, or that gangly scholar Priscus and his tribune friend from Constantinople.'

'That's because they were representing an emperor, not a general. I come to you not with offers of concessions, but with an offer of war. It may not be this year, or next year, but it will be soon, at a place of your choosing. The mother of all battles.'

'The mother of all battles,' Attila repeated slowly, eyeing him.

'I couldn't have put it better myself.' Flavius remembered too late that the expression had come from Priscus, who had quoted it from Attila himself. He suddenly felt on a knife-edge, not daring to look at Bleda. Priscus and Maximinus had left under a cloud, and if Attila guessed that he had been in contact with them, things might go wrong very quickly. He tried not to look tense, but his heart was pounding and he could feel the sweat trickling down his back.

Attila narrowed his eyes. 'There were two others with you. Who are they?'

'My centurion, Macrobius, and my manservant and armourer, a Gaul from Armorica. Your daughter is taking them to find a grinding wheel in your armoury. Our swords need sharpening.'

Attila thought for a moment, grunted, and then got up, putting the book carefully aside and walking towards a shuttered window in the side wall of the room. 'I'm told that in Rome and in Constantinople the military *scholae* include dioramas for mock-ups of battles,' he said. 'Well, here's my playground.' He pushed open the wooden shutters and led Flavius out onto a balcony, into the blazing light of the sun. Flavius shielded his eyes, blinking against the glare, and began to make out features that they had seen on the way in, the surrounding cliffs with the steppe-land above, the road leading out to the palisade and the entrance formed by the ravine.

From this height atop the citadel he could appreciate the immensity of the bowl, at least a mile across, with their position commanding views in all directions. Attila opened his arms expansively. 'When I exercise my warriors, we play war games for real. From my last excursion against the Persian Empire we have a thousand captured Parthians, infantry and cavalry, fully equipped and armed. If they survive until sundown, they gain their freedom. If my warriors fall to their arms, that is their lot. I can ask my men to recreate any battle I choose, using the flat land of the plain to the east or the undulating land to the west.

Sometimes I watch it from here alone, sometimes with my daughter, sometimes with my commanders. Today, I will go down and join them.'

He turned and bored his eyes into Flavius. 'Let me see what a nephew of Flavius Aetius Gaudentius is made of. Ride with me.'

The next four hours were the most exhilarating Flavius had ever experienced outside real battle, and also the bloodiest since that morning ten years earlier before the walls of Carthage. Attila had set up two scenarios to replicate successful encounters with the Parthians during his campaigning season the previous winter, as a way of introducing his younger warriors to Hun battle tactics and to give them a taste for killing. Flavius and Attila had observed the first one on horseback from the west side of the citadel, where they saw a Parthian force take a ridge blind, without forward observation of the Hun positions; they had been shot down by a fixed line of Hun archers below their side of the ridge as they bunched above, unable to retreat because further Parthian troops pressing behind were unaware of their dire situation. The few survivors had been mercilessly cut to pieces by the Hun infantry soldiers who had sprung forward from behind the archers to finish them off, and the victors had then run and galloped in review order past Attila and Flavius, ululating and clashing their arms as they sped east to the next killing ground.

The second scenario was on a larger scale, involving at least a thousand mounted archers, lancers and swordsmen, and the remaining five hundred-odd Parthians. The prisoners had been told to defend a wagon laager that was too small to contain an adequate number of defenders or to provide protection for the Parthian troops in the field, allowing them to be broken apart and encircled by columns of Hun cavalry who then shot them down and laid into them with the sword, finishing off each cluster of men one by one.

This time, to Flavius' astonishment and delight, two men

under instruction from Attila rode up and slipped a cuirass of segmented armour and chainmail over Flavius' tunic, fitting him with gloves and helmet and greaves and slinging a long Hun cavalry sword over the flanks of his horse. When they had finished and Flavius had flexed himself and drawn his sword Attila slapped the back of his horse and it reared up, galloping at high speed into the fray. Attila caught up and rode beside him, keeping close by as they joined the great wheeling movement of the cavalry, seeking prey among the Parthians who were now panicking and running around wildly to escape the horses.

Flavius rode at a group that was making a stand and cut down two of them, men with bows who were aiming at him, the great slashing sweeps of his sword decapitating one man and splitting the other almost in half across his chest. Attila had watched approvingly, and then had leapt off his horse, scooped up gore from the second man's wound and splashed it over Flavius' horse and body, pulling him down and smearing it over his face. He had pushed him back upright, his face creased with pleasure, and then had tensed himself and roared, a great bellow that was taken up and repeated by all of the Hun riders around them until they sounded like a herd of raging bulls. Attila stood back, panting and sweating, the blood dripping from his face. 'I bet your uncle Aetius can't do that,' he bellowed, roaring again.

Flavius's horse had reared up, and he brought it under control, the adrenalin coursing through him. He reached down and picked up a spear and rode at another Parthian, skewering him where he stood, and then dropped the spear and rode off with a group of archers who had galloped around him, enveloping him and driving him on. One of them threw him a bow with three arrows attached, and he let go of the horse's reins, riding only with his knees, strung an arrow and released it at another cluster of Parthians, hitting one in the leg but nearly falling off the horse as he did so, his legs clamped tightly to the animal as he pulled himself on again.

The Huns around him shouted their approval and ululated, a strange howling sound above the battlefield, and then they were off again, heeding the call of a commander for a massed wheeling movement to bring as many bows to bear as possible on a belea-guered group of Parthians sheltering behind the wagon laager. Flavius had released his two remaining arrows, not knowing whether they found their mark, and then he slung the bow over his shoulder and pulled out the great sword once again, riding in a great sweep round and round the laager with the bowmen, seeing them release arrow after arrow until none of the prisoners was left standing. He was breathing in the smells of battle, of horses and the dust, of his own sweat and adrenalin, of blood and fear from the Parthians. He realized that he was yelling at the top of his voice, bellowing, the sound completely submerged by the din around him, but he did not care. He was having the time of his life, and he was learning what it meant to be a Hun warrior. He was learning what it was that made Attila tick.

As the dust settled and the field cleared, the ground thick with Parthian corpses, Flavius cantered off in the direction of the citadel, sheathing his sword and looking for Attila. Bleda came riding up to him, pulled up short and then circled around him, a sneer of contempt on his face. 'Attila has other business to attend to. He told me to take you to your friends and see you on your way. And don't expect any favours from me, Roman. I'd have killed you there and then in the throne room, regardless of your tall tales and flattery.'

Flavius doffed the armour, dropping it on the ground along with the sword, and followed Bleda as he sped off. He began to cool off after the excitement, taking a deep draught from the water skin that was hanging from the neck of his horse and pouring some on his face, seeing the blood from the Parthian he had killed come off when he wiped his chin with his hand. It had now been over five hours since he had left the others, far longer than they had imagined it possible to keep Attila's attention, and he could only hope that they had managed to get into the strongroom. But the involvement of Bleda was an unwelcome development, as this was a man who was suspicious and volatile by nature and who, with any hint of what they had been up to, might terminate their mission with terrifying rapidity.

They reached the entrance to the citadel, tethered their horses and went in through the same route that Erecan had taken. At the point where Flavius had previously gone on alone to the audience chamber they now veered left, dropping down a stone-floored passageway that seemed to penetrate the deepest recesses of the citadel. After about a hundred paces they turned right, and Flavius froze. Ahead of him on the ground were the bodies of two Hun warriors, clearly the guards of the armoury that was now visible ahead. In the split second that it took him to register them, Macrobius had launched out of the shadows at Bleda, forcing him back against the wall. The two men tumbled to the ground, locked together, Bleda snarling like a dog and Macrobius desperately trying to get him in a neck lock. Flavius had whipped out his sword and was trying to find an opportunity to use it, but the two men were rolling across the floor in a single mass. Suddenly Macrobius was on his knees, holding Bleda's head and bringing it down against the floor with a crack, moving back as the Hun staggered and reeled. Then the Hun shook himself and came on again, charging like a bull. Macrobius pulled out his own sword just in time and brought it down with full force on Bleda's right bicep, slicing through the thick muscle and bone and severing his arm just above the elbow. He bellowed in pain, his arm spurting red, and fumbled for his sword before slipping on his own blood and falling heavily on a raised wooden revetment along the side of the passageway, his lower back breaking with a sickening crunch of bone.

Erecan appeared in the passageway, bow in hand, followed by Arturus, and Bleda tried to move, swinging wildly at them with his left hand, his face contorted with rage and pain. Erecan lowered her bow and Bleda dropped his sword, clutching at the stump of his right arm, his legs paralysed. He looked up at her, breathing heavily, his lip curled in disdain. 'Go on, daughter of a whore. Kill me.'

'I would rather not waste the arrow.'

'Your mother was not so lame when I killed her. She kicked and screamed like a real Hun.'

'So it *was* you,' she hissed.

'Your father did not wish to sully his hands with a woman's blood. For me, doing his dirty work was no problem.'

'I thought you were enraged with me because I had told Attila that I knew she was my mother, and because he ordered her – your mistress – killed.'

'Pah,' Bleda said, spitting. 'Whores are ten a penny. I was enraged because I had the Hun bloodlust, which means that when you kill a woman you want to kill all of her offspring as well.'

Erecan was still for a moment, and then bared her teeth like an animal and said something ferocious to him in the Hun language, a snarling, guttural noise that made Bleda pick up his sword with his remaining arm and elbow himself upright. In one swift movement Erecan took the bow off her back, strung an arrow and shot it clean through his head, the arrow clattering away down the passageway with a piece of skull attached to it and the hole in his forehead pumping blood. She stared at him, watching his eyes glaze over and his mouth droop, the puddle of blood rapidly spreading over the floor. 'Now I *really* can't stay,' she said.

'Suits me,' Arturus said. 'I could use a Hun archer in my army.'

'Are you really going back to Britain?' Macrobius said, leaning on his sword and breathing heavily.

Arturus nodded. 'I've done all I can for Rome.'

Flavius looked at the three of them. 'Well?'

'Well what?' Erecan said.

'Shall we show him?' Arturus grinned at her.

'Why not.' She led them quickly down the passageway past the dead guards to the armoury, a vast chamber full of weapons and armour of every description, rack upon rack of Hun swords and bows, past two more sprawled bodies to an opened metal grille at one end. She waved a heavy iron key. 'Only the daughter of Attila knows where he hides it, in a secret chamber beneath the big kettle drum on top of the citadel that's used to raise the alarm,' she said.

'It looks as if you had a little resistance,' Flavius said, picking his way over the two blood-drenched corpses, then leaning over and pulling himself towards the entrance of the strongroom.

'There are three more dead on the far side of the room.'

Flavius squeezed inside and gasped in astonishment. It was a dragon's lair of gold, vast quantities of coin, some of it spilled onto the floor, as well as loot in precious metal from everywhere that Attila had taken his army, from Parthian gold plaques to heavy silver dishes from Gaul decorated with classical scenes and Christian motifs. But it was the object that Erecan lifted off a platform in the centre that took his breath away, that made every-thing else fade to grey. It was a great sword of cavalry length, like the one he had just been wielding against the Parthians, but with a hilt decorated with a sparkling black pommel and a blade shining with an extraordinary pellucid lustre. 'The sword of Attila,' Erecan said, handing it to him. 'Look after it well.'

Flavius felt the heft of the blade, its perfect balance, and shook it, sensing the slight give. Whoever had made this, the smiths from the island far to the east that Priscus had talked about, were master craftsmen, able to forge a blade of surpassing beauty but also a perfectly honed weapon of war. He stared, hardly believing that he was holding it, and then he remembered where they were and how little time they might have before the alarm was raised.

He took the leather sheath that Erecan handed him, slid the sword into it and turned to the entrance. 'We need to get out of here.'

Macrobius had followed him in, and looked wistfully at the spilled gold on the floor. 'A down payment on a small farm in the hills of Etruria, that's all I ask for.'

Flavius slapped him on the shoulder. 'All right, centurion. Everything you can pick up in the next two minutes, provided you take it back and share it out evenly among the men of the *numerus*. But not so much that they'll go soft and give up fighting. And the same goes for you.'

Macrobius gave him an uncomprehending look. 'Since when did we ever fight for gold? I can't remember the last time I was paid.'

'I hear you. Just get on with it.' Macrobius knelt down and scooped coins into his pack, slinging it on his back and following Erecan and Flavius out. They joined Arturus, and the three men then quickly gathered their weapons and bags and made their way behind Erecan down another passage to the outer wall of the citadel, through a small gap that led out to the plain. In the shadows outside two Hun warriors stood with half a dozen horses. Macrobius reached for his sword, but Erecan halted him. 'They're Optila and Thrastilla, my bodyguards,' she said. 'I've ordered them to escort you back to Rome. As soon as my father finds that I've gone and Bleda is missing he'll send riders out along the main routes, but we'll have a head start leaving now and travelling in the dark. If he catches up with you after this, his reception won't be quite so friendly. Most thieves get flayed alive, but stealing that sword would demand a unique punishment.'

'Understood,' Macrobius said, slinging his and Flavius' bags over two of the horses and tying them onto the saddles. Flavius wrapped the sword in the cassock from his bag and strapped it to his back, then sprung up onto one of the horses. The others followed behind, and together they swung west, towards the setting sun, leaving the citadel and its king behind in the haze, then hearing the clamour and the beating of the great drum as the alarm was raised.

They began to ride for their lives.

PART FOUR

THE CATALAUNIAN
FIELDS, GAUL
AD 451

15

Flavius and Macrobius stood with their horses in the courtyard of the monastery at Châlons, once the villa of a wealthy Gallic nobleman with Roman tastes but after the conversion of Constantine given over to the Church as a house of God. The monks had offered it as a headquarters to Aetius in the expectation that they would lead him in prayer before battle, but he had brusquely swept them aside, cleared out the main rooms as accommodation for his staff and set up his operations room in the convocation hall, once the atrium of the villa. They were still moving in, bullock carts bringing all of the clerical equipment of Aetius' secretarial and logistics staff, and Flavius knew that they were going to have to be patient before they had a chance to see the general himself.

He thought back over the events that had led them here, and realized that they had been on campaign now for nearly three months. It had been almost two years since he and Macrobius had arrived exhausted back in Rome after their escape from Attila, having parted ways with Arturus and Erecan in the southern Alps and watched them ride west towards the Atlantic shore and Britain. Erecan's Hun bodyguards Optila and Thrastilla had come south and entered Aetius' service as his bodyguards when he was in Ravenna, an appointment engineered by Aetius so that they could be his eyes and ears in the court. What he had discovered there had dismayed him, but it came as no surprise. The eunuch Heraclius had encouraged Honoria, Valentinian's increasingly deranged sister, to pursue a fixation on Attila with an offer of marriage, an embarrassment for Aetius which became worse when Valentinian himself became involved, sending his own emissary to refute the marriage and protest at the dowry Honoria had offered of half the western empire.

Rather than remaining safely caged in Ravenna, the lunatics had flown the nest, but they had only been released as a ploy by Heraclius to undermine Aetius' plans. The farce of the western Roman emperor's sole contact with Attila during a time of crisis and build-up to war being about his patently insane sister had convinced Attila of a fundamental weakness in the empire, something that made him foreshorten his own plans for conquest. For months afterwards everything had hung in the balance, Aetius becoming increasingly desperate to shore up his allies and create new alliances, with the spectre of Visigoth refusal hanging over everything. But finally the work of Pelagius in persuading the clergy of Gaul to push for an alliance had paid off, and Theodoric had come on board in the nick of time.

Flavius remembered the gauntlet he had thrown Attila, the invitation to battle. Then, it had been a way of occupying time, a provocation more amusing to Attila than the platitudes and attempts at appeasement that he was used to receiving from other emissaries, but now it had a prophetic air to it, with all of the events of the last two years leading inexorably towards a showdown. All of the planning and expectation and fear had come to a head three months before when Attila had come bursting out of his homeland, reaching Gaul and taking Aurelianum before heading north towards the rolling grasslands of the Catalaunian Plains. Some thought that the arrival of Aetius and the *comitatenses* had driven Attila out of the city on an unruly flight towards northern Gaul, and it suited Aetius for them to think so. But Flavius knew the truth. He remembered what he had offered Attila, when they had talked that day in his stronghold in the steppes: *a battleground of your own choice.* Attila had not fled, but he was leading them on, drawing them to a place where the two armies could meet in the contest of his dreams, the mother of all battles.

Flavius had last seen Pelagius four months earlier when Pelagius had handed him the sword, having kept it in secret since Flavius had passed it to him for safekeeping after his escape from the court of Attila; now Flavius carried it day and night swathed in the same old cassock he had worn on their adventure up the Danube. Pelagius too had been on his way to Britain, his work for Aetius done. Flavius had remembered Arturus' parting words below the Alps, an invitation for him to join him as well in Britain, if Rome became too dangerous and soldiering for the empire had become too thankless a task; it was something that had been on Flavius' mind over the last days as he contemplated what the future might hold in terms of Roman service for Macrobius and the surviving men of his *numerus*, all of them here today geared for the coming battle that for any of them could be their last.

He reached up and twisted his thin leather necklace that he had worn constantly since Una had given it to him on the beach two years before, feeling the lump of polished blackstone that was hanging below. It was as if touching it stopped him from worrying about her, made him simply remember the warmth of her presence, took his mind from the voyage she had undertaken and the dangers and uncertainties that she must have faced on the way. Macrobius, the grizzled bachelor, had always told him that soldiering and long-term relationships were doomed never to work together, but it still did not make the parting any easier or help him when he lay awake at night wondering whether he should have done things differently. He let go of the stone and squinted up at the sky. Soldiering at least had the benefit of keeping your mind on practical issues of the moment, and right now he needed to ensure that he was primed and ready to give Aetius the best possible advice on Attila's likely tactical plan. It might be the last task of any consequence that he ever carried out in the service of Rome, but it was a daunting responsibility as well as something that he was determined to do to the best of his ability.

And still he wondered about Attila. How had he reacted when he realized that his sacred sword was missing? It was impossible to know; there had been no reliable intelligence from the Hun court since their departure. The death of Bleda would have been a blow – he had been a volatile, mercurial man with a savage temper, but an experienced adviser in war and Attila's own brother; yet violent death was commonplace in the Hun court, and others would be there to replace him. Flavius had felt a chill of doubt course through him when he had first heard word of the Hun army rolling west three months ago – something that surely could not have happened had Attila lost his own confidence and that of his people in him. Flavius had steeled himself not to think of these things again until the time was right. The sword was a weapon of war, a symbol that could sway the outcome of a battle, and if it had the power that was claimed of it, then it was in battle that the test would lie, the proof that their mission had been worth the lives of Uago and others who had fallen along the way.

A soldier wearing the insignia of a tribune came out of the entrance to meet them, Flavius having announced their arrival to one of the *milites* guarding the courtyard, who had then gone in to inform Aetius. The tribune saluted and gestured, and Flavius nodded in return. He let his horse finish drinking from the bucket he had been holding in front of it, and passed the bridle to Macrobius. It had been a long, hot journey, and watering the animals and the men would be a priority for the coming day. He took off his sword belt and handed that as well to Macrobius, leaving him to seek food and drink, and then picked his way among the piles of horse droppings in the courtyard and followed the tribune inside.

Aetius was standing at the head of the room contemplating a charred wooden cross that the monks believed was one of the very crosses of the crucifixion set up on the hill of Calvary on the day of Christ's judgement. Five other men stood around the table in front of him: Thorismud and two other Goths on one side, and

180

on the other the two Roman *magistri* of the *comitatenses* armies that were present in the field, Flavius Aspar and Gaius Petronius Anagastus. Aetius saw his nephew entering and, stepping down from the altar, went over to the head of the table. 'This council of war is convened. The two *comitatenses* commanders you all know. Flavius Aetius, my nephew, is a tribune who has ridden with Attila. Theodoric is not able to be present.'

Thorismud turned to the Roman commanders. 'My father and brother are walking among our men. It is the tradition of kings on the eve of battle, to be followed by a feast in the mead hall for the King and his captains, and around the campfires for the men. Oxen for the men and boar and deer for the king have been brought in for slaughter and roasted in preparation. I am here at this council to represent my father, along with my cousins Radagaisus and Thiudimer.'

Aetius unrolled a soft vellum sheet that was lying on the table, and the two generals weighed down the ends with drinking cups. It was a map, the course of the rivers clearly marked in black, the disposition of the armies as blocks in other colours. The convention was instantly familiar to Flavius from map-making classes in the *schola militarum* in Rome almost fifteen years before; it brought to mind the last time he had been with Thorismud poring over a map like this, studying the Battle of Adrianople and the tactics of the Goths in defeating the Romans on that fateful day almost seventy years before. Aetius pointed out the features on the map as he spoke. 'This was prepared in the past few hours by my *fabri*, and is based on their own survey as well as on the reports of the scouts from the reconnaissance *numerus*. You can see the river Aube, trending north and defining the west side of the battlefield, and to the south the point where it joins with the river Seine. The triangle of land created by that intersection is a potential killing ground if an army were to be trapped there by another pressing down from the north-east. Otherwise, the topography comprises low-lying, undulating plains, with a ridge in the middle bisecting the battlefield, and to the east open rolling countryside.'

Aspar tapped the map. 'Our army is to the west of that ridge with the river behind us, the Hun army to the east with open land beyond. Other than the one place where the river Aube can be forded, we have no escape route.'

Aetius gave him a grim look. 'Then we must fight to the death.'

'*Ave, magister militus.*'

'What of the terrain?' Flavius asked. 'Where my centurion Macrobius and I have just ridden, the ground was very hard, almost like rock.'

'It has not rained for weeks,' Aetius replied. 'There will be no mud to contend with, though the hard ground will pose other problems. It will become slippery where it pools with blood.'

'That is how it will be after I and my men have fought there,' the Goth Radagaisus said, his voice guttural and his Latin heavily accented. 'A place slippery with Hun blood.'

Aetius carried on. 'The only trees are along the line of the river. The fields are planted with wheat, but it is not high enough to provide cover. There is a stream running through the centre of the battlefield below our side of the ridge, fed by a spring, but the ditch is narrow enough for a man to leap across. There are no particular advantages to either side of this landscape from a tactical viewpoint, except that ridge that rises to a height of fifty to seventy feet above the floodplain. It's not much, but whoever holds it might be able to dominate the battlefield.'

'What of the dispositions of the troops?' Flavius asked.

'My scouts tells me that the Huns are concentrated with their wagons immediately beyond that ridge, with Valamer and his Ostrogoths to the north and Ardaric and his Gepids to the south. On our side, the *comitatenses* are ranged to the north and the Visigoths to the south, with the centre of the line opposite the Huns divided equally between Romans and Visigoths.'

'That division was not necessary,' Aspar grumbled. 'My *comitatenses* alone could hold the line against the Huns.'

Aetius glared at him. 'Your faith in your men is commendable, *magister*, but you have not been ranged against a Hun army like this before. The Roman *milites* are more skilled as archers than the Visigoths, but the Visigoths are better at single combat. We cannot afford a Hun breakthrough in the centre of the line and we must strengthen it to our maximum advantage, regardless of the sensitivities of the commanders. If that means *comitatenses* share the task with Visigoths, then so be it.'

'We have agreed to another compromise,' Thorismud said, looking at the two Roman commanders. 'We wished the main flank of our Visigoth army to confront the Ostrogoths to the north, but my father Theodoric agreed that instead we should face the Gepids to the south, and leave the Ostrogoths for the *comitatenses*.'

'Your father may once have been my mortal enemy, but he is a wise and experienced general,' Aetius said. 'The blood feuds you doubtless have with your Ostrogoth cousins may stiffen your resolve against them, but blood feuds have no place in war. One chieftain may divert his men in order to encounter a particularly reviled cousin, whereas another might avoid a group with whom he has kinship ties and no animosity. To have placed your army opposite the Ostrogoths as some of your Visigoth chieftains wished could have created inconsistency in the line, whereas against the Gepids you can fight as one force.'

'And Sangibanus?' Flavius asked.

Aetius pursed his lips. 'I have placed Sangibanus and his Alans between the Romans and the Visigoths, but as soon as battle is joined we will close up and they will be forced back to form a reserve. They are our one liability. I offered Sangibanus a bribe of more land around Orléans for his Alans to settle as well as a place for his men in my army in return for his allegiance, after he had threatened to turn Orléans over to Attila and revive the traditional alliance of the Alans with the Huns.'

'These are not Alans as we saw them with Gaiseric's army at Carthage,' Flavius said. 'Macrobius and I passed Sangibanus and his men on the way up from Nîmes. The warriors who were once a tower of strength are now fat and indolent, softened by settled life and self-indulgence.'

'Exactly what we had hoped for when we offered them land in the first place years ago. Give some enemies an easy life, and soon they are no longer a threat. But when I was forced to negotiate terms with Sangibanus, I did not yet know whether Theodoric would join us against Attila, and I needed every ally I could get. Had I known then that I could rely on the Visigoths, I would happily have kicked Sangibanus and his pigsty back to Attila.'

'If they're to be a reserve beside the river, we could use them to bring water up to the troops,' Anagastus suggested.

'They're too unfit even for that,' Aspar said. 'In this heat, they'd probably collapse before they marched ten paces.'

'I am more confident of the barbarians in the *comitatenses*,' Aetius said. 'As I formed my army on the way here I enlisted Salian and Ripuarian Franks, Burghundians, Armorican Celts, even a few exiled Britons. Because we had no time for training I only accepted veterans, offering them enlistment in the *comitatenses* and rank appropriate to their experience, as well as the all-important payout when the battle is over. Valentinian has assured me that the gold will be available, but these veteran *milites* know well enough how far they can trust the word of an emperor when it comes to pay. I gave them five gold *solidi* apiece on enlistment out of my own purse, and will probably be making up the remainder myself when it comes time for the survivors to demand it.'

'What are the overall numbers?' Flavius asked.

'Almost evenly matched,' Anagastus replied. 'Nearly thirty thousand men of the *comitatenses* and twenty thousand Visigoths, against twenty thousand Huns and thirty thousand Ostrogoths. The *comitatenses* have more infantry archers, the Huns more mounted archers.'

Aetius turned to Flavius. 'I invited you here because you have ridden into battle with Attila, because you know the man. What is your assessment of his tactics?'

Flavius stared at the map, remembering the Huns in their homeland and imagining what their encampment would look like now on the Catalaunian Plains. He thought hard, and then looked at Aetius. 'Attila has never fought a pitched battle like this before. Most of his battles have been clashes of movement, of an army constantly on the move overtaking and bearing down on an advancing or retreating enemy, quick and ferocious encounters with little preamble or tactical forethought. Because he has no supply chain and is used to campaigning in the barren wastes of the East where the pickings from foraging are slim, war on the hoof is a matter of necessity, not choice. Unlike many of the Goth commanders, men like our own Theodoric and Thorismud, or his Ostrogoth general Valamer, Attila did not attend the *schola militarum* in Rome or Constantinople, so he has no training in the tactics of pitched battle. He has had no need of them before; all he has needed is the whirlwind terror of the Hun mounted assault, and that has carried him this far. But now it is different.'

'Does he have good advisers?'

'Valamer is a competent tactician. But like most of the Goth officers who went through the *schola* at Constantinople, he is obsessed with the Battle of Adrianople. After all, it was a Goth victory, and the battle site is just a stone's throw from Constantinople itself. But Adrianople was a more close-run thing than many have been led to believe, and if Valamer does influence Attila, that obsession with Adrianople could end up being his biggest tactical weakness tomorrow.'

'You mean the laager!' Thorismud exclaimed. 'The wheeled fortress of wagons.'

'Precisely,' Flavius said. 'If our scouts are right, Attila has shown his limitations by going to the opposite extreme from the fluid, mobile warfare in which his warriors rule supreme, opting instead this time for the fortified compound behind wagons that allowed the Goths at Adrianople to resist repeated Roman assaults and then sally forth. But we too have learned from Adrianople, and that is precisely *not* to make the same mistake again: not to make frontal assaults on a hot day against a wagon laager, wearing down our men with exhaustion and casualties to the point where they can be overwhelmed by a force erupting from the compound.'

'So instead you surround them and starve them out,' Thorismud said.

'And you force him to sally forth, to send out his mounted archers in lightning attacks in an effort to keep up the morale of his men and to erode ours,' Anagastus said. 'But by maintaining our defensive line in strength, we resist his attacks and keep our line unbroken, and his casualties mount up higher than ours.'

'Our *sagittarii* in the *comitatenses* use bows that have a greater range than the Hun cavalry bow,' Aetius said. 'I have made a special study of them at the butts on the Field of Mars in Rome with the emperor Valentinian, who exercises his fascination with archery whenever he allows himself out of the clutches of that eunuch Heraclius. If we can reach high ground and rain arrows down on the laager, then we might win the day.'

Anagastus stood back, put his hands on his hips and shook his head. 'This is still going to be a battle won mainly by attrition. We have been talking about a scenario where Attila has already been forced back into his laager, and for that to happen we still have to confront his army in open battle and drive the Huns back over that ridge. It may just be a bump in the ground, but for many men tomorrow that ridge will seem like an insurmountable mountain.'

'We do have one crucial advantage,' Aetius said. 'We can keep our supplies coming, and he cannot. If we can avoid outright defeat and hold a stalemate for more than twenty-four hours, then his army will begin to suffer. Attila has depended on foraging as his army has made its way east, whereas we can still call on the military stockpiles in the diocesan and provincial capitals. When I was a young candidate in officer school we were taught that the three pivots of battle were strategy, tactics and supply, and this could be one of those battles where that third pivot is decisive. I must go now to meet my quartermasters.'

'And we go to feast,' Thorismud said, rising from his chair, the two Goths beside him doing the same. 'In your absence, I ask that Flavius Aetius take your place in the tent we have laid out as a mead hall.'

Aetius nodded at Flavius, who turned to Thorismud and bowed. 'I would be honoured to attend king Theodoric and feast alongside his sons and captains.'

The two Roman *comitatenses* commanders got up. 'The sun is near its zenith,' Anagastus said. 'Tomorrow will be a long day, the longest of the year so far.'

'The longest of our lives, for those of us who see it through,' Aetius said, reaching for his helmet. '*Milites*, we have had our last council of war. The next command I issue to you will be on the battlefield. I will be riding at the head of the *comitatenses*, and King Theodoric will be at the head of the Visigoths. Relish the sight of two bitter enemies joined together to fight the greatest foe that any of us have ever faced. My command will be to engage the enemy, to fight to the last drop of blood to vanquish Attila the Hun.'

Four hours later Flavius sat in the improvised mead hall of the Visigoth king, having downed his fourth cup of watered-down wine in a toast and eaten his fill of roast boar and venison. He knew that for some here the drinking would go on until dawn, that their engagement with battle would be in a drunken haze, but he was determined to rise with a clear head and not be debilitated by the dehydration that came from too much wine. Such reasoning seemed far from the minds of Thorismud's companions, who were passing along an ancient aurochs' horn embellished with gold, each of them downing its contents in one, the horn being filled to the brim with ale for each new drinker from a wooden keg. At the head of the table Theodoric was sitting next to an ancient uncle he had brought along as his adviser, a silvery-haired man with skin like leather who bore more scars than all of the rest of them put together. It was said that he had fought against the Romans more than seventy years before at the Battle of Adrianople, and he had been regaling Theodoric and those closest to him who could hear above the boisterous noise with tales of wars of the past, of battles where myth and reality seemed intertwined. Flavius could hear him now, his low, deep voice incanting in the old Gothic dialect of the East, telling of a battle he had fought somewhere in a mountain fastness of the North: *Hand to hand we clashed, in battle fierce, confused, prodigious, unrelenting, a fight unequalled in accounts of yore. Such deeds were done! Heroes who missed this marvel could never hope to see its like again.*

Flavius strained to listen, but a huge roar came from the opposite side of the table as the last of the captains downed his ale, dropped the horn on the bench and threw up over the ground. The rest of the men began to crash their hands on the table, drumming in unison, and the servant filled up the horn again and handed it to the same man, who tossed it back in one but held it down this time, belching and joining in the noise. Flavius saw Thorismud eyeing him and then raising his hand for quiet. 'So, Flavius Aetius,' he said loudly, lifting his cup and gesturing towards him, the wine spilling over the side. 'Your grandfather Gaudentius was a Goth warlord, and yet your mother is descended from Julius Caesar. Are you a Goth, or are you a Roman?'

The bellowing and table-thumping died down, and all eyes

were on Flavius. He looked around, seeing the red-faced chieftains, bearded and long-haired, adorned with the neck torques and arm rings that were the badges of rank and prowess among their men, their helmets on the table in front of them. They looked the very image of the barbarians of old, the foes of the Caesars whom he had first seen as a boy on the great sculpted columns and arches of Rome. Drink had made them boisterous and bawdy, but it had also made them appear as what they really were. Some barbarians had become Romanized, men like Flavius' grandfather, but the court of Theodoric was still a court of Goth chieftains, and in this place Flavius was the odd one out. He remembered Aetius' last words before leaving the council of war. Until the rise of Attila he and Theodoric had been mortal enemies, and the men around this table would have been bent on nothing but the destruction of Romans, whether or not those Romans had Goth grandfathers. They were drunk, but that was all the more reason to be careful now in what he said.

He raised his right forearm on the table, conscious of the eyes watching him, and rolled down his sleeve, revealing the four parallel scars where the Alaunt had gouged into him twelve years earlier before the walls of Carthage. 'I am neither,' he said, looking at Thorismud. 'I am a warrior.'

There was silence among the men, the only noise the crackling of the fire. Then someone bellowed approval and banged the table with his fist, and the others joined in. Thorismud held up his hand. 'You are a warrior, but who do you serve?'

The table went quiet again, and everyone watched expectantly. Flavius picked up his cup and looked at Theodoric, who was sitting impassively at the head of the table, enjoying the rowdiness of his men but not joining in. Flavius raised his cup towards the king, drank it down and then slammed it on the table. 'I serve,' he said, wiping his lips, 'whichever king shows the greatest prowess in battle, and whichever leads his men to victory or glorious death.'

Thorismud stared at him, his eyes unfathomable, and then brought one hand crashing down on the table, picked up his cup and raised it. 'To our king,' he said. 'To Theodoric, King of the Visigoths. May the god of war shine on him.' He drained his cup and the others followed suit, belching and bellowing for more. Flavius let the slave refill his cup, but he left it brimming, stood up and bowed to the king, and made his way out of the tent. In the time that they had been feasting the sun had gone down, and in the twilight he could see the fires of the Goths and the Romans flickering along the banks of the river. He walked towards the edge of the water. The low clouds broke and the half-moon shone through, causing myriad ghostly reflections on the ripples in the river and bathing the scene in an eerie light. The trees along the bank rustled, and he felt the warm breeze on his face. If battle were truly to be joined tomorrow, it would be hard fought in this heat, with thirst as big a foe as the enemy. He would need to make sure that the men of his *numerus* were well watered and had filled their skins before the order came for the advance.

He heard movement behind him, and turned to see Theodoric coming towards the river bank. He was wearing his two swords, the shorter *scramasax* on his left side and the long sword of the Goths on the right, and he held his hands on the gold and jewel-encrusted pommels as he stood by Flavius and stared into the waters. The clouds had closed up again, and the waters looked dark, forbidding, like an image of the river Styx from the ancient accounts of the voyage to the underworld. Theodoric took a deep breath and exhaled slowly, the smell of wine and the smoke of the mead hall coming off him. 'Tomorrow, this river will run red,' he said quietly. 'Men will slake their thirst on their own blood.'

Flavius remembered the mantra of the Goths on the eve of battle. 'Tomorrow will be a good day to die,' he said.

Theodoric turned and looked at him, placing a hand on his shoulder. 'My time draws to an end,' he said. 'This battle will be my last, and soon Thorismud will take over my mantle. If you survive, Flavius Aetius, you must look to yourself. Allegiance neither to a Roman emperor nor to a Goth king will see you through to old age. If it is to be the god of war that you follow, choose your god with care.'

Flavius watched him walk away and disappear back into the tent, and then he looked to the north-east and the undulating treeless plain where they knew that Attila had his encampment. Attila would be there too, around an open fire, his lords of war intoxicated and telling tales just as the Goths were doing, his encircling laager of wagons providing a wooden fortress like the palace far off in the folds of the steppe-lands that Flavius had once visited. He remembered his time there, the scarred cheeks and piercing eyes of Attila as he had sat beside him, and for a fleeting moment he missed it, wishing that he too was over there by the fire sitting next to the emperor, seeing battle not in strategy and tactics but in the adrenalin and exhilaration of a people who had been born for war.

The clouds broke again, above the Hun lines, and for a second he thought he saw something extraordinary, a ball of white with a streaking tail reaching high into the night sky. It was blotted out almost as quickly as it had appeared, and for a moment he wondered whether it had merely been a strange effect of the moon, reflected against the clouds. But he remembered as a boy studying the course of comets with Dionysius the Scythian in Rome, and hearing the monks in Chalôns predict that this year the great comet recorded by the Babylonians would reappear. Even the men of God believed that this would augur momentous events: the birth or death of great kings, defeat or victory in battle, events that would shape the world to come.

Dionysius had scoffed at augury, and Flavius knew better than to believe in fate. But, staring across the plain, he wondered whether Attila's shamans had seen it too, or whether they were too busy reading the cracked shoulder blades of oxen beside the fires, preparing their own rituals of divination. He stared at the sky again, seeing only darkness. If it was an omen, it could only mean one thing, but he did not have to believe in augury to know what lay ahead. He had seen the preparations around him, the two sides resolutely encamped, the bleak plains ahead, the perfect killing ground.

It was an omen of war.

16

The wind rustled through the wheat on the plain, a whispering, haunting sound that seemed to set the men on edge, their heads rising above the flattened patches along the river bank where they had been lying since dawn waiting for the order to move. All that morning the air had been still, the heat rising inexorably until they were dripping with sweat under their armour; at least the breeze had brought them some respite. Flavius watched it now, eddying and gusting up the stalks of wheat on the slope in front of him, and yet again he scanned the ridge to the east for any signal from the scouts who had crept up there during the night, seeking concealed positions to overlook the enemy encampment on the other side. The wait all morning for a signal had seemed interminable, but at least the sun had risen high enough that it would no longer be in their eyes when the assault took place; the enemy had lost an obvious tactical advantage there, but they were probably playing the same game, waiting to see which side would draw the other into battle, all eyes on that ridge where the commanders knew that the key to any victory must lie.

Flavius felt for his *gladius* and then shifted the shoulder belt that held the additional sword he was carrying on his back, its long blade sheathed and the hilt concealed beneath a woollen cover. He took a water skin from one of the Alans who were trudging to and from the river to keep the men replenished. Sangibanus, their leader, was skulking somewhere behind, miffed at not being invited to join the council of war; but he was the least of Aetius' worries, the Alans in their present state of fitness posing no threat to world order after the battle and serving a useful purpose today as water-carriers. Aetius came up to him, took a swig from the proffered skin and then stared at the ridge himself, his eyes narrowed. 'Walk with me, Flavius.' They made their way out of the flattened patch that served as headquarters and twenty paces or so into the wheat in front of the Roman lines, out of earshot. Aetius turned to him, speaking quietly. 'You still feel certain that Attila will break? It has been eight hours since dawn.'

Flavius nodded. 'Attila is a cunning tactician, but he is not a patient man. He will order his troops to the assault before you do, *magister militum*.'

Aetius took another swig, wiped his mouth and handed the skin back to Flavius. 'All right. We shall continue to wait for the signal from the scouts. We can hold out for another day if need be.'

'Attila will not wait that long. He has no stockpiles of food as we do. To delay for another day he would have to send men out foraging, weakening his force and making him more vulnerable. He has no choice but to attack today.'

Aetius nodded and went back to confer with his two *comitatenses* commanders, Aspar and Anagastus. The disposition of their forces was based on intelligence received earlier from scouts about the spread of the enemy below the other side of the ridge and the likely order of battle. When the time came they would lead their two armies up the northern flank of the slope to confront the Ostrogoths under Valamer, as well as Attila's Huns in the centre, while to the east the Visigoths were ranged against the Gepids under Ardaric. Flavius recalled Aetius' negotiations the day before with Theodoric and Thorismud to ensure that the two Goth armies did not meet in battle. It was wisdom that might have escaped a lesser commander than Aetius, one without his political nous and good judgement born of his own Goth background; he knew what made his people tick. Modern generalship, Flavius had realized, was a far more complex business than it had been at the time of the Caesars, when there had been a rigid chain of command and the legions were rarely allied in battle with a force as powerful as themselves, particularly one that had been their sworn enemy only a few weeks before.

The Visigoth king and his sons were not with Aetius, but were in their own separate headquarters with their chieftains half a mile to the south. That too had been a careful strategy on the part of Aetius, underlining a promise he had given to Theodoric that he would be an equal ally in the field, not a subordinate. By keeping the Visigoth commanders away from his *comitatenses* staff he had also avoided flare-ups that could easily have arisen between former enemies and destroyed in an instant their chances of success in the coming battle. Aetius was playing a balancing act on many levels, yet even so in this waiting game it could only be a matter of time before the Visigoths questioned his strategy, potentially launching an independent attack of their own and disastrously weakening his plan. Flavius could guess what was running through Aetius' mind, why he had taken him aside and questioned him again about Attila. The sooner the Huns attacked now, the better.

He looked at the expanse of wheat on either side, a wavering sea of gold that held more than fifty thousand men poised for battle, the largest army ever fielded by Rome in the western empire. For a brief moment he felt overwhelmed, as if the crucible of battle were in his hands alone. Aetius had made him his special adviser because of his first-hand knowledge of Attila, and had appointed Macrobius and the rest of the *numerus* as his personal bodyguards. It was a huge honour, but also a daunting responsibility. What if he had been wrong? It was he who had advised Aetius not to make a pre-emptive assault but to wait until the Huns themselves were charging, to meet them head to head on the ridge, to fight a bloody battle of attrition and hope to win the day there; a pre-emptive charge might find Attila's bowmen ranged below ready to pour a deadly storm of arrows into the Romans and Visigoths and force them back over the ridge, weakening them and making them less able to resist the Hun assault that would inevitably follow. It was a tactic that Flavius had seen Attila deploy in Parthia three years before, goading the enemy into an assault over a desert ridge and meeting them with a fixed line of Hun archers.

Flavius remembered the great sword, and holding it for the first time with Arturus in the strongroom of Attila's palace. If he were right today, the legacy of that extraordinary adventure might not only be the absence from Attila's hands of that sword, that potent symbol of Hun kingship, but also what Flavius had learned riding alongside him in the mock battle in the Hun stronghold, absorbing knowledge of the great warrior's strengths and weaknesses that could now be brought to bear against him this day on the Catalaunian Plains where the fate of the western world would soon be decided.

Along the line to the right he saw his cousin Quintus Aetius, shouting orders at the mixed *numerus* of Visigoth and Roman troops that he had honed into one of the finest shock formations in the army over the past months. Quintus was muscular and bronzed, a thick scar running through his stubble and down his neck, a far cry from the inconsolable boy Flavius had seen leaving the *schola* after he had accidentally killed his friend Marcus Cato two years ago. The others of that class were here too, those who had survived this long: one on Aetius' staff, two among the *fabri* tribunes who were overseeing camp fortification behind the lines, the rest leading cavalry and infantry *numeri* up the slopes. Flavius saw Macrobius watching Quintus too, and they exchanged a smile. For all the bravado and toughness, they both knew that Marcus Cato was with Quintus today, that with every step he took up the slope now his ears would be ringing with those words that Macrobius had bellowed at him beside the bloody corpse in the *palaestra*, that he owed it to his friend to stand up to what he had done like a man and carry the honour of Rome forward.

Flavius squinted up at the sky. The sun was lost in the haze, but the humidity was rising, and he felt a trickle of sweat down his cheek. He looked at the ridge again. Suddenly he saw something, a man in the far distance running through the wheat towards them, cutting a trail from the ridge down the slope. Another one followed, and further along he saw two more raise themselves out of concealment and wave their flags. The scouts were all supposed to remain on the ridge after the assault began to signal any changes in the enemy movement, but he did not blame the two who were fleeing, seeking relative safety in their own lines rather than certain death between the two opposing armies.

Aetius and the two generals quickly stood up, helmets on, and Flavius did the same. All along the line a huge mass of men had risen, spears and sword flashing, the *comitatenses* cavalry saddled up and mounted, the horses snorting and stomping. The head of the monastery at Chalôns who had been waiting with vestments and holy water for this moment tried to anoint Aetius, but he pushed him aside; this was no time for God. He stormed out ahead of the line, and then turned round. 'Gird for battle,' he bellowed, and then began charging up the ridge, sword in hand. Flavius drew his *gladius* and glanced at Macrobius. 'Are you ready, centurion?' He turned to the others of the *numerus*. 'Apsachos? Maximus? Cato? All of you men? Are you ready?'

They clashed their swords together. '*Ave*, tribune.'

Flavius pointed his sword after Aetius. 'Then to war.'

At first the army surged forward with no certainty that the enemy was doing the same, their view of the Hun lines completely obscured by the ridge and with only the signals of the scouts to go on. Then one of the men who had come racing down from the ridge tore past Aetius, shouting '*The Huns are coming, the Huns are coming!*' Aspar caught hold of him, dragging him stumbling and panting back up the slope as he questioned him, and then let him go. 'Attila comes in a line up the slope just as we are, his infantry first,' he shouted to Aetius. 'You were right.'

Flavius looked from side to side. The cavalry were cantering behind the infantry, ready to gallop into the melee or around the flanks. To have sent them forward on a headlong charge would have been to risk their arrival on the ridge exhausted and in full view of the Hun archers who might by then be ranged up on the other side. Attila had clearly decided the same, to keep his cavalry in reserve, knowing that his mounted archers in particular were too valuable to send ahead up the ridge, sitting targets in that moment of uncertainty as they saw that there was no cavalry charge from the Romans to counter and only an enormous wave of infantry advancing towards them. As he ran forward, Flavius felt his mouth go dry, the sign of fear and adrenalin that he had first experienced before Carthage. The Battle of the Catalaunian Plains was to be a clash of foot soldiers, battle of the most brutal kind, thousands of men surging together and fighting with sword and club and fists for possession of that ridge and control of the battlefield.

Immediately to Flavius' right the left flank of the Visigoth army was advancing under Radagaisus and Thiudimer, with Theodoric and Thorismud out of sight several *stades* further south, where the main thrust of Ardaric's Gepids was expected. One man, a Roman *milites* who had boldly run forward behind Aetius but then baulked, overwhelmed perhaps by the enormity of the army behind him and his own visibility in front of it, was weaving and staggering and straying too far to the right, ahead of the Visigoth lines; he suddenly fell to his knees and dropped his weapon, clapping his hands to his ears and curling up in a ball on the ground. Radagaisus strode up to him, his face contorted with rage, then picked the man up by his hair and lopped his head off with a single stroke of his sword, turning and holding it high so his men could see. 'This is what happens to cowards,' he bellowed, hurling the head in the direction of the ridge, gobs of blood flicking out around it.

Aetius was too far ahead and too intent on the ridge to have witnessed the event, but even if he had done so, Flavius knew that he would not have tried to stop it; keeping up the momentum was all that mattered now. For first blood in a battle to be a disciplinary act on your own side was not necessarily a bad omen, as it was something that could stiffen the resolve of the soldiers who followed, but in the circumstances of this alliance, a Goth leader executing a Roman soldier in full view of the army could be seen as an act of lethal provocation, something that could lead to total disintegration of the line as the man's comrades sought vengeance by attacking the Visigoths. Fortunately the event seemed to have been forgotten as quickly as it had been played out and the man's body was trampled and left far behind beneath the advancing army. Flavius himself knew that Radagaisus would have had no intention of being provocative, and would undoubtedly have done the same to one of his own men if he had shown hesitation or gone to pieces, probably dealing with him with more savagery and fury than he had inflicted on the Roman.

The ridge was no more than three hundred paces ahead now. Flavius was panting hard, the sweat pouring off his face, his heart beating like a drum. The dry ground beneath the wheat shuddered and vibrated with the pounding of thousands of armour-clad men running up the slope. Everything in the past, all of the planning and strategy, the thoughts that had occupied the long hours of the morning, seemed to recede like the flattened field of wheat behind them, and all he could focus on was the present, on a world of sensation and action that allowed little room for reflection. It was the age-old mechanism of the soldier about to go into battle, a locking down of thought processes that would otherwise only seize up at the enormity and horror of what was about to happen. All that mattered now was his grip on his sword, the pounding of his feet, the training and instinct that would kick in as soon as he made first contact with the enemy.

Macrobius was ahead, running forward with the others of the *numerus* to surround and protect Aetius, to try to slow him down and draw him back behind the leading edge of the army. He was no longer needed out in front to encourage and lead the troops forward, and it was more important that he survive the initial clash in order to direct the battle as it unfolded. Aetius knew this too, and he fell back with them, letting the *numerus* envelop him as the infantry flowed around them and thundered up the slope. The leading elements were less than two hundred paces from the crest of the ridge, and still they saw nothing ahead, just the wavering line of wheat and the haze of the sky beyond. For a fleeting moment Flavius wondered whether the whole thing were just a dream, whether Attila and his army were just figments of their imagination, a mirage seen by the scouts in the heat haze. It was as if they were running up to a ridge where all that lay beyond was the edge of the world and a tumble into the abyss.

Then he heard it. The drumming of their feet seemed to magnify twofold, a throbbing noise that hammered into his ears. The ground was no longer just vibrating but was shaking, blurring the line of the ridge ahead. And then the Hun army burst into view, thousands of black-clad men bellowing and swaying on the line of the ridge, no more than ten paces ahead of the leading Roman soldiers. He barely had time to register it before the two armies crashed together, the huge momentum of each side causing the men to concertina forward until the centre was a solid mass of human flesh, crushing the men in the middle with a force that rebounded back on either side, knocking the men ahead back into Flavius and pushing those behind him sprawling into the wheat.

As he picked himself up and the line shook itself out the pounding noise was replaced by a cacophony of shrieking and bellowing, by the clash of steel and the thud and crunch of maces and clubs. The tangle of bodies from the initial crush had become the front line, the Huns on one side and the *milites* and Visigoths on the other, swinging and hacking at each other, also taking out men of their own side who were too tightly packed to avoid their own comrades' weapons. Bodies piled on bodies until the two sides were too far apart to make contact, and then they were climbing and slipping over the mound, no longer able to wield their weapons but gouging at each other with hands and teeth, going for the eyes and throats as they had been taught. The press of men coming up the slope forced more and more into the meat grinder, thousands fighting desperately for their lives in a strip of land no more than ten paces wide and already piled high with bodies. Blood came pouring down the slope past Flavius in viscous rivers of red, as if the ridge itself were bleeding, bringing with it hacked-off fingers and limbs and worse, hunks of meat that looked as if they had been torn from living flesh by wild animals in a feeding frenzy.

Flavius was stunned by the ferocity and speed of the attack, and he knew that the thousands of others poised along the line just behind the fighting must feel the same. But he knew that they must keep their nerve and hold their ground, ready to counter any breakthrough and prevent the Huns from storming down the Roman flanks. Already he could see men from both sides who had made it over the pile of bodies, fighting desperate duels before being overwhelmed by sheer force of numbers. He saw Huns using the weapon that had most struck fear into the Parthians three years before, the weighted lasso, flicking out of the enemy line like snakes' tongues, instantly killing the Romans and Visigoths who took the full force of the lead weights in the face, and wrapping around the necks of others who were pulled off their feet and dragged helplessly into the Hun lines to be finished off with swords and clubs, their hands clutching at their necks and their noses and eyes spurting blood as the nooses tightened.

Out of the swirling mass a Hun warrior came staggering towards them, one eye missing and the side of his face horribly mutilated, as if a dog had savaged him. Aetius raised his sword, but Macrobius leapt ahead and ran the man through the neck, twisting him aside with the sword still embedded and dropping him to the ground as he gargled out his last breath. Another man came into view behind him, but this time it was the Goth chieftain Radagaisus, a gory mess of skin hanging from his mouth and an eyeball swinging from a tendril below, the grisly results of his struggle with the Hun; he staggered by, lurched and fell to the ground wide-eyed, an axe embedded deep in his back. Along the line to the left Flavius could see blood and pieces of meat flying through the air like mud from a speeding cartwheel where a *numerus* of Iberian axemen had entered the fray, their weapons flashing above the melee as they raised them up and swung them down with sickening noises of splintering bone and pulverized flesh.

Flavius wondered how many of the Hun warriors opposite were men he had ridden with alongside Attila two years before. He remembered how he and Attila had talked about what the Greeks called *kharme*, battle lust. He wondered whether Attila had it now, or whether he truly was unable to feel it without the sacred sword in his hand. As he looked along the line, searching for any sign of the Hun leader, he sensed a fall-off in the ferocity of the battle, the men who moments before had been throwing themselves at each other across the piles of corpses now drawing back in ragged lines on either side of the ridge. The last of the surge that had pulsed through the Roman lines since the initial assault, pushing men forward wave after wave, had finally expended itself, like a huge sea-swell that had crashed against a shore but was now falling back boiling and in disarray. He could sense the same on the Hun side too. It was as if the casualties and the exhaustion and the shock of the clash had caught up with the survivors and left them stunned, the momentum from behind no longer being sufficient to force them forward over the bodies against each other. They were like two great beasts mauled and torn after a duel, snarling and slavering but no longer able to lock themselves together in mortal combat, the will to fight still there but the energy dissipated and their limbs unable to respond.

The battle seemed to hang in the balance. Flavius knew that the smallest event could now sway the course of history: a renewed burst of ferocity from a few soldiers in the line, the shouts of an officer leaping forward to encourage his men, a celestial sign that might suddenly take on huge significance. He knew that there would be those on the other side watching too, waiting for the right moment to make their move. And then he saw the form of a mounted warrior rising from the dark line of the Hun army, the horse slavering and stomping, tossing its head from side to side, the man on top solid and imperturbable, staring forward with both hands on his hips. Even before he recognized him Flavius knew that it could only be Attila. He was less than fifty paces away, closer than Flavius had ever imagined getting to Attila again, so close that he could see the lines of his moustache and the three white scars on each cheek. He rose in his saddle, tensed himself and bellowed like a bull, an extraordinary sound that rumbled and crackled down the line like a rolling thunderstorm. The rest of the Huns took it up, gesticulating and leering at the Romans and Visigoths only a few paces in front of them.

The noise of bellowing was drowned out by a huge clash of arms, sword against shield, axe against greave, like the sound of a great mountain waterfall crashing into a gorge. Flavius could sense a sudden apprehension along the Roman line, could smell the fear. It was too late for Aetius to respond in kind; Attila had the advantage. But Flavius knew that Attila had also taken a big gamble; he had appeared without a weapon in hand. Perhaps by appearing unarmed he had intended to taunt the Romans, to reveal his invincibility even without weapons, and to empower his Hun army, to show them that he trusted their own force of arms to win the day. But there was a truth behind Attila's gamble known only to Flavius and Macrobius and Aetius, a truth that could now be used devastatingly against him. Flavius sensed those in the Hun line becoming jittery, restless, girding their weapons again, preparing for a renewed assault. He glanced at Aetius, who nodded. *Now was the time.*

'Macrobius!' Flavius shouted, looking around at the *numerus*. 'You other men – raise me up on your shoulders.'

Macrobius immediately came forward, sheathed his sword and cupped his hands for Flavius to step into, the *optio* Cato on Flavius' other side and Sempronius and Maximus behind him. When he was high above their shoulders, above the surrounding *comitatenses* and Visigoths and clearly visible to Attila and the Hun line, he reached back and opened the flap over the long sword that had been strapped to his back, feeling the irregular hard stone on the pommel and closing his hand around the grip. He drew it in one sweep and held it high, looking around and seeing that all eyes were on him. 'We have the sword of Attila,' he shouted. *'We have the sword of Attila.'*

Macrobius had polished it the night before, and the precious metal that had been bonded with iron to make the blade stronger than steel gave it added lustre even in this haze, as if it had absorbed what sunlight there was and radiated it out over the men assembled on the ridge. As he looked at it himself, squinting in the reflection, Flavius remembered what Erecan had told Priscus about the sword, that its secret, its mastery over men, lay not in some magic of the shamans but in the cunning of the metalsmiths, in the age-old skill of those who fashioned weapons of war: those who knew that the power of a great sword made for a king lay not just in its heft and sharpness, but in the special qualities of appearance that made others rally to its bearer or cower before it.

A huge cry went up from the Roman side, resonating up and down the line. Attila bellowed again, but this time in dismay, his horse rearing up and nearly throwing him, kicking back and disappearing down the slope in a storm of dust. The Huns in the front line turned to watch him, taking their eyes off the enemy, the adrenalin that had been stoked up for the attack now leaving them confused and in disarray. Aetius seized the moment and leapt forward, sword in hand, followed by Macrobius and the others of the *numerus*, breaking through the front line with the *comitatenses* surging behind him, scrambling over the mounds of bodies and falling on the Huns. Within seconds the entire Roman and Visigoth line had closed the gap and taken the crest of the ridge, hacking down scores of Huns pressing back against the bulk of their army in a desperate attempt to escape. All along the line the Roman trumpets sounded, the signal for the *comitatenses* to stand their ground and halt on the ridge; Aetius had instructed his commanders to consolidate and wait for reinforcements rather than pursuing the enemy down the slope and risking running into a reformed line strengthened with archers from Attila's reserve.

Flavius re-sheathed the great sword, took out his *gladius* and watched the Huns retreat down the slope, towards the wagon laager that he knew lay somewhere in the haze and dust beyond. The noise had changed, the din of combat replaced by the shrieks of the wounded and the moans of the dying, a chorus of pain from thousands of stricken men along the line. The carnage was appalling, on a scale that he never would have thought possible in such a brief space of time. The men of his *numerus* had escaped unscathed, having been held back as a cordon around Aetius, but those who had been thrown forward into the churning horror of the ridge had paid a fearful price. Most of the tribunes of the leading *comitatenses* units were gone, as well as many of their senior officers; Aspar lay drenched in blood against a pile of corpses being ministered to by the first-aid men of his personal *numerus*, somehow still alive despite his neck having been ringed by a lasso and his head nearly severed.

Attila had suffered a blow to his prestige but was still alive, and his mounted archers were still a formidable foe. He would know that the Roman army had been severely weakened, and that the casualties would include chieftains like the Goth Radagaisus who would have led from the front and would have never allowed themselves to be pulled back and protected as Aetius had. The course of the fighting to the north and south against the Ostrogoths and the Gepids was still unclear; Aetius had immediately sent out runners to inform their commanders of the success in the centre, to try to boost their resolve. But with the centre of the ridge now in Roman hands they were in an excellent position both for defence and for offence, able to counter Hun attacks up the slope as well as harass the enemy from long range. Already Flavius could see the *sagittarii* climbing the slope from their reserve positions, ordered up by Aetius once the ridge had been secured and ready to pour down arrows into the enemy. Along the ridge the *fabri* tribunes were organizing the *milites* to pile up the bodies, those of their companions and of the enemy alike, in a long mound along the forward edge, creating a fortress of flesh from the carnage of battle.

Flavius turned to Aetius. 'Congratulations, *magister militum*. It is the greatest feat of arms of all time.'

Aetius' face was set like stone. 'The battle is not over yet. The tide of war may still turn against us. I need you by my side, tribune, to tell me what Attila will do next.'

'*Ave, magister militum.*'

17

As Flavius and Aetius stared out from the ridge an extraordinary scene met their eyes. The slope dropped down to a monotonous plain similar to the one they had just traversed, only here there was no river in the distance to break the view. The heat of the sun and of so many men and horses in such a confined space, breathing and sweating and bleeding, had created a haze that floated above the battlefield and obscured everything more than a few *stades* distant. But out of the haze some five hundred paces below the ridge loomed the leading edge of Attila's wagon laager, the wheels facing outwards and the sides of the wagons forming a nearly continuous screen of wood like the wall of a fort. From their vantage point on the ridge they could see down into the laager, but their view was blocked by a huge dust cloud that rose above; all that Flavius could see was an occasional flash of steel and a blur of hooves and legs, and he could hear whinnying and snorting above the noise that rose out of the laager like the roar of a crowd in a stadium. He turned to Aetius, raising his voice above the din. 'I saw this in Parthia. Attila is stoking up his mounted bowmen, riding them round and round in a circle so that they are wound tight like a coil, ready to spring to the attack.'

Aetius turned to Aspar. 'Tell the tribunes of the *sagittarii* to line up their men in close formation in two ranks for volley fire. They are not to shoot their arrows in a high arc to fall among the enemy, but must wait until they are at point-blank range, until they can see the whites of their horses' eyes. They must only shoot on my command.'

Aspar shouted the orders down the line. Flavius turned and saw the first men of the two *numeri* of *sagittarii*, each about five hundred strong, reach the crest and unsling their bows. They had been kept in reserve behind the main force, too valuable to expend in the initial assault, but now it was essential that they establish their position as fast as possible to take advantage of the high ground. More of them arrived, panting hard, their quivers full of arrows, the iron tips shining where they had been filed to extra sharpness the night before. Another sound came from the laager, a sound that Flavius had heard before, the eerie throat-singing that had filled the night air on the steppe-lands of the East three years earlier. It was the last sound the Hun horsemen on the plain of Parthia had made before charging, and he saw the first of them appearing now, bursting out of an opening in the laager and leading a stream of riders that spread out over the plain and began to thunder up the slope towards them.

Apsachos the Sarmatian turned to Macrobius. 'Permission to join the *sagittarii*, centurion.'

'Permission granted,' Macrobius growled, his eyes on the Huns. 'Just save the last arrow for me in case you see me being captured.'

The ground began to shake as the Huns charged closer. Flavius glanced to either side along to the ridge. Far to the right he glimpsed Quintus, bloody but upright, the surviving men of his unit forming a defensive perimeter at the end of the ridge. There were still too few *sagittarii* in position, less than a hundred from each *numerus*, the rest still out of sight making their way up the slope from the west. But the weakness of the position in front of the first Hun charge could work in their favour. At their current speed of attack the Huns would wheel and shoot before the bulk of the men had taken up position, restricting the casualties to the men already on the ridge. Those who followed would have to keep their nerve, stepping over the bodies of their comrades and reforming the line, but they would be there in sufficient numbers. Flavius gripped his sword hilt tightly. The Huns were less than two hundred paces away now, near their favoured range for wheeling and presenting their bows.

He knew that Aetius would not give the order this time for the *sagittarii* to shoot, that those now in position would be sacrificed to ensure that maximum effect was achieved when the rest of the men had arrived. To shoot a depleted volley now would be to send the wrong message to the Huns, would make them redouble their efforts when they swung around for another charge, believing that the ridge was poorly defended and Aetius unprepared for an assault. To stand any chance of defeating such a formidable enemy, Aetius would have to ensure that he delivered the maximum possible blow when the line was at its greatest strength.

The Huns were within range now, swinging parallel to the ridge, the horses lunging forward and their archers turning and raising their bows. The nearest *sagittarii* tribune looked to Aetius, his face ashen and drawn, but Aetius was unmoved, standing his ground and staring impassively ahead. With a great shriek as the horses wheeled around the Hun archers released their arrows, the tips hurling through the air with a shrill whistling sound and bringing down the men on the ridge as if they were a slashed stand of wheat, every second or third man of the *sagittarii* falling dead or wounded. The tribune who had looked so desperate was sitting with an arrow through his upper thigh, the blood pulsing out from the artery in great jets until he sank slowly to the ground, and behind Flavius the *optio* Cato of his own *numerus* had dropped his sword and was struggling vainly with an arrow that had gone through his throat, gurgling and frothing blood and then falling back dead, his eyes wide open in disbelief.

The Huns had wheeled round close to the line of their wagons ready for another charge, the air in between a maelstrom of dust from the horses' hooves. Aetius turned to Flavius and gripped him by the shoulder. 'You and Macrobius must take over the southern *sagittarii numerus*. Their centurion has also fallen.

You must rally the men as they arrive and get them into position. With the heavy iron tips I ordered them to put on their arrows last night, their bows will give them an advantage of twenty paces in level flight over the Hun bows. Wait for my command.'

Macrobius was already among the men, bellowing orders to those who had newly arrived, and helping to pull aside the dead and the wounded to make space to reform the line. Within minutes there were two hundred, then three hundred men spaced along the ridge, protected at the far end by Quintus and his men, the archers matched by a similar number in the *numerus* on the other side. It was the critical mass needed to make volley fire effective, but even so it was going to be a close-run thing. The Huns were already pounding up the slope again, their horses slavering and wide-eyed and galloping under their own momentum, leaving the archers free to hold their bows ready to draw as they came within range. Macrobius stomped up and down the line, shouting orders. 'Choose your man as they wheel around, and stay with him. When the order comes the first two men on the right of the line shoot at the first rider, and then on down the line in pairs as the Huns wheel round and come in range. Remember, they are moving targets, so aim just ahead of them. Wait for the command of Flavius Aetius.'

The ground thundered and vibrated as the first Huns began to wheel. Macrobius roared again: 'Tense your bows.' Seconds passed, long seconds as more of the Huns wheeled round. 'Let fly!' Aetius yelled. The first pair of *sagittarii* loosed their arrows point-blank at the leading rider, bringing him down tumbling over his horse, and in rapid succession the remainder of the *numerus* loosed as the Huns came in range . What had seemed an unstoppable charge became a scene of utter chaos, the first fallen horses having blocked the rest, and within moments dozens of horses and men lay piled in a heap on the slope, the riders behind them careering off in all directions in an attempt to avoid the carnage and then falling prey to arrows themselves. The *sagittarii* were now shooting at will, pouring a continuous stream of arrows into the Huns. Hundreds now lay dead and wounded, with the surviving horses that galloped back towards the laager mostly riderless. Flavius took a deep breath and looked back at Aetius. His plan had worked. Without a single casualty to the Romans during the second assault the Huns had been routed and slaughtered, the survivors forced back into a laager too ill-supplied to withstand a siege for long.

He made his way back along the ridge towards Aetius, pausing to kneel down over Cato, breaking and removing the arrow from his neck and closing his eyes. He felt nothing, no regret or grief, as if the passing in battle of a man he had known for twelve years was as inevitable as the cycle of the moon, and then he remembered Cato's little boy in Rome and wondered whether he would ever hear how his father had died: facing the enemy and laying down his life in the greatest contest Rome had ever fought in any of their lifetimes against a barbarian force.

He got up and went over to Aetius, and together they stared at the carnage of men and horses down the slope, watching as the *sagittarii* picked off the Hun wounded who were trying to hobble and drag themselves out of range. 'Attila will be enraged, but he will know that he has lost any hope of tactical advantage,' Flavius said. 'He can try a sortie again, but he knows it will have the same result. Eventually, they will be driven out by hunger and thirst. This part of the battle may be won, but the killing is not yet over.'

Aetius jerked his head to the south, where a slogging match was still going on between the main Visigoth force and the Gepids under Ardaric. 'The *sagittarii* will remain here along with the rest of Aspar's *comitatenses* to keep Attila at bay. Anagastus can now move his *comitatenses* to reinforce Theodoric and Thorismud against the Gepids. That is, if Theodoric and his sons are still alive, and if they are willing to take a *comitatenses* army under their wing. With the battle now swung in our favour, the intentions and balance of power among our allies may have shifted,

Flavius. What began as an alliance of necessity between Roman and Visigoth may now become a competition to fill a vacuum left in the northern empire as the spectre of Attila recedes. For a general, orchestrating the tactics of battle quickly shifts to the strategy of politics and power-play. You should count yourself lucky that you are still a tribune and can focus on the fighting. I must now play a different game.'

Another noise came up from the laager, a hollow, booming noise, echoing from the circle of wagons into the humid air above the ridge. The soldiers stopped what they were doing, the *sagittarii* who had been replenishing their quivers, and Macrobius and the others of the *numerus* who had been squatting around Cato's body, and stared at the extraordinary scene that was unfolding below. The dust from the riders had settled and the interior of the laager was now clearly visible, the survivors of the Hun army crouched and lying in disarray around the edge, their horses corralled around them. In the centre was a mound of saddles from the dead horses that rose to five times the height of a man or more, surrounded by piled-up planks and wheels from dismembered chariots. Standing above on a platform was a man, black-cloaked and black-armoured, his feet planted firmly apart, facing the ridge. Each time he bellowed he raised his arms and clenched his hands, as if his body were knotted in rage. Flavius stared, transfixed. *It was Attila.*

'What's he doing?' Aetius muttered.

'He's built his own funeral pyre,' Flavius said. 'He's telling us that we may have him caged, but he will not remain so for long. The Hun is a warrior of the steppes, of vast open spaces, not used to being cooped up in fortresses and cities. He is telling us that he would rather die by his own hand or die fighting than waste away in a siege.'

Macrobius came over and stood beside them. 'He is like a lion brought low by hunting spears that paces back and forth in front of his den and dares not spring, but never ceases to terrify those around him by his roaring.'

Aetius narrowed his eyes. 'As soon as the Visigoths and Askar's *comitatenses* have destroyed the Gepids and there is no longer any threat of counter-attack from the flanks, I will order the *sagittarii* down the slope to a position where they can rain down arrows into the laager. The *comitatenses* cavalry will draw up on the ridge, ready to counter any last-ditch Hun foray. I am not in the business of allowing Attila his wishes, but I will either see him and his army destroyed this day or I will allow him to leave as a vanquished foe. My decision will rest on the Visigoths, on who survives among Theodoric and his sons and where their futures lie.'

Another sound reached them, this time from the muffled noise of the melee between the Visigoths and the Gepids to the south: the deep, resonating sound of a horn blasting, one long blow followed by a shorter one, as if abruptly cut off. Flavius felt the hairs on the back of his neck rise, every muscle in his body tensing, an instinctive reaction from somewhere deep within his soul. He had heard that sound once before, when his grandfather Gaudentius had been cornered by wolves while they had been hunting in the forest, and he and his Goth cousins had ridden to the rescue. It was the war horn of the Gothic kings, blown only in times of greatest peril. He remembered Thorismud's question about his allegiance the night before in the mead hall. His Roman side told him that there was little he could do for Theodoric now, that his place was here beside Aetius, that the king would already be beyond help. But his Goth side told him that even if Theodoric had fallen it was his duty to join Thorismud and his brother and stake claim over the body, to fight to avenge those who had brought down the king. He knew that despite his bitter past enmity with Theodoric, Aetius must feel the same ancestral draw of the sound of the war horn, for he was even closer than Flavius to their shared Gothic ancestry, but that as general he must wrench himself away from instinct and remain rooted to this place, lord of the battlefield.

Flavius turned to him, but did not even need to ask. Aetius pointed south: 'Go.' Flavius shouted to Macrobius, who had gone back to the *sagittarii*, 'Centurion, follow me.' He sheathed his sword and began to run, followed by Macrobius and the other men of the *numerus*, Apsachos and Maximus coming hard behind, weaving and jumping over the corpses that lay strewn on the battlefield, leaping over the blood-filled stream just below the ridge and making their way as fast as they could towards the fighting. Flavius could pick out individual Visigoths coming up from the river bank, surging forward behind their chieftains to join the fray, shrieking and bellowing as they reached the swirling clash of arms in the centre; the Gepids were holding a line and resisting each Visigoth attempt to break through and separate them, to make it easier to overwhelm and kill them. Two hundred paces further on, with the bodies piled up ever higher, Flavius drew his *gladius* and yelled as he ran, leading Macrobius and the others through the outer Gepid line and towards the melee in the centre of the fight.

Flavius slashed and thrust, catching one man in the throat and slipping with him on the bloody ground, jumping back to his feet just as a flight of arrows from the Visigoth archers thudded into the line of Gepids to his left. He was running to the place where he knew that Theodoric was most likely to be leading his men forward, and then he saw something that made him stop in his tracks. The Gepids were close kin to the Ostrogoths, but were smaller, stockier, and used shorter swords; the men that Flavius saw ahead were not Gepids but Ostrogoths, taller and more muscular than the men around them. Aetius had done his best to keep the Visigoths from fighting their Ostrogoth cousins, but somehow it seemed that an Ostrogoth unit had become incorporated into the Gepid force.

As he got closer he realized that it was more than that. Several of the men wore embellished helmets and Hun segmented armour. These were not Ostrogoths separated from Ardaric's army that the *comitatenses* had faced on the ridge to the north – they were from Attila's own bodyguard, an elite unit, perhaps the best troops at his disposal. For these men not to be guarding Attila now was extraordinary; they must be on a mission of great significance, under orders from Attila himself. Flavius realized that Attila may have had the last play in the battle after all: once he knew his own Hun forces had been defeated and Aetius was inviolable on the ridge, he would have been bent solely on trying to kill Theodoric and would have committed his best resources to this one last act.

Flavius' mind raced as he lurched forward, slipping on blood and stumbling over bodies as he searched for the Visigoth king. He remembered what Aetius had said about the power vacuum after the battle, about the uneasy alliance between Romans and Visigoths. Attila had known of that too; the king they had seen in the laager bellowing above his funeral pyre was a master strategist as well, not just a warlord. Flavius realized that Attila's melodrama on the pyre after the failure of his archers had been a distraction to keep their eyes off the Visigoths, off the dispatch of his elite bodyguard into the fray. By ordering his bodyguards to kill Theodoric, Attila may have been trying to secure a lifeline, knowing that Aetius might think twice about allowing the Visigoths under an ambitious new prince to pursue and destroy the surviving Huns and create a momentum of their own, potentially turning back against their Roman allies and Aetius himself.

Macrobius came up alongside him, panting and dripping with blood. He pointed with his sword. 'That's Andag. I remember him from Attila's bodyguard at the citadel.'

Flavius stared at the hulking form about twenty paces in front of them standing beside a pile of Visigoth bodies and goading others to try him on. A huge ball-and-chain mace hung from his left hand, the ball covered with vicious spikes. The Visigoths had fought around him as they pushed the Gepid line back, leaving plenty of room as he swung the mace provocatively. The reason he was standing his ground and not flailing into the advancing Visigoths lay on the ground in front of him: it was a crushed hunting horn. He was like a predator with a kill, standing over the body of his victim, making sure that his enemy saw that he had been victorious. The Visigoths were a hundred paces and more beyond him now, pushing the Gepids back down the slope, but still Andag stood there, glaring and circling. Flavius gripped his sword, walking forward.

Macrobius came after him. 'He is isolated now and cannot survive. We need just wait and he will be brought down by an arrow.'

Flavius shook his head. 'Thorismud and his brother are nowhere to be seen. The other chieftains are dead or are leading their men on the flanks. I am the one who must take vengeance.'

A cry came from behind them, and Flavius turned to see Maximus encircled by a group of Gepids who had turned back from their retreating line for a final fling at the enemy. Apsachos had been searching for arrows to fill his empty quiver, but drew his sword and ran to help, Macrobius and the others following close behind. Flavius turned from them and went forward until he was only a few paces from Andag, separated only by a platform of exposed rock and surrounded by Gepid and Visigoth corpses. He saw the horn again, and then in front of the mass of mangled bodies in a pool of blood he saw a sword with a golden hilt that he recognized from the night before, when Theodoric had come and stood with him beside the river bank.

Andag was a monster of a man, two full paces at least in height, and he had stripped off his armour to reveal a barrel chest and shoulders and biceps as big as any Flavius had ever seen. He suddenly heaved up his ball and chain and brought it down with sickening force on the head of one of the corpses sticking out of the pile, mashing it into a bloody pulp and then raising the mace and swinging it round his head, the fragments of skull and gore that had been caught on the spikes flying off around him. He let the mace down and stared at Flavius, panting and slavering like a dog. 'The king is dead,' he sneered, his Latin thick with a Gothic accent. 'Long live the emperor.'

'Your emperor is trapped in his laager, ready to light his own funeral pyre,' Flavius said. 'His mounted archers have been destroyed by our *sagittarii* on the ridge. Beyond that, the Ostrogoths have been vanquished by the *comitatenses*, and you can see what has happened to the Gepids. We are all that is left, Andag. You and I *are* the battle.'

'Then why do you confront me? Why do you not let me be finished off by one of your archers, or leave me to skulk away and disappear?'

Flavius replied in the Goth tongue. 'Because I know you are no coward. Because you will stand over your trophy until you are challenged. And because he was my king, and I will have vengeance.'

He gripped his *gladius* and leapt forward, avoiding a slippery slick of blood that had pooled on the rock, and thrust hard into Andag's abdomen, feeling the muscles grip the blade as he slid it in up to the hilt. Andag had been caught off guard by the speed of his attack, and bellowed with rage and surprise, bringing up his mace and swiping it across the old scars on Flavius' forearm. Andag fell back, staggering, the *gladius* pulling free as he did so and the wound in his abdomen welling up with blood. Flavius knew that his thrust had missed the spine and would not be enough to fell Andag immediately, and he stood tensed and ready, his sword dripping in front of him. He remembered his first kill all those years before, the Alan in front of the walls of Carthage, the point of vulnerability that Arturus had taught him to anticipate. Andag was visibly weakening now, his abdomen and legs glistening with blood from his wound, but he swung the mace behind him and suddenly bounded forward, his torso and neck exposed just as the Alan's had been. This time it was Flavius who was caught off guard by the speed of the assault, unable to do anything except throw himself forward and hold out his sword with both hands at arms' length, locking it into his body so that he became a human spear. He felt the crunch as the sword drove into Andag's forehead, the huge man unable to stop himself because of the momentum of his arms, the mace flying out of his hands and whirling away over Flavius' head.

The two men slipped together on the pool of blood and Andag crashed into Flavius, the huge body knocking the wind out of him and snapping his head backwards. In the split second as he struggled with consciousness he knew that it was not the absence of Attila's great sword that had won this battle, but sheer force of arms, the brutal struggle of men in individual combat, fighting for their lives as he and Andag had just done.

Then he saw nothing but blackness.

18

Flavius recovered consciousness face down in a puddle of gore, the blood having pooled on the hard ground and trickled under his head and body. With one eye open he could see the rivulet of blood feeding the pool from the pile of corpses beyond, their wounds drained and open: partly severed heads, gaping slices through limbs and torsos, dark holes where bowels had spilled out and lay glistening in lurid cascades over the bodies beneath. He tried to move, but his body seemed paralysed, a feeling he had not had since being tackled by his Goth cousins while playing their ball game as a boy. Then he remembered Andag, the brutal body-blow as he had thrust his sword forward, the funnel of Visigoths who had run up screaming to support Theodoric, the bellowing and chanting of the Huns, the last lunges of the stricken king. He tried to move again, and felt his knees bend, and then his arms. As he did so he saw an arm lying out from the pile, half-submerged in blood, the attached torso pulverized beyond recognition and the head a mess of bloody hair and bone and brains. He kept the hand in his sight as he slowly raised himself to his knees, and then he saw it: the gold ring, unmistakably, on the index finger. *It was Theodoric.*

He stared, his mind reeling. He could see the letters engraved on it: HEVA. He remembered the feast in the great hall in the forest when Theodoric had shown it to him, the heady laughter and tales of derring-do in battle, their intoxication from honey liqueur and wine and the meat from the hunt. Theodoric had explained the meaning of the letters: *Hic est victoriae anulus. Here is the ring of victory.* Flavius looked around, seeing the blood beginning to congeal, the flies already settling on the eyes and mouths of the corpses. If this truly was victory, then Theodoric had secured his place in the great mead hall in the sky. Flavius saw the king's short sword poking out of the gore, and the longer one impaled in a Hun warrior a little further away. He pulled the torn chainmail on the forearm up over the hand, concealing the ring from any scavengers, and drew the sword hilt down and clasped the lifeless fingers around it. He would find Thorismud and his brother and bring them to this place, and the ring would prove that the mangled corpse was their father. And they would see that he had died sword in hand, facing the enemy, in the bloodiest battle that had ever been fought in the name of their kingdom and of Rome.

He slowly raised himself to his feet, seeing the fresh wound on his forearm across the four white scars where the Alaunt had torn into him all those years ago before the walls of Carthage. He remembered the raging thirst he had felt after that battle, and he felt it again now, only this time it was as if his soul itself needed replenishing. He took a few hesitant steps forward, swaying on his feet, and then saw the colossal form of Andag lying contorted among the corpses just ahead of the pool. The weight of Andag's own body as he had slipped in the blood and fallen on Flavius' sword had driven the blade through the back of his neck and out of his forehead, and yet he had lived on for a few tormented moments, somehow heaving himself up and staggering back before falling, his hands clasped against the sides of his head and his eyes wide open and distorted with horror.

Flavius put one foot on Andag's head, reached down and pulled out the *gladius*, holding it unsteadily and looking around in case any more of Attila's warriors were ready to spring up and attack him. But the only living forms he could see on the battle-field were dazed Roman *milites* and Visigoths wandering among the piles of corpses, occasionally reaching down to check a fallen comrade, sometimes delivering a sword or spear thrust to end the agony of a friend or dispatch an enemy. Macrobius was there, and behind him Flavius could make out half a dozen men of the old *numerus*; Astragos the Sarmatian was supporting Maximus, his head wrapped in bloody fabric. Macrobius had removed his felt hat, and he looked old, his hair white and his face etched with lines, but as he came closer he seemed the timeless image of a Roman warrior. Flavius held up his arm and the two men clasped hands, the survivors of the *numerus* gathering around them. For once, there were no quips, no attempts at battle humour. They were all exhausted and caked in blood, and the scale of the carnage seemed to leave even Macrobius dumbstruck.

'I need to find Thorismud,' Flavius said, his voice hoarse. 'His father lies slain beneath that pile of corpses.'

Macrobius pointed to a cluster of men and horses over a fold in the ground to the west. 'He is conferring with Aetius. Thorismud wishes to pursue Attila, but Aetius is warning against it. Attila is a spent force, and Thorismud as the Visigoths' new king needs to secure his throne in Tolosa before he sets off on campaign again.'

'I will go to him. Before that, we need to find water for our men.'

'The stream through the battlefield runs red with blood. The nearest source is the river above the point where the stream flows into it, about two *stades* to the west. We will need to leave now to reach there before sundown.'

Flavius rested his hand on Macrobius' shoulder. 'Make it so, centurion. The last great battle of Rome is over. We have done our duty and upheld our honour. Now is the time to look after our men.'

'*Ave*, tribune.'

That evening Flavius stood in the darkness beside the river Aube, just outside the flickering circle of torches that surrounded the burial pit. Below the bank at the fording place the horses whinnied and stomped, already saddled up and watered for the long journey they would begin that night to the Visigoth capital of Tolosa ten days to the south. To the east over the battle-field the sky glowed orange like a false dawn, lit up by the pyres that the Romans and the Visigoths had made from the mounds of their own dead; the fallen Huns and Ostrogoths would be left on the battlefield to be picked over as carrion, a last great feast for the vultures that had followed the armies of Rome since they had first set out on their wars of conquest more than a thousand years before.

It had begun to drizzle, and through the spluttering of the torches Flavius could see the Visigoth chieftains around the grave, their heads bowed and their swords drawn and held point down in front of them. The only other Roman present was Aetius, standing in the shadows beyond the far side of the torches, his helmet in his hands and his gaze grim and resolute. After Flavius had taken Thorismud and his brother to their father's body, they had carried it to this spot and dug the grave themselves, easily removing the soft sand that had built up against the river-bank at this place; only once they had laid out the corpse did they send word to the chieftains to make their way from the encampments. The burial had been hasty and in secret to keep it from the eyes of the scavengers who would already be lurking around the battlefield, waiting to strip the corpses and pick the blood-soaked ground clean of anything of value. But there had been another reason for Thorismud's urgency. He had used the ceremony to secure oaths of fealty from the chieftains, the men whose backing would be vital if he were to strengthen his claim to the Visigothic throne. Some of them would go back to the encampment to drum up loyalty among their men, while others would ride that night as Thorismud's personal bodyguards to Tolosa, hoping to reach the capital before news of Theodoric's death did and to assert Thorismud's right to kingship over any claim from his brothers. The ceremony over Theodoric's grave had not been one of grief and mourning; it had been a new council of war.

Flavius looked at Aetius, trying to assess the strategic game he was now playing. Before Attila, Theodoric had been Aetius' greatest enemy, and Thorismud knew that. The alliance between the Visigoths and the Romans had been one of necessity, against a common foe. With the Huns now vanquished, Aetius would know that the old enmity with Rome might resurge through Theodoric's sons. Aetius too was not here to mourn Theodoric, but to ensure that Thorismud got off that night for Tolosa with his army. Had Thorismud pursued Attila as he wished and crushed the remnant Hun army, he might have been tempted to take up Attila's mantle, renege on his alliance with Rome and carry on to Ravenna itself. With Gaiseric's Vandals from Carthage now assembled like a pack of sea-wolves off the coast of Italy, Aetius knew that Rome could not withstand a simultaneous assault from two barbarian forces. Persuading Thorismud of the threat in Tolosa and of the need to secure his kingdom would take the pressure off Rome, allowing her forces that had been so depleted after the battle to regroup and Aetius to develop a new defensive strategy.

Of all the sons of Theodoric, Thorismud was the one most likely to be well disposed towards Rome once he had settled as king, the one most worth cultivating. He had trained in the *schola militarum* in Rome, and had just fought victoriously alongside Rome in the greatest battle either of the allies had ever experienced. Theodoric, the youngest son, had also been at the Catalaunian Plains, but he was far down the line of succession and was too much in his brother's thrall to be a contender; his time might come later. Of the four other brothers, Frederic, Euric, Retimer and Himnerith, none of them had been at the battle and none had strong ties with Rome. If Thorismud fell to their machinations, whichever of them survived the inevitable war of succession that followed would be more likely to forge an alliance with Gaiseric than with Valentinian and his weakened army under Aetius.

Flavius looked at Thorismud standing at the head of the grave and remembered the eager young man in the *schola* ten years before when they had studied the Battle of Adrianople. Though all of the boys in the *schola* had known the ugly reality behind war, having grown up with intrigue and assassination and precarious alliances among their fathers and uncles and brothers, for them war had been about battles and tactics in the field; the backdrop that interested them had been logistical – the movement of armies, the size and specialism of units, keeping open lines of supply, how to organize recruitment and training. In the years that followed they had been drawn into a darker, more complex business, far removed from the point of the blade and the glory of arms. The Battle of the Catalaunian Plains itself had been a new form of war, something that few of their game-plays could have allowed, a battle in which the overview of generals and tactical nuance barely mattered and in which victory in the end was down to physical prowess and bloody attrition.

And now Thorismud was burying his father, and faced a future as king in which there could be no place for four of his brothers. Flavius did not envy him the price he would have to pay for assuming his rightful inheritance: the squalor of internecine fighting, the murders, the distress and hatred of his sisters-in-law and their children, the guilt that would fester with him until his dying day. Today was the last day of Thorismud's youth; the burden of kingship would weigh heavily on him. That was the reality of war, of the power struggle that lay behind it. Flavius was glad that all of that now lay behind him, that his days of fighting for the grand strategy of Rome were now over.

The chieftains sheathed their swords and moved away. It was the signal for the two Romans to pay their respects, and Flavius and Aetius stepped within the ring of torches, standing beside the grave with Thorismud at the head and his brother at the foot. Flavius looked into the shallow pit, remembering the crushed corpse he had found on the battlefield; he saw that the head and torso had been covered with a blanket, the arms folded over on top and the golden ring clearly visible. Along with the corpse were the items that Theodoric and his brother had been able to assemble to ensure that their father did not reach the afterlife empty-handed: several bronze drinking cups, the gold and gilt-bronze horse trappings from Theodoric's own harness, the neck torque of twisted gold that he had worn into battle, and laid alongside him his two swords, their hilts encased in gold and decorated with garnets. The smaller sword, the one that Flavius had placed in Theodoric's hand on the battlefield, was still smeared with blood, the highest mark of honour in the grave goods of a Gothic warrior who had died facing the enemy in combat.

Thorismud turned to Flavius, his eyes dark and unfathomable, already dwelling on the future. 'Flavius Aetius, you fought along-side my father and you tried to save his life on the battlefield. I will not forget that. I salute you.'

Flavius bowed his head in acknowledgement and as a farewell to the fallen king. He glanced at Aetius, and the two Romans withdrew from the circle and made their way to the river bank, leaving Thorismud and his brother alone with their father. Aetius turned and put a hand on his nephew's shoulder. 'You have fought well, Flavius Aetius, and upheld the honour both of Rome and of your grandfather's Goth ancestors. And by taking the sword of Attila and removing his symbol of power you may well have swayed the battle in our favour. I too salute you.'

'But now I cannot return to Rome.'

Aetius took his hand away and stared back at the burning torches, at Thorismud and his brother just visible filling the grave from the pile of sand alongside. 'The court is a dangerous place. It is for me too, but I am *magister militus* and have lived with it all my life. For you, the fact that you have carried out subterfuge against one emperor, even though he was a mortal enemy of Rome, might suggest to another that you could do the same to him. Valentinian is easily swayed by Heraclius, who knows what you and your men think of court eunuchs. And there are others who influence Valentinian – the Augustinian bishops of Rome and Ravenna, who know of your association with the heretic Pelagius. There is already talk of public burnings, of Christians purging Christians. If you returned to Rome you would be walking into a maelstrom as dangerous as any battlefield, but less easy for you to navigate.'

'Then I must ask that you absolve me of service to Rome.'

'Thorismud will accept you into his inner council. You could do great service there for me, as my eyes and ears in the court of Rome's last remaining ally. One day soon, in your lifetime if not in mine, a Goth prince will be emperor in Rome.'

Flavius stripped the gilt embellishments from the side of his helmet, the marks of his rank as a tribune that he had ordered to be put on by the metalsmiths of Ravenna before sailing out to Carthage all those years before. He handed them to Aetius. 'I have learned what it means to be a soldier. I will not be a spy, nor a schemer. My place is with my sword in hand in front of my men. And I will not serve Rome if her emperor is to be swayed by a eunuch.'

Aetius took the strips of gilt, weighing them in his hands. 'It is done. You are relieved of all further duty to Rome. But I will keep these as honoured reminders of one of the last true warriors of Rome.'

'And my men? Macrobius?'

'They too are released from service, if that is their wish.'

'They are waiting with the horses. I will ask them.'

'And you? What will you do, Flavius Aetius?'

Flavius looked up into the drizzle, feeling the drops form on his lips, tasting the salt from the sweat and the blood that were still on his face. Above them the low clouds still reflected the pyres on the battlefield, as if the blood of that day had stained the heavens themselves. He pointed along the line of the river beyond the battlefield. 'I ride north tonight, along with those of my *numerus* who wish to join me. We will find a ship to take us to the western British shore where Arturus has a stronghold. I will offer my services to him as a soldier.'

'War is in your blood, Flavius Aetius.'

'In Britain I can fight still for Rome, not for the Rome that abandoned her under Honorius, but for the Rome that once forged a bond between the legionaries and the people of that land, the ancestors of Arturus and his men. It is a cause where Rome does not mean intrigue and murder and eunuchs, but a place where a soldier can fight as a soldier.'

Aetius turned his hand up into the drizzle. 'If you are going to Britain, you will have to get used to more of this.'

'I've been to the deserts of Africa to fight the Vandals, and ridden on the steppes with Attila. In the desert, on the barren wastelands that lead to it, everything of history litters the land around you, barely covered by the dust. The constant reminder of past glories becomes a burden, a vision of battles that we have come to believe we could never emulate. Carthage was won by the exploits of Scipio Aemilianus, but his legacy weighed us down as much as it inspired us. With Attila it was different. Riding with him was like riding out of a blank canvas of the past, with no Caesars or Scipios to emulate, no victories to better, heading into an unknown future. It was exhilarating. I feel that up here too, in the north, where the rain cleanses us of the past. Soon enough the blood on the Catalaunian Plains will wash away into the cracked earth, the crops will ripen like never before, and people will forget that a battle ever took place here. One day I may be an old warrior dwelling on past glories. But as a soldier now I yearn for a place where people look only to the future.'

Aetius cracked a smile. 'Well then, Britain could be for you. And Arturus has the makings of a king. You could do worse.'

'He needs all the help he can get if he is to succeed against the Saxons.'

'Does he still have that Hun woman with him? Erecan?'

'She left with him for Britain after we made our escape from the Hun capital across the Danube. I have heard little of them since.'

Aetius shook his head. 'A granddaughter of Mundiuk. A daughter of Attila. That would give any enemy pause for thought.'

'Do you remember when you used to teach me archery when I was a boy on the Field of Mars? I never believed your stories of Hun archers being able to pin together two enemies through the head with a single arrow, until I saw her do it with my own eyes.'

'I've been meaning to ask,' Aetius said. 'That sword. What will you do with it?'

'The sword of Attila? Its day is over. It is time for new kings, and new swords. But by rights it should go to the next in line, to the Hun warrior who will perpetuate the blood line of Attila.'

'This also is why you go to Britain?'

'Until then the story will be unfinished. It is my last duty to Rome, begun when you sent me east to find Attila and the sword beyond the Danube.'

They watched as Thorismud and his brother swept sand over the ground of their father's grave and then picked up the torches and hurled them into the river, extinguishing the last of the flames and plunging the bank into darkness. A horse whinnied and then a dog howled, a thin, piercing noise from the direction of the battlefield that echoed across the river banks. Flavius stepped back and raised his right arm. '*Ave atque vale*, Flavius Aetius Gaudentius, *magister militum*. I salute you.'

Aetius raised his hand in return. 'Godspeed, Flavius Aetius Secundus, last true tribune of Rome.'

EPILOGUE

Flavius cupped his hands and blew into them, feeling the warmth of his breath against his palms and watching the condensation swirl away above him. The snow was falling harder now, but he could still make out the craggy peaks that rose around them like a great amphitheatre, opening only where they had come up the rocky trail the evening before from the valley to the east. They had passed lake after lake, each one higher than the next and joined by rushing torrents of white water, the edges frozen in cascades of ice that lapped the trail and made the going treacherous for horses and men alike. Finally they had reached the highest one of all, the pool that Arturus called Glaslyn, its dark waters just visible below him through the swirl of snow and morning mist.

Like most of the others, Flavius had spent a fitful night curled up under his cloak inside the entrance to one of the copper mines that peppered the slopes, as protection against the mountain more than against any Saxon foolish enough to have followed them up to this place. Climbing in the howling wind the night before, he had been astonished to see chunks of rock come flying off the peaks, and had cowered with the others behind a jagged slab as an avalanche of scree came tumbling down around them. The Britons told him that a giant stalked these crags, a monster called Rhitta Gawr, trapped up there since the time when sheets of ice had covered the mountains and shattered the rock, leaving jagged chunks for him to hurtle down when the storm winds stoked his rage and he crashed and bellowed around the peaks.

Macrobius, though, had told a different story, passed down from soldiers of the legion who had once occupied the ruined fort at the head of the valley, built there in the time of the early Caesars to provide protection for the miners. They said that when the emperor Constantine converted to Christianity the war god Mars had stormed off in disgust to this place, and it was he who paced the peaks and clashed the rocks together, tossing them down into the valley below. Since Constantine had spurned him, no Roman soldier who came this way was safe from his rage. The men in the fort had refused to come up from the valley any longer, and the mines were abandoned. When Flavius had heard the story, he was bowed down against the wind as they all trudged up the path, the crags looming forbiddingly above, and he had pulled his heavy woollen cloak around him, concealing the last vestiges of his past allegiance, the heavy *cibanius* sword belt that his uncle Aetius had given him in Rome a lifetime ago. He felt distant from Christ out here, and he was willing to give the story the benefit of the doubt. For once, he had felt pleased no longer to be fighting for Rome.

Now Macrobius made his way up the slope from the cooking fires, carrying a full skin in one hand and a leg of cooked meat in the other. He clambered over the rock in front of the mineshaft and sat down heavily on the loose slate beside Flavius, handing him the skin. 'Weak beer and mutton. It's all they've got.'

Flavius unstoppered the skin and took a deep draught, raising the skin high. It was ice cold, but refreshing. He set the skin down and eyed the mutton. 'Do you remember the venison we ate before Carthage? Close your eyes and imagine it's that.'

Macrobius took the skin and drank noisily, gulping the beer down and spilling it over his beard. He stoppered the skin and wiped his mouth. 'If we're lucky, we'll be having venison again before too long. The last of the warrior bands of the Britons came in a few hours ago, and Arturus is conferring with them now. Rumour is that we'll be going back down to the borderlands and the valley of the river Dee, to the old hunting forest of the Twentieth Legion. We'll feast like kings.'

Flavius pursed his lips. 'If we're going there, it won't be deer that we're hunting.'

Macrobius looked dejectedly at the meat. 'Only barbarians eat sheep.'

Flavius squinted at him. 'Barbarians? Have you looked at yourself recently? That pigtail is long enough to tether a wagon, and your beard would do any German warlord proud.'

'It was your uncle Aetius' advice, remember? Blend in with the natives, or someone will single you out. Anyway, you can hardly talk.'

Flavius cracked a grin. 'Well then, if we're barbarians after all, we *can* eat sheep. I'm starving.'

Macrobius took the leg of mutton in both hands and ripped it in half, handing one part to Flavius and noisily eating his own, the fat spurting into his beard to join the beer. A horse whinnied loudly, the sound echoing around the mountainsides, and he got up, still eating. 'Time to tend the animals,' he said, his mouth full. He lurched forward, his scabbard tip clattering on the rocks, and headed down to the jumble of boulders by the lakeshore where they had corralled the horses for the night; the horses had been terrified in the storm and had refused to come into the tunnels, and Macrobius had stayed with them behind what little shelter the boulders could afford. Flavius could just make out Arturus and the dozen or so British chieftains further along the lakeshore, gathered around the circular slab of rock that was the ancient conferring place for those who rallied here. Flavius was not among them by choice. He was Arturus' battle companion, not his adviser, and Macrobius was Arturus' horse master, and nothing more. Flavius' role as a strategist and war tactician had ended on the Catalaunian Plains, the moment when he had handed his badges of rank to Aetius and walked away from the Roman army for ever. Out here, he was a mere soldier, and another man was king.

He tore the last bit of gristle off the bone with his teeth and let the fat drip on the blade of his sword that was lying across his knees where he had been burnishing it when Macrobius had come up. He rubbed the grease into the blade and then turned it over, making sure to get it into the gap at the hilt where the damp air had caused the steel to rust. He wiped off the excess with the hem of his cloak and then ran his finger along the dents that had been too deep for the grinding stone to remove. He stared down at their route from the valley, marked now in white where the snow had stuck on the unbroken ground of the trail between the tumble of rocks. The four years since the Catalaunian Plains had been a time of almost unbroken fighting, and they had been continuously on the move. Of those men from the original *numerus* who had chosen to follow him and Macrobius across the sea to Britannia, only a handful now remained. They were no longer Roman *limitanei*, but were knights of a new liege, battle-hardened, Arturus' chosen guard, each man the equal of any champion the Saxons could throw against them. It had been a war of duels, of skirmishes, of bloody ambushes as they and the other warrior bands of the Britons had fallen back before the relentless advance of the invaders, the survivors joining together under Arturus' leadership as word spread that he had been accepted by the chieftains as their overlord, their king.

And now in this desolate mountain stronghold they had reached the end of the trail. Further west lay Mona, the ancient island of the Druids, flat and indefensible, and then Hibernia; beyond that was only open ocean, the edge of the world. They had reached the last place where the Britons who had resisted Rome four hundred years earlier had holed up, and now Arturus and his men faced the same fateful decision as their forebears: whether to stay in these mountains, in this place that no invader could subdue, to see a future for their children only under the baleful eye of the god of these crags, or to turn and sally forth, to use the few hundred men of their bands to try what had never been tried before – to confront the Saxons in pitched battle using tactics of the Romans that the enemy had not yet experienced. The decision was being made now by those gathered at the lakeside around the circular slab. But Flavius knew which course Arturus would take. He would not disappear into history like the last of the British warriors four hundred years ago, living like trolls in the mountains, forever on the move, always hunted. Those were Arturus' ancestors, but so were the Roman soldiers who had come to Britain and married British women, and Flavius knew it was Arturus' Roman blood that would win the day. If they were to go down it would be as soldiers on the field of battle, holding their ground alongside the shadows of their Roman ancestors, the legionaries and *milites* of a thousand years of warfare, a history that could not end with the last of them turning away from their rightful place as warriors sworn to fight to the death to protect their honour and that of their comrades.

He stared out into the swirl of snow. *Four years since the Catalaunian Plains.* The affairs of Rome seemed like ancient history now, as remote as the great events of the Punic Wars that he had read about as a boy in the books of Polybius and Livy. For a long time after arriving in Britannia they had heard little news, and nothing first hand, only rumours from captured Gothic mercenaries who had crossed the sea to Britain to fight alongside the Saxons. And then his cousin Quintus, his former student in the *schola* in Rome, had joined them after a perilous journey from Italy, and had been killed only a week ago while single-handedly holding off a Saxon charge in the bloody skirmish near Viroconium that had finally pushed Arturus west through the mountains to this place. Quintus' news had shown that Flavius had been well advised to leave Rome when he did. The hated eunuch Heraclius had persuaded Valentinian that Aetius coveted the imperial purple, and together the two men had caught Aetius unawares and stabbed and bludgeoned him to death. Flavius had known that Aetius would one day fall foul of court intrigue, but to die in such a way at the hands of men who had never once seen an enemy in battle was an ignominious end for a Roman soldier, for the finest general Rome had produced for generations and the last hope for the western empire.

Flavius had bowed his head when he heard the news. What had happened after Aetius' death had seemed as inevitable as the cycle of the stars. Aetius' Hun bodyguards Optila and Thrastilla, Erecan's former guards who had become fiercely loyal to their new master, had wreaked bloody vengeance, murdering Valentinian as he was practising archery on the Field of Mars outside Rome. They had been acting out of loyalty to Aetius, not Attila, but it had seemed preordained that Hun warriors should bring down the last Roman emperor in the West who mattered; after Valentinian they could only be weaklings and puppets. Fearing for her own life after his murder, the empress Eudoxia had offered herself and her two daughters to the Vandal king Gaiseric. In an incredible twist of fate, the barbarian whose army had given Flavius his first taste of battle more than a quarter of a century before outside Carthage had now been invited to the gates of Rome itself. It was as if the goddess Roma, expelled by the priests and bishops of Christ, had risen one last time from her place of banishment and beckoned Rome towards self-destruction, refusing to allow her city to diminish further but opening a crack in the underworld for her to be swallowed up and for her thousand-year ascendancy over the affairs of men to end.

And Quintus had also brought news of Attila. The man who had yearned to die by the sword, whom Flavius had heard with his own ears bellowing for it on the Catalaunian Plains, had also met an ignominious end, drowning in his own blood after a haemorrhage brought on by too much drink while celebrating yet another marriage. After retreating from the battle he had regrouped his Hun survivors and marched on Rome, sacking the

towns of northern Italy on the way, but his army had been a
spent force and the warriors had turned back to their steppe fastness beyond the Danube. Attila may have failed to conquer the
western empire by force of arms, but he had won in the end.
Spies who had watched his *strava*, his funeral celebrations, had
said that he was buried with a vast treasure of Roman gold coins,
all of the tribute that he had exacted from the emperors, sucking
the coffers of Rome dry. The loss of that gold had impoverished
the empire, making it impossible for the emperors in Ravenna
to pay the army. After that, Flavius knew that it could only be
a matter of time before the Goths, Attila's strongest remaining
vassals, swept into Italy and deposed the last of the rulers who
had succeeded Valentinian, the puppet emperors who were overseeing the final disintegration of the Roman army in the West.

Flavius wrapped his cloak around him, remembering how he
had done the same all those years ago on that last frigid morning
outside Carthage before the Vandals had swept in. He remembered Arturus that morning too, how he had seen him for the first
time walking out of a dust cloud in the desert, and then how they
had predicted the future together as they had waited for the ships
to evacuate them from the burning city. History had proved them
right in one crucial respect. From being marauding forest raiders,
the Vandals in their new port city had become skilled navigators
and warriors of the sea. Just as Rome had once learned from the
barbarians, adapting their weapons and tactics, so the barbarians
had learned from Rome, taking the one strength that everyone
had thought was unassailable and making it their own. For the
first time since Pompey the Great had quashed piracy half a
millennium before, Rome had lost control of the Mediterranean.
Within a few decades of his first encounter with the sea, crossing
from Spain to Africa in his march on Carthage, Gaiseric had
become the strongman of the oceans, adapting the tactics of
forest raiding to the sea, avoiding fleet actions with the remnant
Roman navy but using his fast *liburnians* to harass and deplete the

Roman ships in hit-and-run encounters in which the Vandals more often than not came off victorious.

With Attila dead and the Vandal war fleet poised off the Tiber, it would be Gaiseric, and not Attila, who would march through the gates of Rome, but it was a finale made inevitable when Attila had blown the horn of war and led his horsemen over the Danube a decade before, taking Rome's eyes off the threat from the sea and setting in train the collapse of the western empire. For all Flavius knew, it could have happened already; the eternal city and all the symbolism that had driven him as a young man might now be burnt and in ruin.

He remembered something else that Arturus had said at Carthage. *What goes around, comes around.* The loss of the rich agricultural hinterland of Africa to the Vandals had fatally weakened Rome, just as six hundred years before the loss of Africa to the Romans had doomed Punic Carthage. He remembered a volume he had seen as a boy in the library in Rome, a collection of Sibylline utterances that predicted the fall of Carthage once again, and that Rome would pay a price for her devastation of the city by Scipio and his army all those centuries ago. Flavius had learned not to believe in pagan prophecies; it was men, and not gods, who decided the fate of cities, and the game of war was not some divine whimsy but a matter of hard strategy and tactics, involving the balance of power and decisions, right or wrong, made by men. With Gaiseric now on the doorstep of Rome, one thing seemed certain. War with Carthage all those centuries ago had made Rome great; now, with Carthage as the headquarters for the final barbarian assault on Rome, the final act in that conflict had broken her.

Flavius sheathed his sword and stood up. He ducked inside the tunnel entrance and retrieved his saddlebag, slinging it over his shoulder and going back outside to stand on the rim of rocks thrown out by the miners. Through the snow he could see movement by the lakeside. The chieftains who had been sitting around the circular slab had left, some of them heading up the slopes to their men and others going over to the horses. Around him, Flavius could see men stirring at the other mineshaft entrances, and closer to the lakeside he saw men who had been huddled around the cooking fires for warmth beginning to gather their weapons and belongings. Macrobius was leading a mottled grey horse along the path towards the slab, and the other dozen or so horses that were all they had left were kicking and stomping on the pathway, each one held by a boy and awaiting its rider. Beyond the slab Flavius could make out Arturus and another figure standing by the shore, looking out over the lake. He knew that they were waiting for him. *It was time.*

Twenty minutes later Flavius slid down the final slope of tailings from the mines and joined the lakeside path where Macrobius was leading the horse just ahead of him, with Arturus and his companion waiting beyond. The main force of men, perhaps three hundred all told, had gathered under their chieftains on an area of flatter ground beside the eastern end of the lake, where the water dropped in a raging torrent towards the next lake far below, on its way down to the river in the valley they had passed on the way up. The other horses under Macrobius' charge were dispersed among the chieftains, their only sign of status among the cloaked forms who huddled together against the snow, and who included the few remaining men from Flavius' *numerus* of four years before.

He quickened his pace now that he was on firmer ground, anxious not to keep the men waiting any longer than was necessary and hoping that the movement would relieve the cold in his limbs. Moments later he stood beside Macrobius in front of Arturus, whose grey-flecked beard was just visible beneath the hood of his cloak. Arturus' companion had stepped down to the water's edge, but now she came back up, her hood thrown back and her face raised to the snow, her long brown hair tied back and the scars on her cheeks showing up livid in the cold. The years of war had toughened Erecan, made her fiercer, more beautiful. Beneath her cloak she still wore the scale armour that her father Attila had given her, and beneath that the fur-lined tunic and trousers made from the pelts of animals she herself had hunted in the steppe-lands of her ancestors. Her bow was swathed in leather on her back, and on her belt Flavius could see her coiled lasso, the metal blades carefully turned inwards so that only her enemy would know their lethal bite.

Flavius turned to Arturus, who had also taken down his hood. He looked gaunt, his face framed by his beard and the long hair that fell to his shoulders, like the images of Christ that the men of the North had begun to make in their own likeness. Flavius put his hand on his sword pommel and stared at his friend. 'Well? Have you made your decision?'

Arturus pointed down the path. 'We can't stay here. The wet snow will be ice in a few hours' time. The cold is creeping down the slopes. The ice would break the legs of horses and men alike.'

'You mean you have chosen to return to war.'

Arturus stared at Flavius, his eyes unfathomable. 'Will you follow me?'

'My men are your men, Arturus.'

'You are still their tribune, Flavius. And Macrobius is their centurion.'

'That is in the past. Rome has receded. The time has come to shed history. You are their *dux*. You are their captain.'

Macrobius reached down and picked up a large piece of old tile from the lakeshore, part of a guardhouse that had once stood below the mines. He brushed off the snow, revealing letters stamped deeply into the surface: LEG XX. 'Twentieth Legion,' he muttered. Flavius remembered all of the vestiges of Roman military power they had seen across the ravaged landscape of Britain: the crumbling walls of the old fortress at Deva, the grassed-over remains of the marching fort at the head of the valley, all of it being absorbed back into the earth. Macrobius turned the tile over, paused, and then tossed it against a rock by the lakeshore, smashing it into small pieces. 'So ends Rome,' he said, squinting up at Arturus. 'Now is your time.'

Arturus stared at him. '*Ave*, centurion. As long as you wear that old felt hat, you're a Roman *milites* to me. Rome may be gone, but her soldiers live on.'

Another figure came towards them, hooded and with a staff in hand, and pointed to the circular rock where Arturus had held his council. 'In the distant days of our ancestors, stones and stone circles had great significance as meeting places. They're all over the place, if you open your eyes to them and know where to look.'

'You're beginning to sound more and more like a druid, Pelagius,' Arturus said. 'I shall have to begin calling you by your old British name.'

'Not yet, Arturus. Not until you are crowned king.'

'Then you may be waiting a long time, my friend. Your beard will become whiter, and will be so long it will be tucked into your belt. And anyway, remember what we believed so passionately with Aetius in Rome. The time for empires is over. The time for republics is on us.'

'Ah,' Pelagius said, crooking his finger, 'That was *Rome*. But this is *Britain*. And I'm not talking about an empire, just a kingdom. Possibly a very small kingdom. But from small shrubs, great and strong trees may grow.'

'There you go again, talking like a druid. Time you drank your mistletoe tea.'

'Barbarians,' Macrobius muttered, stomping off. 'Can't live with them, can't live without them.'

They turned and stared out over the lake. The water was a strange colour, a shimmering metallic red, tainted by the copper that had been worked in the mines on the slopes, long abandoned but still seeping red every time it rained, as if the mountain were bleeding. The view across was obscured by the mist and snow, but Flavius could sense the great walls of rock that lay beyond, rising from the far shore to the crags high above. It was said that a second giant of the mountains lurked here, in the lake: Afanc, monster of the deep, brother of Rhitta Gawr, cast down here after the two fought a titanic battle on the crags at the dawn of time. Others said that the lake was bottomless, that a stone cast into it would fall into the underworld. For the ancient Britons it had been a sacred pool, a place of offerings like the rivers and bogs that Flavius had seen them venerate throughout Britannia, watery boundaries between this world and the next. Warriors who knew that their end was near would cast their shields and swords into them, knowing that their weapons would be waiting to gird them when they themselves breathed their last and passed into the next world, ready for the battles to come.

Arturus nodded at Macrobius, who took a long bundle from the horse's saddlebag and handed it to him. Arturus drew a sword out of the bundle and handed it to Erecan. It was the sacred war sword of Attila, the sword of the war god, kept with them since they had taken it from the citadel of the Huns under Attila's nose almost five years ago. It had not seen the light of day since the Catalaunian Plains, and the blade was dull grey, pitted with rust. Looking at it, and looking at the fierceness in Erecan's eyes, Flavius wondered whether their mission to take the sword and deprive Attila of his symbol of power had changed the course of history after all. His cousin Quintus had said that when Attila had died, the new emperor in the East, Marcian, successor to Theodosius, had dreamed not of a broken sword but of a broken bow. Hun warriors had no need of a sacred symbol to propel them into battle, any more than Roman soldiers had needed a Christian cross or an eagle. He glanced at Macrobius, at the weather-beaten face, lined, grizzled, and remembered the Catalaunian Plains. Perhaps the greatest battle of all time had been decided not by the absence of the sacred sword in Attila's hands but by Roman force of arms, by the blood and sweat and determination of men like Macrobius, bringing all the force of a thousand years of military prowess to bear on the last battle to be fought in the western empire in the name of Rome.

Flavius turned to Arturus. 'Are you sure about this?'

Arturus nodded and shrugged. 'After all, it's a cavalry sword, too long for us. We fight as foot soldiers, as *pedes*. It's deadweight.'

'Too right,' Macrobius muttered. 'Give me an old-fashioned *gladius* any day. The *equites* have always been overrated.'

Arturus put a hand on his shoulder. 'Spoken like a true *milites*, my friend.' He turned to Erecan. 'Anyway, the decision is not mine.'

Erecan hefted the sword, looking at the dull gold bands around the hilt, and then spoke in Greek. 'I am sending this to my father, so that it can lie alongside him in its rightful place in the underworld.'

Arturus bowed slightly and they all stood back. Erecan took the hilt in her left hand, let the tip trail on the ground behind her and then aimed with her other hand out into the lake. With a harsh cry she leaned back and hurled the sword over her head, sending it cartwheeling high into the air and then down beyond their line of sight, in the swirl of mist. They heard it slice into the water and then it was gone, leaving barely a ripple. She turned, clambered back up to the path and took the bridle from Macrobius, jumping on the back of the horse and patting its neck, leaning close to its ear and talking softly in the language of her people. The horse stomped and snorted, and she sat upright, took the lasso from her belt and snapped it above her head, the rope swirling and coiling in the falling snow, and then pulled it up and tucked it back away. 'When my father found that sword, he knew he would become a lord of war,' she said. 'After that, they called his army a whirlwind. Follow me into battle and you will see why.'

Flavius caught the glint in her eyes. He had seen exactly that look before, far away on the harsh plains near the Maeotic Lake, riding alongside Attila as he thundered forward with his bowmen towards the Parthian prisoners. He felt suddenly lightheaded, as if he were living for the moment, for a sign like the glint of a freshly whetted blade that battle was in the offing, that the enemy was near. He turned to Macrobius. 'Are you ready, centurion?'

Macrobius pointed at the men waiting ahead of them. 'Just thinking of our boys. Whether they've had enough food. Can't march an army on an empty stomach.'

Flavius cracked a smile. 'You will have seen to it.'

Macrobius took a deep breath, nodded, and then took out his battered old helmet and rammed it onto his felt cap. 'Forward, *milites*,' he said, marching ahead along the path towards his men. Flavius lingered for a moment, staring at the smashed tile on the ground in front of him, remembering all of those Roman soldiers who had gone before. 'Forward, *legionarii*,' he said under his breath.

Erecan reined up her horse and looked down at him. 'Where is she?'

Flavius looked up at her, bemused. 'Who do you mean?'

'You keep touching that stone around your neck. A woman must have given it to you.'

Flavius realized that his finger was hooked around the jet necklace that Una had given him. He let go of it, tucking it quickly back under his tunic, and peered at her. 'She is with God.'

Erecan gave him a determined look. 'Then you must find another woman.'

'No,' Flavius said. 'I didn't mean it like that. I mean she's spreading the word of God, among her own people.'

Erecan looked unimpressed. 'Can she use a sword?'

Flavius thought for a moment, peering up again. 'She can run. Very fast, and for a very long time.'

'Then we have use for her. When this next battle is over, you must go and get her.' She pulled her horse around to follow

Macrobius, and then turned back. 'And she can bring God with her if she wants. We could use all the help we can get.'

She galloped away and Arturus came up beside Flavius. He was carrying the helmet that Aetius had given Flavius when he had been appointed tribune, and that Flavius had given to Arturus when they had crossed the sea to Britain. A gilded helmet had no place on the head of a foot soldier who was no longer fighting for Rome; out here, it was a helmet fit only for a king. Flavius remembered when he had first met Arturus, striding up the African desert dressed in a monk's cassock, a man who had foresworn fighting and earthly pleasures for a life of contemplation, who had turned his back on his people as the barbarians were sweeping in. He smiled to himself at the memory, seeing the battle-hardened warrior-king in front of him now. 'Are *you* ready?'

Arturus put the helmet on and took a deep breath. He unsheathed his sword and pointed it down the valley. '*To war.*'

Author's Note

The following pages provide a brief historical companion to the novel, including an account of the late Roman world in the West, the administration of empire, Christianity, St Augustine and Pelagius, and the Roman army in the fifth century AD, and end with a summary of the historical and archaeological sources for the novel.

The Late Roman World in the West

Almost six hundred years have passed since the time of *Total War Rome: Destroy Carthage*, my first novel in this historical series. From being a fledgling republic flexing her muscles in the Mediterranean, Rome had become the centre of the greatest empire the world has ever known, her influence stretching from the Strait of Gibraltar to the Bay of Bengal and from the edge of the Sahara to the northern tip of Britain. At the centre of it all had been the army, Rome's pillar of strength as the centuries rolled on, as dictators became emperors and the empire wavered under corruption and personal ambition, as the barbarian pressure on the frontiers became too much to contain and as the populace came under the sway of a new religion. A crucial turning point came during the reigns of the emperors Diocletian and Constantine the Great at the end of the third century and through the early fourth century AD. Diocletian reformed the army, making it less easy for potential usurpers to persuade soldiers to rally to their cause and also making it more effective on the frontiers, and split the empire administratively in two; Constantine officially adopted Christianity as the state religion and moved the

main imperial capital from Rome to the new city called Constantinople, formerly the Greek colony of Byzantium, on the Bosporus.

The period of the late Roman Empire in the West refers to the
century and a half following these emperors and up to the fall of the
last western emperor in AD 476. The first half of this period was a
time of revived prosperity and security as the reforms of Diocletian
and Constantine took positive effect. A visitor to Rome would have
seen a city grander than it ever had been before, with magnificent
new basilicas, including St Peter's. But the second half was another
matter altogether. No amount of strategic flexibility, treaties and
concessions could contain the barbarian threat from the Rhine and
the Danube frontiers, and a rupture in the fabric of empire was
inevitable. In AD 376 at the Battle of Adrianople a combined eastern
and western Roman army was defeated by the Goths, who then
moved inexorably forward through Greece and Italy until they
sacked Rome itself – a devastating psychological blow from which
the West never truly recovered. Despite able commanders, the
Roman army was hamstrung by weak emperors more concerned
with deploying the army to bolster their own security than using
it to defend the frontiers. Other barbarian armies followed the
Goths, from Vandals to Saxons, the former marching through Gaul
and Spain and the latter forcing the final Roman withdrawal from
Britain. The stage was set for the extraordinary historical backdrop
to this novel, a story of tragedy and inevitability but also of courage
and military prowess against the odds that puts the achievements of
the late Roman army alongside those of its illustrious forebears
of earlier centuries.

By the decade beginning in AD 430, the time of the opening of
this novel, Rome was a changing place. A significant proportion
of the administrative classes now had some barbarian ancestry, a
result of pacified Germanic chieftains sending their sons to Italy to
be educated, Germanic mercenaries in the army rising to high rank,
and intermarriage. Although people were living in more fear than
ever of barbarian invasion, the ethnic distinction between Roman

and barbarian was becoming blurred. Stilicho and Flavius Aetius, the two most able Roman military commanders of the fifth century AD, were respectively of Vandal and Goth ancestry, and many among the common soldiery had ancestors who had been mortal enemies of Rome in the forests beyond the Rhine and the Danube only a few generations before.

Significant changes in lifestyle and material culture were also taking place. Scrolls were being replaced by codices – books as we know them today; togas were being discarded in favour of trousers and tunics. The old monetary system based around the silver *denarius* had been replaced by a new gold standard in the form of the *solidus*, with silver and base-metal coinage no longer having such widespread acceptance as a result of debasement and economic instability. The city of Rome, no longer the capital of the empire, was changing in appearance too. At the time of my first novel, set in the second century BC, the Colosseum, the Pantheon and the imperial palaces had yet to be built; by the fifth century AD they were already monuments of the past, the last gladiatorial display in the Colosseum having taken place in AD 386 and the palaces now being secondary to the new imperial capitals at Constantinople in the East and Milan and Ravenna in the West. The buildings that were to survive – temples and law courts and amphitheatres – often did so only because they had been converted to places of Christian worship. The fifth century thus saw the beginnings of a new order, but it was one that was to come crashing down before the world that we would recognize as medieval really took hold; and behind that descent into darkness lay one barbarian warlord more than any other, the fearful figure of Attila the Hun.

Administration of Empire

The first emperors liked to claim that they were merely caretakers of the Republic, that the title *princeps* was just another version of the old emergency title *dictator* assumed by Julius Caesar to tide the Republic through the civil wars. This of course was a fiction; after Augustus, ancient Rome was never again a republic. But the main administrative institutions of the Republic did survive, particularly the Senate, and the devolved form of provincial management established in the late Republic provided a blueprint for the empire. The success of this system in the new provinces depended on empowering the native elite – encouraging them to take up administrative roles in the towns and to see the attractions of Romanization. If we think of the great monuments around the Roman Empire, of the amphitheatres and aqueducts and basilicas, few were actually ordered and funded from Rome; many were the result of competitive munificence among the Romanized native aristocracy, men keen to bolster their prestige and secure election to office. In a province such as Britain the majority of people living a Roman lifestyle were natives, with retired soldiers making up the only sizeable immigrant population, one integrated through marriage – and those veterans were not always Romans themselves or even from Italy. This system proved an effective means of maintaining peace and prosperity in the provinces, encouraging enough wealth generation to sustain a high rate of tax and providing the basis for its collection through the development of towns and road networks.

The circumstances that prompted the emperor Diocletian's reforms were a massive breakdown in this administrative system during the third century AD – a period that saw more than thirty emperors in as many years, as well as increased barbarian pressure on the frontiers and an economic collapse that threatened both the supply of food for the army and the bullion needed for their pay. Rather than attempting to reconstitute the old system, Diocletian and his advisers created a tighter structure based around smaller provinces arranged into 'dioceses'. The old province of Africa Proconsularis, for example, became the three provinces of Byzacena, Zeugitana and Tingitana; Britain became Britannia Prima and Britannia Secunda. Most dramatically, Diocletian divided the empire into West and East, with a ruling tetrarchy made up of a senior 'Augustus' and a junior 'Caesar' in each. By so doing he paved the way for Constantine to create the new imperial capital on the Bosporus and for the shift in Italy away from Rome to Milan and Ravenna, which became the new administrative hubs of the West. As well as being a matter of administrative practicality, Diocletian's division recognized deep-seated social, economic, linguistic and religious differences between East and West, and eventually led to their formal creation as separate empires in AD 386. By the time of this novel, therefore, soldiers in the western army would have been swearing allegiance not to a 'senior' emperor in Constantinople, but rather to their own emperor in the new western capital of Milan.

The later Roman emperors often seem to us to have been more autocratic and despotic than their predecessors. Partly this was a consequence of greater state control of economic activities, including the production of foodstuffs and equipment for the army as well as the obligation for people to stick with their occupations, making many jobs hereditary by law. Another factor was the shift in focus to the East, where the tradition of semi-deified kings was more deeply embedded. Whereas in Rome the emperor and his family had been a visible presence, in Constantinople and the new capitals in Italy the imperial court was more remote and regal. This remoteness is embodied in the statue of Constantine erected in his new basilica in the forum in Rome: colossal, highly stylized and gazing to the heavens rather than to the people, ironically commissioned just as he was about to renounce pagan religion and the imperial cult. If we look at the coin portraits of the western emperors over the following century the picture is varied, with some showing the gritty realism of soldier-emperors for whom despotism meant being hard-nosed and brutal, rather than depicting any kind of elevated self-image. Problems arose through attempts at dynastic succession where weak emperors were propped up by men of nefarious ambition; capable army commanders such as Stilicho and Aetius could spend more time battling court intrigue than staving off barbarian invasion. This as well as dynastic strife was to play a major part in the undoing of the Roman West as an administrative entity in the fifth century AD.

Christianity

A huge change in late antiquity was brought about by the emergence of Christianity as the state religion. Its adoption was born out of war – a vision in battle had caused the emperor Constantine to convert to Christianity, leading to its acceptance by the state on his death in AD 331. Christianity appeared to offer much to the common people that pagan Roman religion did not. In its earliest form, three centuries before Constantine, Christianity was less a *religio* – in the original Latin meaning of the word, an 'obligation' – than it was a course of moral teaching, more philosophical, interactive and relevant to day-to-day life than pagan religion. It was inclusive, welcoming all into its fold, whereas pagan religion at the state level had been exclusive and remote, restricting participation in ritual to the priests and the privileged. At a time when whimsical cruelty was commonplace, the Judaeo-Christian tradition offered a code of morality that had little precedent in the classical world; there had been no equivalent to the Ten Commandments in pagan Rome, only obligations to sacrifice and worship and threats of divine retribution against those who failed to do so. Christianity attracted the downtrodden by showing them how to gain strength by living an overtly moral life, and thus offered consolation to less privileged people who were severely restricted in the ancient world in their scope for social betterment or material gain.

It would be mistaken, though, to think that those in power in Rome who made Christianity the state religion were swayed by these factors. For Constantine the Great it was more a matter of *realpolitik* than personal revelation, despite his claim to have 'seen the light' in the battle against his rival Maxentius in AD 312. Constantine would have known how the Sassanid rulers in Persia – Rome's arch-rivals in the East – had used monotheism to their advantage, harnessing the Zoroastrian religion to strengthen their own power base. Already the Roman emperors in the third century had encouraged the worship of Sol Invictus, 'invincible Sun', similar to the worship of the sun god in ancient Egypt, and had aligned it with the imperial cult. In doing so they paved the way for the transition to the single Judaeo-Christian God after AD 331.

The conversion to monotheism lost the emperor his divine status, the basis for the imperial cult – he could no longer be a god – but that was swiftly replaced by the notion of the emperor as divinely appointed, as Christ's chosen one, equal to the Apostles. As a result, the early Christian emperors could be even more god-like in their behaviour than their predecessors, some of them exerting this new image powerfully, but the weaker ones existing as little more than symbols, living remotely in their palaces, puppets in the hands of the strongmen who really ran the empire.

In other ways too the transition to state Christianity represented less of an upheaval than might be imagined. The old 'Capitoline triad', the gods Jupiter, Juno and Minerva, translated into the Holy Trinity of God, the Son and the Holy Ghost. Mater Magna became embodied in the Virgin Mary, and the many saints that soon proliferated in Italy and elsewhere took over from local pagan gods. The idea of priests as divinely ordained, as necessary intermediaries between the people and God, gave the clergy a status similar to the old priesthood, enhanced by the development of arcane rituals and liturgies that further set them apart from the common people. Christianity began to take on many of those features that had turned people away from pagan religion. As Constantine had foreseen, the inclusivity of Christianity – the size of its congregation – meant that the population could be controlled through the Church. Christian morality being rooted in poverty and abstinence suited an empire of high taxation, hereditary jobs and servitude that for many citizens bordered on slavery because, as Christians, these citizens were more likely to accept their lot. Far from being a transition to enlightenment after a cruel and amoral pagan past, Christianity became a means for a totalitarian administration to control and oppress a population that otherwise might collapse into anarchy and turn against the emperor.

At the time of this novel, a hundred years after Constantine, many of the institutions of later Christianity were becoming well established, including the papacy, bishoprics and monasteries, the earliest of which were sited in the fortified rural villas characteristic of this period. The Roman dating system changed from *ab urbe condita*, 'from the foundation of the city', to *anno domini nostri iesu*, from the year of the birth of Our Lord, a date fixed by the Thracian monk Antesius. In the cities, a pressing need was for buildings large enough to take big congregations, to provide 'Houses of God'. In Constantinople this need was met by the great church of Hagia Sophia, its domed form influencing the design of many churches in the East as well as the first mosques in the seventh century. In Rome, it was the old law courts or 'basilicas' – a term originally derived from the Greek for 'king', and meaning 'palace' – that provided the blueprint, their oblong colonnaded design with an apse at one end being seen in the early basilican churches such as St Peter's. In addition, many pagan temples became churches – for example, the Pantheon in Rome – and other buildings such as the Colosseum were consecrated as holy places because of their association with early Christian martyrdom, ironically ensuring their survival to modern times.

Despite the earlier history of Christianity, before Constantine, as a persecuted religion, there was no systematic retribution against those who continued to practise pagan religion after AD 331; we would be wrong to project backwards to the Roman period a view conditioned by our picture of extreme religious intolerance by the western Church in the medieval period. On the whole, Christianity was attractive enough to the masses for forced conversion to be unnecessary. Pagan sacrifice was banned, but not polytheism. Pagan religion continued to have enough cachet for the emperor Julian 'the Apostate' in the mid-fourth century to return to polytheism and to persecute Christians during his reign. Of the four main historians of the fifth century, the earliest of them, Eusebius, was profoundly anti-Christian, blaming the woes of the empire on the rejection of the old gods and the adoption of Christianity. Among the Roman army, there can be no doubt that deeply embedded pagan practices continued, including the worship of gods traditionally favoured by soldiers such as Mithras, Isis and Sol Invictus.

Within the Church, differences in the style of Christian worship were becoming increasingly apparent between East and West, resulting in the distinctions that exist to this day between the Church of Rome and that of Constantinople. As these differences became institutionalized, theologians became entangled in debate over matters of doctrine and practice that became increasingly obscure – a parallel to the sophistic tradition of philosophical debate in the late classical period, about style more than substance. Despite their often recondite nature, these debates resulted in 'schisms' that led to the adherents of one or another position being branded as heretics and persecuted, often to death; more Christians were killed by fellow believers in this way than were ever thrown to the lions by the pagan emperors; a dark side of Christianity in the West that was to blight its history for many centuries to come.

St Augustine and Pelagius

Two scholars in the early fifth century AD who figure in this novel stand out for their impact on early Christian thought, and on the relationship between Roman Christianity and the conduct of war in the final decades of the western empire. The first was Bishop Augustine of Hippo Regius in North Africa, later canonized as St Augustine; the second was a monk of probable British origin named Pelagius. We know a great deal about Augustine because his ideas became part of mainstream Christian thinking in the West through his two greatest written works, *Confessions* and *City of God*; Pelagius, on the other hand, was branded a heretic and nothing of his original writing survives.

Augustine's *City of God* can be seen as a response to the barbarian invasions of his lifetime as well as the endemic weakness he saw in the Roman state, leading him to dismiss earthly empires and assert that the only triumphant one would be the spiritual kingdom of the Church, his 'City of God'. It was a position that would have found few followers among the army leadership looking for a militant church to provide a rallying point for troops on the ground, rather than one that had abandoned earthly matters and looked only to heaven. On the other hand, many of Augustine's other assertions pleased the clergy and state because they served to strengthen the hold of the Church over the people, including his belief that bishops and priests were divinely ordained and that divine favour or 'grace' was a prerequisite of human action – that is, human action was something that required the intervention of priests and the rituals of the Church that were becoming established at this period.

It was this latter point that put Augustine at odds with Pelagius, who argued that human actions did not need divine or priestly guidance and that people could behave according to their own free will. Pelagius' thinking may reflect an undercurrent of individualism in the spiritual life of Roman Britain and the old Celtic world of north-west Europe, among people attracted to the teachings of Jesus when they first reached Britain in the early empire but who were less amenable to the Roman Church as it later developed. The legacy of this distinctive north-west European tradition, at odds with the Roman Church, can be seen a thousand years later in the Protestant revolution and the spread of non-conformism in Europe and beyond. The development of religious thinking in the fifth century therefore has a direct bearing not only on military strategy at the time – on whether or not an 'earthly' empire was worth fighting for – but also on our understanding of the Christian world today.

The Roman Army in the Fifth Century AD

The late Roman army was very different from the Republican army of my previous novel in this series, *Total War Rome: Destroy Carthage*. The danger in looking at past eras where generalization seems possible, such as ancient Rome, is to foreshorten them and apply one well-documented image – of soldiers, of lifestyle, of building types – to the entire period, when in fact huge expanses of time are involved; the six-hundred-year period between the siege of Punic Carthage in the second century BC and the Hun invasions of the fifth century AD is almost exactly the same span of time as that between the Battle of Agincourt and the present day. The changes we see in the late Roman army partly reflect the developments we should expect to see over such a long time period, but they also owe much to the reforms under the emperors Diocletian and Constantine mentioned above.

In many respects we know less about the late Roman army than we do about its Republican predecessor. For the army in the second century BC we have the extensive military treatise of Polybius, whereas none of the fifth-century AD historians whose work survives were themselves soldiers or much interested in military detail. The *Notitia Dignitatum*, a fourth-century AD catalogue of offices in the Roman Empire, tells us much about the upper structures of command but little about organization at the unit level. Unlike in the earlier empire, there are few tombstones in late antiquity inscribed with details of a soldier's military career, and little accumulation of archaeological and inscriptional evidence from forts where occupation by individual units had been sustained over long periods. Moreover, fewer sieges and battles of late antiquity were outright victories for the Romans, and even those that were are rarely recorded in eyewitness accounts or in more than a few lines of text, often with no detail of the tactics or units involved.

Again, because of our tendency to foreshorten, to draw together fragmentary evidence that is in fact quite widely dispersed in time – even in the context of the late Roman army in the West, we are talking about a period of a century and half, from Constantine the Great to the fall of the western empire in AD 476 – some modern accounts of the late Roman army can present a bewilderingly complex picture, whereas if we were to know the picture in detail at any one point in time it might seem more orderly and rational. What the apparent diversity of ranks and unit titles does show, particularly as we move into the fifth century, is an army rapidly evolving and reshaping in response to external threat, internal discord and the increasing incorporation of barbarian units within its fold, all of it overshadowed by the knowledge that the army would soon have to face an enemy from the steppe-lands of Asia in a showdown as decisive as any in Rome's long history.

Our adjective 'Byzantine', meaning excessively detailed and complicated, comes from the name of the old Greek colony on the Bosporus where Constantinople was built, and the term 'Byzantine' is often used to refer to the eastern Roman Empire from its creation in the fourth century AD until Constantinople finally fell to the Turks in 1453. At first glance the late Roman army might seem 'Byzantine' in its organization, over-administered and paralleling the complexity of the new provincial governance created in the fourth century. However, delve deeper, come closer to the soldiers themselves, and it is possible to see how this picture might give a misleading impression of its effectiveness as a fighting force. In many respects the early imperial army was more tightly controlled and less flexible, with the legions having something of the intractability of European infantry regiments in the eighteenth and early nineteenth centuries. If we leave aside the apparent complexity of higher-level organization, we can see an army in the fifth century where greater tactical responsibility was devolved to smaller units, with more flexibility given to commanders at a lower level and more initiative expected from the individual soldier. It was this that gave the late Roman army its strength, and this is something I have tried to bring across in this novel.

Officers and Other Ranks

Gone in large measure was the *'cursus honorum'*, the succession of military and civil offices that formed a fixed career structure for a Roman of senatorial or equestrian rank in the early empire. In the early fifth century the sons of aristocrats would still be 'commissioned' as junior officers, but only after having gone through tribune school. Whereas the officer academy of the second century BC in my first novel in this series was conjectural, the *schola militarum* in the late empire is attested historically, a forerunner of modern academies such as Sandhurst and West Point. A crucial difference from my earlier academy is that students in the *schola militarum* included many former 'non-commissioned' officers, men who had been recommended by the *magister* of their field army or the *dux* of their frontier unit, meaning that the officer corps of the late Roman army included more men risen from the ranks than had been the case in the early empire. This gave a very different flavour to army service, where any *milites* could aspire to high command and where many of the soldier-emperors and *magisteres milites* were themselves men of humble origin who had risen up the ladder through military merit rather than through privilege of birth.

The old rank of *centurion* still existed in some units, including those that still carried the title *legio*. However, the familiar legion of the early empire, numbering up to seven thousand men and divided into cohorts and centuries, had ceased to exist by the fifth century, and units that still carried that title were no different from the other smaller units, often called *numeri* – many with nominal strengths of perhaps a thousand or five hundred men – that formed the building blocks of the late Roman army. The role of the centurion in commanding a company-sized unit was now taken by a tribune, who as we have seen could either be a young officer or a veteran promoted from the ranks. The prevalence of veterans as unit commanders would have placed a particular onus on a newly appointed tribune with no field experience, his men being less deferential to his social status than they might have been in the early empire and expecting him to earn their respect the hard way through leadership in battle.

'Tribune' is best understood not as an actual rank but as a title meaning 'commander of a unit', the relative status of the tribune being determined by the unit involved – so that the tribune of a *limitanei numerus*, perhaps 80 or 100 men, would be understood as junior to the tribune of an *equus comitatenses* or a *pedes homoerari*, respectively an elite cavalry guard unit and a larger infantry unit of hundreds of men. In modern terms, a tribune might be the equivalent of anything from a platoon to a battalion commander, from lieutenant to lieutenant-colonel. For lower ranks, the many titles attested in late antiquity for junior NCOs and private soldiers could represent a collation from different time periods, as suggested above, though like the modern British army there may have been different titles for the same rank according to specialized roles or traditions within that unit, similar to sapper, gunner, trooper, fusilier, rifleman or Guardsman. In this novel I refer to private soldiers by their most commonly attested title, *pedes*, literally 'foot soldier', or *milites*.

Weapons

The armour and weapons of the Roman soldier had also changed dramatically from the early empire. Gone were the *lorica segmentata* plate armour, bare legs and sandals of the legionary; soldiers were now more likely to wear chainmail, tunics and trousers, an image that to us would appear more medieval than Roman. The short thrusting *gladius* sword and the *pilum* spear of the legionary had been replaced by an array of weapons that sometimes reflected the barbarian origins of their users, including the composite bow. Sword types that had been copied by Germanic smiths centuries before from Greek, Etruscan and early Roman examples, and had then evolved to suit barbarian fighting tactics – such as the long sword from a fifth-century warrior's grave in Hungary that illustrates this novel – had in turn become the basis for late Roman swords; weapons technology had thus come full circle by the middle of the fifth century AD, when soldiers fighting for Rome were pitted against barbarian invaders as never before, in a confrontation where Roman military might and the reputation of Rome in her heyday could no longer be counted on to hold sway against a man who saw himself as the next emperor of the known world.

Organization

The army of the early empire can be divided broadly into legionaries – citizen-soldiers – and auxiliaries, men from the new provinces who would be awarded Roman citizenship after a term of service; it also included irregular units from newly allied frontier tribes, the *foederati*. After the emperor Caracalla granted universal citizenship to free men within the empire in AD 212 the distinction in status between legionaries and auxiliaries became blurred, though the legions continued in their role as units garrisoned within the provinces ready for deployment, and the auxiliaries as frontier units.

The reforms of the emperors Diocletian and Constantine did away with this old army structure, replacing the legions with *comitatenses*, literally 'companions', and the frontier units with *limitanei*, border troops. These new units broadly continued the distinction in role between the legionaries and auxiliaries, but there were big changes in internal organization, particularly between the legions and the *comitatenses*. The legions had been large units of five thousand men or more, with the *esprit de corps* of a modern regiment but a tactical role more akin to that of a brigade; they were suited to the set-piece battles typical of the late Republic, for example during the Punic Wars. The *comitatenses*, by contrast, comprised units of about eight hundred or a thousand men, more like a modern battalion.

Reducing the size of the units made the field army more mobile and flexible, better suited to a range of actions against barbarian invaders who might be less likely to engage in set-piece battles. But the main reason for the change may have had little to do with field tactics, and more to do with the emperor's security; legionary commanders intent on threatening the imperial purple could call on the loyalty of large bodies of men, whereas smaller units loyal to their own commanders might be more difficult for a usurper to marshal and easier for the emperor to keep under control.

Confusingly, as we have seen, some units continued to be called legions – for example, *Legio II Adiutrix* and *Legio XX Valeria Victrix*. However, these appear to have been legions in name only, and probably represent a conscious attempt to retain some continuity of tradition from the earlier formations in order to boost morale and recruitment. A comparison could be made in the British Army today with the retention of the name The Black Watch, the old Royal Highland Regiment, for a battalion of the recently formed Royal Regiment of Scotland, meaning that the traditions and symbols are retained even though the Black Watch has ceased to exist as a regiment.

Along with the new organization came new structures of command. Gone were the old legates, the commanders of legions, with armies in the field being led by consuls or members of the imperial family. The frontier *limitanei* were now led by a *dux*, the origin of our word 'duke', or by the lesser *comes*, 'count'. The *comitatenses* field armies were commanded by a *magister*, and the army as a whole by the *magister militum*, the emperor's right-hand man and in effect the second-in-command of the Roman Empire.

To further bolster their security the emperors marshalled a special *comitatenses* force as their personal army, taking strength away from the provincial armies in the process, and replaced the old Praetorian Guard with a new elite palace guard, the *praepecti comitatente*. This decision to prioritize the emperor's security over provincial and frontier defences counterbalanced the tactical advantages of the new *comitatenses* organization, and was to be a weakness that helps to explain the western empire's vulnerability to invasion during this period.

Recruitment

The army of the early empire was largely a volunteer force, continuing the tradition of the citizen-army of the Republic and including soldiers from martial backgrounds in the newly formed provinces. To be a legionary was an honourable and esteemed occupation, and could lead to the all-important grant of land on retirement; to be an auxiliary was a route to citizenship. Crucially, soldiers were paid well enough for salary to be an incentive to recruitment as well, allowing a man to save enough to develop his plot of land on retirement and to provide for a family, improving his social standing and the prospects of betterment for his children.

Much of this picture had changed by the late empire. The grant of universal citizenship under Caracalla in AD 212 reduced the incentive for men to join as auxiliaries. The third-century crisis, a time of anarchy that saw more than thirty emperors in as many years, saw successive emperors debase the silver coinage until soldiers' pay was nearly worthless. Even after a gold standard was recreated, the pay for soldiers in the fourth and fifth centuries was notoriously irregular and often non-existent; soldiers instead came to depend on the emperors or on affluent commanders for lump-sum handouts, a system that could allow the loyalty of an army to be bought by the emperor or an opposing faction at a time when the army should have been independent of politics and marshalling all of its resolve against the barbarian threat.

As this would suggest, the traditional basis for volunteer recruitment had largely disappeared by the fourth century, and many of the *comitatenses* and *limitanei* were soldiers under some form of compulsion – some of them in lieu of tax, whereby a father might send one of his sons to the army as a substitute for his dues in cash or goods-in-kind. As with any conscript army, morale and *esprit de corps* were not to be taken for granted; fewer men would have fought for the glory of Rome than was the case with their legionary ancestors, and there would have been plenty of cynics and individualists. Yet it is sometimes those men in a conscript army under duress of war who prove the most capable and imaginative soldiers, so conscription in the late Roman army was not necessarily a weakness. However reluctant they may have been to begin with, conscripts could develop resolve in the face of total war where their homes and families were threatened – as was certainly the case in Italy after the sack of Rome by the Goths in AD 410 – as well as a pride in their ability and in that of their units. The greatest loyalties of these men would have been to their comrades and to commanders who had fought alongside them and earned their respect, reinforcing the devolved, small-unit focus of the late Roman army, in contrast to the legions of old.

As well as the 'direct-entry' officers – young tribunes of aristocratic background – the remaining professional aspect of the Roman army lay in the continued voluntary recruitment of soldiers from regions with strong martial traditions, particularly Pannonia near the Danube and the northern Balkans, and above all in the influx of barbarians who had recently been Rome's enemies. In the early empire, offering newly pacified enemies favourable terms of service in the army had been a way of Romanizing the natives and giving them an outlet for martial fervour that might otherwise lead to unrest and rebellion. In the late empire, by contrast, the Germanic warlords newly settled by treaty in Gaul and Spain had not been defeated or disarmed, and saw service in the Roman army as an admirable occupation for their sons as well as a means of defending their own newly acquired territory against further barbarian threat. Barbarians in the Roman army could range from units of *foederati* on the frontiers, some of them little more than roving bands of warriors, to officers up to the rank of army commander, something unheard of in the early empire.

The warrior abilities of those men of barbarian background, as well as of the toughened, cynical conscripts from Italy and the old provincial heartlands, helps to explain the extraordinary resilience of the Roman army in its final battles in the West; these were battles won less by strategy and manoeuvre than by the ability of the individual soldier to stand up to a ferocious enemy in hand-to-hand combat, the nub of any reconstruction of warfare at this pivotal period in ancient history.

Sources for the Novel

The 'Sword of Attila' is a genuinely attested artefact, as described by Priscus of Panium in the quote at the beginning of this novel. Priscus, who is a character in the story, is our main source for Attila and the Huns in the fifth century AD, and virtually everything that can be said about Attila derives either from his surviving account or from later sources that can be attributed to him. Priscus was born at Panium on the Propontis Sea near Constantinople in about AD 420, and with his friend Maximinus – a young army officer – went to the court of Attila on behalf of the eastern emperor Theodosius in AD 449, only two years before Attila's great offensive in the West. Priscus was a scholar first and foremost, the author of works of rhetoric as well as extensive histories of the eastern empire and of Attila, and the surviving text on his expedition to Attila provides one of the most vivid first-hand narratives to come down to us from classical antiquity. From him we learn details of the Huns for which there is no other evidence, in, for example, his descriptions of the 'seamless' wooden construction of Attila's fortress, the ritual scarring of a warrior's cheeks, and the role of the shaman. Priscus also gives a sense of the huge complexity of this period, a time of continuous intrigue and machinations in the courts both of the eastern empire of Theodosius and the western one of Justinian.

Because the Huns were a nomadic people and only ever built in wood, if at all, the archaeological evidence for them is very limited other than through the chance finds of burials. Some of these have produced skeletons of men and women whose skulls show clear signs of flattening, resulting in the description of Huns as having sloping foreheads in this novel. One outstanding discovery was a burial found in 1979 close to the Benedictine monastery of Pannonhalma, not far from Budapest. Among the finds were magnificent gold-foil horse trappings, the basis for Mundiuk's horse decorations described in the prologue of this novel, as well as the beautiful sword that appears on the cover of this book, its grip surrounded by decorated gold bands and the scabbard also embellished with gold.

It is clear that Hun swordsmiths were highly skilled craftsmen, and that veneration for the sword was deeply rooted; almost a thousand years before Priscus, the Greek historian Herodotus described how the Scythians worshipped their god of war in the form of an iron sword, set up on a mound made of brushwood, and how not only cattle and horses but also captured enemies were sacrificed in front of these altars: '. . . they cut their victims' throats and collected the blood, and carried it to the top of the mound and poured it over the sword. At the foot of the altar they cut the right arm and shoulder from the body, and tossed them in the air, each arm left to lie where it fell. The torsos lay separately' (*Histories*, 4.62).

Unfortunately for us, Priscus was no military historian, giving few details of campaigns and battles, and his surviving work contains nothing on the two huge contests that feature in this novel. Despite being the culmination of one of the most extraordinary military campaigns in history, the conquest of Roman Carthage by the Vandals under Gaiseric in AD 439 is known only from a few lines from other historians, none more than a sentence long. We fare better when it comes to what was probably the greatest military contest of classical antiquity, the Battle of the Catalaunian Plains in AD 451 between the Romans and Visigoths on one side and the Huns and Ostrogoths and Gepids on the other, with numerous other allies on both sides representing most of the warlike peoples in Europe of the period. All modern accounts of the battle derive from the *History of the Goths* ('*Getica*') by Jordanes, a minor official in Constantinople in the mid-sixth century who based much of his work – including a history of Attila and the Huns – on lost volumes of Priscus. Jordanes' account of the battle takes up over two thousand words, though there is much that is formulaic – a speech from Attila, for example, that must be fictional – and there are only a few topographical and tactical details, including the appearance of the central ridge, the disposition of the armies, the stream running with blood and the Goth king Theodoric's fate, '. . . thrown from his horse and trampled underfoot by his own men . . . though some say he was slain by the spear of Andag of the host of the Ostrogoths, who were then under the sway of Attila' (*Getica*, 40). He also tells us of the comet that was supposedly seen on the eve of the battle. In evaluating Jordanes as a historical source, it is important to remember not only that he was writing a century after the battle but also that his main source, Priscus of Panium, was neither an eyewitness to the battle himself nor a military historian.

In the case of Carthage, the sheer humiliation of defeat and the absence of an eyewitness historian – such as a man like Polybius, who had watched the Roman conquest of Carthage almost six hundred years earlier – helps to account for the lack of written evidence from the Romans, with the Vandals themselves having no literary tradition. For the Catalaunian Plains, shock and exhaustion may have overwhelmed anyone attempting to describe the scene, though there were other factors. The main historians of the period whose work survives, men such as Priscus and Jordanes, were from Constantinople and were more focused on eastern affairs. In Ravenna and Rome, any cause for celebrating the battle, at best an ambiguous victory for the Romans, was soon lost in the march of history; Attila himself may no longer have been a threat, but only twenty-five years later in AD 476 his erstwhile Ostrogoth allies invaded Italy, took Ravenna and declared their chieftain Odoacer king, effectively ending the Roman Empire in the West.

The Catalaunian Plains probably lay in Champagne in northeastern France near Chalôns, a name by which the battle is sometimes known. For some, a clinching factor in this identification was the discovery nearby, in 1842 on the south bank of the river Aube, of a burial containing a skeleton with two swords and gold and silver ornaments datable to the fifth century AD – one of them a ring with the inscription HEVA, perhaps to be interpreted as described in chapter 13 of this novel – consistent with the grave goods of a Goth warrior chieftain. The idea that this may have been King Theodoric, hastily buried after the battle, was first mooted in the nineteenth century, and this is the basis for the scene in chapter 16 in this novel. You can see the so-called Treasure of Pouan today in the Musée Saint-Loup at Troyes.

A central figure in this novel is Arturus, a renegade Briton with Roman blood who serves in the *foederati* in Gaul, works as an intelligence agent for the *magister militum* Aetius and then returns to Britain to lead his people against the invading Saxons. The decades after the Roman withdrawal from Britain in AD 410 have always seemed to me the most likely context for such a man, at a time of turmoil in Britain when the outcome of the invasions was uncertain – when a single charismatic leader on either side might have swayed the balance – and also when Gaul was probably awash with British veterans and adventurers, some of them with one eye on the situation back home. At the Catalaunian Plains, for example, it is impossible to believe that the armies of both sides did not include British mercenaries, some of them with legionary ancestry, fighting alongside Saxons, Angles, Jutes and men of all of the other warrior tribes whom their brothers and cousins were fighting against in the borderlands of Wales and western England. Whether Arturus really existed and was able to establish a kingdom, one lost to history but preserved in mythology, is another question in this shady but fascinating period of ancient history, at a time when modern Europe as we know it was being born.

The quotes from Ammianus Marcellinus in chapter 7 include phrases on the Huns translated from his *Res Gestae* (Book XXXI), and Una's comment in chapter 8 on the prayer by Bishop Quodvultdeus of Carthage paraphrases a sentence in a sermon attributed to him called the 'Holy Innocents'. In chapter 9, the inscription seen by Flavius is the actual one visible today at the base of Trajan's Column in Rome; and in chapter 11, the inscription carved under Trajan's orders in the cliffs of the Iron Gates on the Danube, the 'Tabula Traiana', can be seen today on the Serbian side opposite a huge modern sculpture into the cliff of Trajan's Dacian opponent Decebalus, my inspiration for the idea that colossal carvings of two generals may have existed in the gorge in antiquity. The rise in the river level from damming that led to the Tabula Traiana being moved to its present position also inundated the island of Adekaleh, a medieval free port and smugglers' den with 'a thousand twisting alleys' that I have imagined already having this appearance by the fifth century AD.

At that time, in Ethiopia, on the other side of the ancient world, the extraordinary Christian kingdom of Aksum was reaching its height, much as recounted by Una in chapter 8; to many like her, Aksum would have seemed a haven from persecution and a place to start Christianity afresh, and it was undoubtedly a basis for the stories of a fabled Christian land in the East – including the legend of Prester John – that persisted into early modern times.

The coin illustrating the part titles of this book is an actual *solidus* of Valentinian in my possession, minted in Rome and dating from about AD 440. For more facts behind the fiction, including my own translation of passages in Priscus on the Huns and in Jordanes on the Battle of the Catalaunian Plains, as well as images of the great sword of the Huns and other artefacts and sites mentioned in the novel, go to www.davidgibbins.com and www.facebook.com/DavidGibbinsAuthor.

Acknowledgements

I am very grateful to my agent, Luigi Bonomi of LBA; to Rob Alexander of The Creative Assembly and Sega; to Jeremy Trevathan, Catherine Richards and the team at Pan Macmillan in the UK; to Peter Wolverton, Anne Brewer and the team at St Martin's Press in New York; to all of my other publishers and translators; and to everyone at The Creative Assembly and at Sega for their input. I am particularly grateful to Martin Fletcher for his excellent editorial work, to Al Bickham of the Creative Assembly for his comments, to Mandy Woods for her copyediting and to Ann Verrinder Gibbins for her proofreading and much useful advice along the way.

When I was at school my father encouraged me to read Robert Graves' novel *Count Belisarius*; that in turn led me to Graves' main source, Procopius, and then to Jordanes and Priscus, the historians who give such an insight into the barbarian invasions of the fifth century AD and the world of Attila the Hun. I first became involved in the late Roman period as an archaeologist, when I spent a summer expedition to Sicily camped in the ruins of Caucana, the site identified as the embarkation point for Belisarius' reconquest of Carthage from the Vandals in the sixth century AD. In Sicily we were investigating shipwrecks of the fourth and fifth centuries AD, an experience that gave me a close insight into the archaeology of the period; later I was able to expand that interest through excavations at Carthage, as well as in Italy, Britain and other places that figure in this novel. Some of this research was made possible through funding from the Canadian Social Sciences and Humanities Research Council, the British Academy, Cambridge University Classics Faculty and Corpus Christi College, Cambridge, to all of whom I'm grateful.

Acknowledgements

I owe special thanks to my daughter Molly for accompanying me on a wild winter climb in Wales past the lake of Glaslyn and up Mount Snowdon where I first had the idea for the epilogue, and to the many students who worked on an excavation I organized beside the river Dee where I once held a tile marked 'LEG XX' just as Flavius does in the final scene in this novel.

About the Author

David Gibbins is a *New York Times* and *Sunday Times* bestselling novelist whose books have sold over three million copies and are published in thirty languages. He is an archaeologist by training, and his novels reflect his extensive experience investigating ancient sites around the world, both on land and underwater. He was born in Canada and grew up there, in New Zealand and in England. He took a first-class honours degree in Ancient Mediterranean Studies from the University of Bristol and completed a PhD at the University of Cambridge, where he was a research scholar of Corpus Christi College and a postdoctoral fellow in the Faculty of Classics. As a university lecturer he taught Roman archaeology and art, ancient history and maritime archaeology; as well as fiction he is the author of many scholarly publications, including articles in *Antiquity*, *World Archaeology*, the *International Journal of Nautical Archaeology*, *New Scientist* and other journals, as well as monographs and edited volumes.

His archaeological fieldwork has taken him all over the Mediter-ranean region, including Turkey, Israel, mainland Greece and Crete, Italy and Sicily, Spain and North Africa, as well as the British Isles and North America. His projects have been supported by, among others, the British Academy, the British Schools in Rome, Jerusalem and Ankara, and the Society of Antiquaries of London, and by a Fellow-ship from the Winston Churchill Memorial Trust. He has worked at Carthage, leading an expedition to investigate the ancient harbour remains. He learned to dive at the age of fifteen and has investigated shipwreck sites all over the world, including a period as an adjunct professor of the Institute of Nautical Archaeology while he worked on an ancient Greek shipwreck off the coast of Turkey.

His fascination with military history partly stems from a long-standing interest in the involvement of his own ancestors in Victorian and earlier wars. As well as a deep interest in the weapons of antiquity, he collects and restores eighteenth- and nineteenth-century military firearms and makes reproduction American flintlock longrifles that he shoots on the wilderness tract in Canada where he does much of his writing. Military interests reflected in his previous novels include the Punic Wars (*Total War Rome: Destroy Carthage*), Roman campaigning in the East (*The Tiger Warrior*), Victorian warfare in India and the Sudan (*The Tiger Warrior, Pharaoh*), and the Second World War (*The Mask of Troy, The Gods of Atlantis*).

More information about David can be found on his website, www.davidgibbins.com and on www.facebook.com/DavidGibbinsAuthor.